Rebecca Makkai's stories have been anthologized in
The Best American Short Stories 2010, 2009, and 2008, and
have appeared in *Tin House*, *Ploughshares*, *The Threepenny
Review*, and on Public Radio's *Selected Shorts*. *The Borrower* is
her first novel. She lives north of Chicago with her
husband and two daughters.

Praise for *The Borrower*

'*The Borrower's* out and out charm is heightened by its furious, righteous heart and conviction that books offer salvation and hope when life is messy and near-unbearable.'

Marie Claire

'The sheer zest and care with which this book is written, as well as the emphasis on children's literature, set it apart... Makkai is an engaging writer.'

Guardian

'The heightening tension throughout their haphazard road trip from Missouri to Vermont is exhilarating... This astonishingly assured novel knows precisely where it's heading, even if the two fugitives don't. By the epilogue, the reader is breathless with hope that Lucy and Ian will find a happy ending.'

Daily Mail

'A tale of the inspirational power of children's books... as an addition to America's long list of books about fictional fugitives, and a homage to children's literature's power to inspire, *The Borrower* is a tremendously entertaining read.'

Financial Times

'Rebecca Makkai has featured in three editions of Best of American Writing selected by the likes of Richard Russo and Alice Sebold. If that isn't enough, her first novel, *The Borrower*, proves she's a great writer... This is a wonderfully entertaining story packed with moral conundrums and beautiful writing.'

Bookseller

'This vivacious, wistful novel has much to recommend it. Makkai, who's an elementary school teacher, is excellent on the language and behaviour of a clever, sensitive boy. Its subjects are somber; emigration and escape, loss and betrayal, and the realization that one cannot greatly change other people's lives. The quality of writing and characters is compelling.'

Sunday Herald

'Funny, charming debut...it's a lovely, inventive novel, smart but not annoyingly wise-cracking, about the power of books and stories to sustain people when life becomes impossible...Makkai's pairing of Ian and Lucy warmly demonstrates that love can come in different and unexpected guises that have nothing to do with romance.'

Metro

'An appealing, nonromantic love story about an unexpected pairing – and a surprisingly moving one.'

The New York Times Book Review

'With her first novel *The Borrower* Rebecca Makkai brings the world of literary aficionados a treasure...Those who love books and the freedom of the written word will appreciate the myriad of issues Makkai incorporates into her engaging and provocative debut.'

The Washington Times

'There's a part of Rebecca Makkai's new novel, *The Borrower*, that feels eerily true to life. The story's sheepishly literate heroine, Lucy, narrates life from the other side of children's librarian desk in a way that suggests the author knows what it feels like to plaster bulletin boards with bright paper cutouts of dinosaurs...Reading *The Borrower* is like taking a bliss-fully nostalgic journey into the bookshelves of American childhood...Pseudo-librarian or not, Makkai is clearly a lover of the public book-lending institution. Her careful, attentive approach seamlessly weaves literary lore into her unusual and touching story of a librarian fighting for social liberty and freedom of expression.'

The Wall Street Journal

'Rarely is a first novel as smart and engaging and learned and funny and moving as *The Borrower*.'

Richard Russo, Pulitzer Prize-winning and bestselling author of *Empire Falls*

'Rebecca Makkai takes all the best features of the children's books her characters love and sweeps them straight into her first novel: their warmth, their vibrancy, their joy at setting their inventions in motion and following them wherever they might lead. She is a generous, original, and arresting writer, and any story she wants to tell, I want to listen.'

Kevin Brockmeier, author of *The Illumination* and *The Brief History of the Dead*

The Borrower

REBECCA MAKKAI

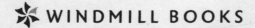

WINDMILL BOOKS

Published by Windmill Books 2012

2 4 6 8 10 9 7 5 3 1

First published in Great Britain in 2011 by William Heinemann

Windmill Books
The Random House Group Limited
20 Vauxhall Bridge Road, London SW1V 2SA

Addresses for companies within The Random House Group Limited can be found at:
www.randomhouse.co.uk/offices.htm

The Random House Group Limited Reg. No. 954009

www.randomhouse.co.uk

A CIP catalogue record for this book
is available from the British Library

ISBN 9780099538127

The Random House Group Limited supports The Forest Stewardship Council
(FSC®), the leading international forest certification organisation. Our books
carrying the FSC label are printed on FSC® certified paper. FSC is the only
forest certification scheme endorsed by the leading environmental organisations,
including Greenpeace. Our paper procurement policy can be found at:
www.randomhouse.co.uk/environment

Printed and bound by CPI Group (UK) Ltd, Croydon, CR0 4YY

For Lydia and Heidi

May all doors—and all books—be open to you both

Acknowledgments

Although I've had to demolish my childhood fantasy that Penguin Books is somehow run by Mr. Popper's penguins, I've happily replaced it with the knowledge that it is populated by wonderful people who were willing to arrange an editing and production schedule around the birth of my second child. Boundless thanks to Kathryn Court, Alexis Washam, Tara Singh, Kate Griggs, and Carolyn Coleburn at Viking, and also to Yuki Hirose for her time and help. Nicole Aragi appeared from the sky one day and turned my pumpkin into a chariot, and I still can't believe my luck or sufficiently express my thanks. David Huddle was an early and supportive reader, and Heidi Pitlor's championing of my short fiction gave me the momentum to keep working and publishing when I might otherwise have lost steam.

Very few writers thank their mothers for keen editorial insight; I'm happy to be the exception. And finally, for most of this book's life, its sole audience was my husband, Jonathan Freeman. Only his students, past and present, will understand how fortunate I am to have such a kind and perceptive man as my first reader.

THE BORROWER

Ian Was Never Happy Unless
There Was a Prologue

I might be the villain of this story. Even now, it's hard to tell.

Back at the library, amid the books and books on ancient Egypt, the picture the children loved most showed the god of death weighing a dead man's heart against a feather. There is this consolation, then, at least: one day, I will know my guilt.

I've left behind everyone I used to know. I've found another library, one with oak walls, iron railings. A college library, where the borrowers already know what they're looking for. I scan their books and they barely acknowledge me through their caffeinated haze. It's nothing like my old stained-carpet, brick-walled library, but the books are the same—same spines, same codes on yellowed labels. I know what's in them all. They whisper their judgment down.

The runaways, the kidnappers, look down from their shelves and claim me for their own. They tell me to light out for the Territory, reckon I'm headed for Hell just like them. They say I'm the most terrific liar they ever saw in their lives. And that one, old lecher-lepidopterist, gabbling grabber, stirring his vodka-pineapple from the high narrow shelf of N-A-B, let me twist his words. (You can always count on a librarian for a derivative prose style): Ladies and gentlemen of the jury, exhibit number one is what I envied, what I thought I could fix. Look at this prison of books.

Before this all began, I told Rocky that one day I'd arrange my books by main character, down through the alphabet. I realize now where I'd be: Hull, snug between Huck and Humbert. But really I should file it under Drake, for Ian, for the boy I stole, because regardless of who the villain is, I'm not the hero of this story. I'm not even the subject of this prayer.

1

Story Hour

E very Friday at 4:30, they gathered cross-legged on the brown
shag rug, picked at its crust of mud and glitter and Elmer's
glue, and leaned against the picture book shelves.

I had five regulars, and a couple of them would have come
seven days a week if they could. Ian Drake came with chicken pox,
and with a broken leg. He came even when he knew it had been
canceled that week, and sat there reading aloud to himself. And
then each week there were two or three extras whose parents happened to need a babysitter. They'd squirm through chapters 8 and
9 of a book they couldn't follow, pulling strings from their socks
and then flossing their teeth with them.

That fall, five years ago, we were halfway through *Matilda*. Ian
came galloping up to me before reading time, our fourth week into
the book.

"I told my mom we're reading *Little House in the Big Woods*
again. I don't think she'd be a fan of *Matilda* too much. She didn't

even like *Fantastic Mr. Fox.*" He forked his fingers through his hair. "Are we *capisce?*"

I nodded. "We don't want your mom to worry." We hadn't gotten to the magic part yet, but Ian had read it before, secretly, crouched on the floor by the Roald Dahl shelf. He knew what was coming.

He skipped off down the biography aisle, then wandered back up through science, his head tilted sideways to read the spines.

Loraine came up beside me—Loraine Best, the head librarian, who thank God hadn't heard our collusions—and watched the first few children gather on the rug. She came downstairs some Fridays just to smile and nod at the mothers as they dropped them off, as if she had some hand in Chapter Book Hour. As if her reading three minutes of *Green Eggs and Ham* wouldn't make half the children cry and the others raise their hands to ask if she was a good witch or a bad witch.

Ian disappeared again, then walked up through American History, touching each book in the top right-hand row. "He practically lives here, doesn't he?" Loraine whispered. "That little homosexual boy."

"He's ten years old!" I said. "I doubt he's *anything*-sexual."

"Well I'm sorry, Lucy, I have nothing against him, but that child is a gay." She said it with the same tone of pleasure at her own imagined magnanimity that my father used every time he referred to "Ophelia, my black secretary."

Over in fiction now, Ian stood on tiptoes to pull a large green book from a high shelf. A mystery: the blue sticker-man with his magnifying glass peered from the spine. Ian sat on the floor and started in on the first page as if it indeed contained all the mysteries of the world, as if everything in the universe could be solved by page 132. His glasses caught the fluorescent light, two yellow disks over the pages. He didn't move until the other children began gathering and Loraine bent down beside him and said, "Everyone's waiting for you." We weren't—Tony didn't even have his coat off yet—but Ian scooted on his rear all the way across the floor to join us, without ever looking up from the book.

We had five listeners that day, all regulars.

"All right," I said, hoping Loraine would make her exit now, "where did we leave off?"

"Miss Trunchbull yelled because they didn't know their math," said Melissa.

"And she yelled at Miss Honey."

"And they were learning their threes."

Ian sighed loudly and held up his hand.

"Yes?"

"That was all two weeks ago. BUT, when last we left our heroine, she was learning of Miss Trunchbull's history as a hammer thrower, and also we were learning of the many torture devices she kept in her office."

"Thank you, Ian." He grinned at me. Loraine rolled her eyes—whether at me or Ian, I wasn't sure—and tottered back to the stairs. I almost always had to cut Ian off, but he didn't mind. Short of burning down the library there was nothing I could do that would push him away. I was keeping *Tales of a Fourth Grade Nothing* behind the desk to sneak to him whenever he came without his babysitter. Almost every afternoon for the past week he had run downstairs and stuck his head over my desk, panting.

Back then, before that long winter, Ian reminded me most of a helium balloon. Not just his voice, but the way he'd look straight up when he talked and bounce around on his toes as if he were struggling not to take off.

(Did he have a predecessor? asks Humbert.

No. No, he didn't. I'd never met anyone like him in my life.)

Whenever he couldn't find a book he liked, he'd come lean on the desk. "What should I *read?*"

"*How to Stop Whining,*" I'd say, or "*An Introduction to the Computer Catalogue,*" but he knew I was kidding. He knew it was my favorite question in the world. Then I'd pick something for him— *D'Aulaires' Greek Myths* one time, *The Wheel on the School* another. He usually liked what I picked, and the *D'Aulaires'* launched him on a mythology spree that lasted a good two months.

Because Loraine warned me early on about Ian's mother, I made sure he read books with innocuous titles and pleasant covers. Nothing scary-looking, no *Egypt Game*. When he was eight, he came with a babysitter and borrowed *Theater Shoes*. He returned it the next day and told me he was only allowed to read "boy books."

Fortunately, his mother didn't seem to have a great knowledge of children's literature. So *My Side of the Mountain* crept under the radar, and *From the Mixed-up Files of Mrs. Basil E. Frankweiler*. Both books about running away, I realized later, though I swear at the time it never crossed my mind.

We finished two chapters and then I stalled until 5:30, when half the mothers would bounce down the stairs in their tennis skirts and the other half would emerge with their toddlers from the picture book pit. "Who is the hero of this book?" I asked. This was easy. It was always the main character. In children's books, there is rarely an antihero, an unreliable narrator.

Aaron sounded like he'd been practicing his answer for days: "Matilda is really the hero, but Miss Honey is kind of a hero, too, because she's very nice."

"Who's the villain?"

"Mrs. Crunchable!" shouted Tessa. "Even though she's the principal! And principals are usually nice!"

"Yes," I said, "I think you're right." Even when the bad guy isn't a man in a black mask, they have a fairly good sense of villainy. A few bright ones understand how broad the category can be.

"Because a villain could be anyone, like a bunny in your garden," Tessa said.

"Could it even be someone's parents?" I asked. I wanted them to think about Matilda's wretched, TV-addicted mother and father, the book's other antagonists.

"Yeah," said Tony, "like if your mom has a gun."

These were wise, modern children, and they knew: a mother could be a witch, a child could be a criminal. A librarian could be a thief.

Let's call the scene of the crime Hannibal, Missouri (Of course there's a real Hannibal out there minding its own business, living on Twain tourism and river water. I only ask to borrow its name.) This Hannibal had no river, but it had a highway straight through town, and if you drove past and saw only the McDonald's, the Citgo, the grime and corn and car fumes, you'd never know the hedged lawns, the schools with untattered flags, the big houses to the west and the smaller ones east with their gravel drives and shiny mailboxes.

And there was the library, right off the main road, its unfortunate '70s brick architecture masked by Fall Fest banners and three waist-high iron squirrels. Noble squirrels, their heads in the air, they stood sentry to the book drop and public entrance. Before pushing open the heavy front doors, every child felt compelled to touch each one, or to brush the snow off the tails, or even to climb up and perch on the tallest squirrel's head. Every child somehow believed these acts forbidden. Thundering down the stairs to the basement, the children's cheeks were red. They passed my desk in bright, puffed-up parkas. Some smiled, some practically shouted their greetings, some avoided my eyes completely.

At twenty-six I was the head children's librarian only because I was willing to work more hours than the other two (much older) women, Sarah-Ann and Irene, who seemed to see the library as some kind of volunteer work, like a soup kitchen.

"We're so lucky they give us their time," said Loraine. Which was true, as they were often busy remodeling entire rooms.

I was four years out of college, had started biting my nails again, and was down to two adult friends. I lived alone in an apartment two towns over. A simple maiden lady librarian.

Observe, for the record, my genetic makeup, indicating a slight predisposition for criminal behavior, a hereditary proclivity for running away, and the chromosomal guarantor for lifelong self-flagellation.

Things Inherited from my Father:

—Taste for mud-thick coffee.
—Two bony knots on my forehead, one above each
eye, just below the hairline. (No trauma at birth, no
drop to the floor, just confused nurses rubbing my
brow, my father baring his own in explanation. If
we two are not the villains of the story, why these
family horns?)

—A revolutionary temperament, dating far past my
great-grandfather the Bolshevik.

—Half a family name, Hulkinov shortened to Hull
by a New York judge, the joke lost on my father's
immigrant ears as he stood in his refugee shoes, a
hull of his Russian self.

—Pale Russian hair, the color of absolutely nothing.

—The family crest my father brought all the way
from Moscow on a thick gold ring, with its carv-
ing of a man—book in right hand, severed head
on pike in left. (This most famous Hulkinov was
a seventeenth-century scholar-warrior, a man who
heard the distant trumpets, left his careful books,
fought for justice or freedom or honor. And here
I am, the end of the line: twenty-first-century
librarian-felon.)

Deep Russian guilt.

Things Inherited from my Mother:

—Mile-thick American Jewish guilt.

These are the setting and main characters. We are nestled into
our beanbags: let us begin.

("Where's Papa going with that ax?" said Fern.)

2

Trouble, Right Here in River City

A woman came down the stairs alone one afternoon early in October, in slacks and heels and a brown silk blouse. Obviously a parent, not a bedraggled teacher or nanny or tutor. Beautiful, with red hair in a ponytail that didn't taper sadly like mine, but ended straight and thick like an actual horse's tail. She put a book on the counter. Her silver earrings swung in sync. I'd never seen her before.

"Are you busy?"

I capped my pen and smiled. "Sure. No."

"I'm Ian's mommy."

"I'm sorry?" She was making such insistent eye contact that I couldn't quite process her words.

"My son is Ian Drake?"

"Oh, *Ian*. Yes, of course. How can I help you?" I was a little astonished to realize that I'd never encountered this woman before. And to realize that I'd never thought about it, even with all the discussion of what books his mother would or would not approve. When Ian was younger, he always came with a babysitter. Now he often came alone on his bike, wearing an empty backpack that he could fill with books.

"Well, he brought home this novel, *Tuck Everlasting?*" She shoved it closer to me, as if I might want to look it over. "And I'm sure this is just a wonderful book for slightly older children, and we *so* appreciate your suggestions. He's just a little sensitive." She laughed lightly and leaned forward. "What Ian really needs right now are books with the breath of God in them."

"The breath of God."

"I know you do such a job of nourishing their minds, but of course we also need reading that will nourish our souls. Each one of us." She smiled, eyebrows raised. "And Ian's still so young, he needs your help. I'm sure you can do that for me, Sarah-Ann."

I must have stared with my mouth open, until I saw that I'd left Sarah-Ann's nameplate on the front of the desk. I was strangely flattered that Ian hadn't told her my name, that our daily conversations were something he wanted to keep private. I wasn't about to correct her. If she thought Sarah-Ann Drummond was the one in charge of selecting books with the breath of God, so much the better.

I smiled, making sure she was done. "Actually, since we're a public library, we don't censor what any of our patrons access. It's our job to make everything available. Although *parents* can certainly choose for their children." I could have gone on at length, but I found myself holding back. I didn't want her to spook and tell Ian he couldn't come to the library anymore, and (as much as I wasn't normally a fan of unaccompanied children in the library) I didn't think his reading experience would be enhanced by this particular mother hanging over his shoulder, making sure all the words Judy Blume wrote were sufficiently God-suffused. So I certainly wasn't going to mention that he could also check out any of the books upstairs in the adult section and access pretty much any Web site in the world from our computers.

"He really does love the library," she said. She was missing a rich southern accent, I realized, one of those charming Kentucky belle ones. It would have complemented her perfectly. She pulled a folded piece of notepaper out of her purse, thick cream with the name *Janet Marcus Drake* in shiny pale blue script at the top. "This is a list of the content matter I'd like him to avoid." She had abruptly flipped from the southern belle and was now putting on the extremely businesslike air of those perfectionist women who'd only worked in the professional world for two or three years before stopping to have children and were now terrified of not being taken seriously. She handed the list over and waited, as if she expected me to read it aloud. It read:

—Witchcraft/Wizardry
—Magic
—Satanism/Occult Religions, etc.
—Adult Content Matter
—Weaponry
—The Theory of Evolution
—Halloween
—Roald Dahl, Lois Lowry, Harry Potter, and similar authors

"You understand what is meant by adult content matter?"

I managed, somehow, to open my mouth and assure her that I did.

"And I neglected to list it, but I also understand that you have candy available for the children." She didn't need to put it so formally. She was staring right at the bowl of Jolly Ranchers on the edge of my desk. "I just don't want him running around here with a sugar high!" And she laughed again, right back to Scarlett O'Hara on the porch.

Because I couldn't think of anything nonprofane to say at that moment, I said nothing. It wasn't so much good manners or restraint as a sort of paralysis of the tongue. I wanted to ask her if she'd ever heard of the First Amendment, if she was aware that Harry Potter was not an author, if she thought we had books about Satanism lying around the children's section, if she was under the impression that I was Ian's babysitter, reading tutor, or camp counselor. Instead I took my pen and added another line to her list: "No candy."

"I'm so glad for your cooperation, Sarah-Ann," she said.

I wanted to get rid of her, and I wanted to placate her, but I couldn't sit there and make a verbal contract to defy the Constitution. So I said, "What I can do is avoid recommending books with this content."

"But surely you understand that he might find it on his own."

I nodded, which she was free to interpret however she wished, and said (reassuringly, conclusively), "I have it all written down here." I patted the list and stood to extend my hand.

A girl came up behind her with a stack of books. Mrs. Drake looked back at her, winked at me as she shook my hand, and walked away.

The girl heaved the stack onto the counter. Seven books, all on Marco Polo.

———

I spent the next few minutes leaning back in my chair, practicing my yoga breathing and trying to figure out if I'd just compromised my morals. I was still clutching Janet Drake's folded list. The next thing I registered was Loraine swaying down the stairs, then lurching forward to lean on my desk with both hands. Her short brown hair was a mess, clumps of it sticking to her forehead in a lacquer of gel and sweat.

"*Lucy*," she said, much too loudly. "Were you able to calm that woman down?"

"Yes." I slid my feet back into my shoes. "She tried to give me this list." I started to unfold it, but Loraine waved her hand. She'd seen it already.

"Just don't let him check out any more wizard books. Leave a note for Sarah-Ann and Irene, too."

I was almost used to Loraine by that point, to her philosophy that if the community was ever going to buy us new chairs, we needed to keep the community happy, civil liberties be damned. She was usually in favor of quickly and permanently removing from the library any book that any patron bothered complaining about. Instead of calling her an alcoholic old bat, instead of picking up the phone to alert the ACLU, I took the path of least resistance. I said, "How am I supposed to do that, exactly?"

Loraine swayed slightly and gripped the edge of the counter. Her fingernails were painted dark red, as was the skin around each nail. "Oh, just tell him it's a reference book or something. Tell him it can't be checked out."

"Sure." I wasn't at all concerned about Loraine enforcing this, or even remembering it a month later. And if she tried to fire me because I'd checked out a book to a patron of the public library, I'd have so much free legal representation within ten minutes that her gin-soaked head would spin.

"Are you feeling ill, Lucy? I only ask because your shirt is so wrinkled."

"I'm just fine."

"Well, yes, I'm sure you are." She took her hand off the counter and walked carefully off to the children's bathroom.

At 6:00 I turned off the computer, re-shelved the books from the cart, and went upstairs. Rocky wheeled himself out from behind the desk as I came up. He wore glasses with black frames and lenses so thick they distorted his eyes, which were already somewhat swallowed by his heavy cheeks. Several patrons had confided in me (as I nodded, somewhat horrified) that they were "surprised he could speak so articulately."

"Coffee?"

"Of course," I said.

We locked up and went across the street to the sandwich place. Rocky waited outside, because there was a step to get in, and I brought his coffee out. I sat down on the sidewalk bench and he wheeled up beside me. I sipped my coffee through the hole in the lid and burned my tongue. "So Ian Drake's mother yelled at me today," I said, which wasn't true but was exactly how I felt afterward. "And then Loraine yelled at me about Ian's mother." I was like an eight-year-old, calling it "yelling" just because I hadn't liked it. "She's telling me to censor his reading. *Loraine* is."

He opened his coffee and blew on it. Why was I always the one to burn my tongue? Why did everyone else think to take these precautions?

"But you know to ignore her. Are you actually letting this bother you?" Rocky's persistent viewpoint was that I took everything too personally. And he was so used to Loraine, after twelve years in the library, that he couldn't be shocked by anything she did. He also seemed, lately, to take a perverse pleasure in pointing out my own naïveté by acting as if he himself had expected, and was even bored by, all unusual human behavior: a four-year-old projectile vomiting on our new Britannica set, Loraine storing an old Sprite bottle filled with vodka in the staff refrigerator, the president of the United States claiming Jesus wanted us to be at war. "Do you have your theme for the summer?" he said. He wasn't going to let me fixate.

"No." I would spend a good part of my winter and spring making flyers and cutting out construction paper race cars or comets to hang on the north wall for Summer Reading Club. There were kits you could order, of course, but I believed they were soulless, and Loraine believed they were expensive. "Loraine wants something about a magic journey again." Two years earlier, the theme had been "There Is No Frigate Like a Book," which was disastrous because none of the children knew what a frigate was, and several parents thought it was something dirty.

"'Devour a Book'? You could have a shark eating a book. A dinosaur."

"Not bad."

"It's better than the frigate."

I turned sideways on the bench and put my feet up. "How about 'Witchcraft and the Satanic Occult'?"

"'Being and Nothingness'! You could give them little Sartre badges!"

"'Civilization and Its Discontents!'"

We kept at this for a while, and at least it made me feel better. Which seemed to be our entire relationship. Probably my fault.

We went to old movies together at the Film Forum—not dates, just movies no one else wanted to see—and we rolled our eyes at each other all day long, till he decided I was overreacting and told me so.

He tugged at the end of my sweater sleeve. "You told me to give you hell if you ever wore a cardigan again."

"It's cold."

"I'm just following orders."

I hated that I'd started to look like a librarian. This wasn't right. In college, I'd smoked things. My first car had angry bumper stickers. I came from a long line of revolutionaries.

I stood up and stretched, and then felt irrationally guilty for doing that in front of Rocky, who couldn't. I got so tired of *sitting* all day, and I was sure it would give me gangrene or hemorrhoids. I made excuses at work to walk through the aisles. The return cart rarely had three books on it, because I was out of my seat to re-shelve them every five minutes.

And for what portion of human history had people even had desk jobs? Maybe the last four hundred years, out of four million? It wasn't natural.

My father's favorite joke: What is one Russian? A nihilist. What are two Russians? A game of chess. What are three Russians? A revolution.

But what do you call a would-be revolutionary stuck at a desk? Antsy, maybe. Trouble. A dormant volcano.

3

The Nothing Hand

On Halloween, I passed out candy from behind my desk to the costumed children whose parents preferred they trick-or-treat in businesses rather than the ostensibly razor-blade-ridden homes of East Hannibal. I had put a poster on the front door that week declaring that children dressed as a character from a book got two times the candy plus a bookmark, but so far we'd had only two Harry Potters, one Dorothy, and a boy who claimed Michael Jordan counted because there were a lot of books about him.

Ian came down the stairs with his mother's manicured hand on his shoulder. I quickly grabbed my nameplate and stuffed it in the top drawer. I wondered if I'd ever see Ian alone again. He wasn't dressed up, just wearing his regular blue coat. I remembered from his mother's list that they didn't do Halloween, but he peered a long time through his glasses at the two children leaving in their space suits before he showed his mother where the C. S. Lewis shelf was. A few minutes later, Mrs. Drake went to the chapter book feature shelf, where I'd put out a bunch of forgotten New-bery winners and runners-up. She was frowning and skimming *The Golden Goblet* when Ian shuffled up to the desk. He pushed his left hand out from where it had been hiding in the sleeve of his coat. His index finger was wrapped in wrinkled tinfoil, with a pointed top and some Sharpie lines indicating a face.

"Miss Hull!" he whispered. "I'm not dressed up, but my finger is the Tin Woodman!"

I laughed and mouthed "Oh my goodness" and gave him two Kit Kats and a bookmark.

He shoved the candy in his pocket and pulled his hand back up his sleeve just as his mother came to the desk with an armload of books. A few Hardy Boys and some biographies, but nothing I thought Ian would like. I stamped them a little vigorously, and smiled back as she wished me a wonderful evening.

In those moments of small-town pettiness, in those moments where I realized I'd forever be on the responsible adult side of the Halloween candy exchange, in those moments where I looked down and saw myself wearing sensible shoes, I might have cursed my ending up in Hannibal. I could have been living in a loft in Brooklyn, or backpacking across Spain with my father's money, or finishing a PhD. But I didn't regret it, at least not totally, because the randomness—the anonymous and insipid randomness—was the appeal. My father would have hooked me up with a hundred good jobs, or at least "good" in the monetary sense. He would have paid for the most self-indulgent, nonfunded MFA in filmmaking at the most expensive university in the country.

But four years earlier, finishing up my English degree, I had stubbornly refused to tell him if I even had a job lined up at all. That April, I'd walked across campus to the Career Development, right next to the health center, and sat in a soft plastic chair until a woman I'd never seen before—a woman with lacquered white hair—welcomed me into her office and asked me a series of increasingly perplexed questions about what I wanted to do with my life. She had a hard time believing that a student graduating magna cum laude could care so very little where she went next. She ended up having her secretary print out a fifty-page list of the addresses and job titles of all the alumnae in the database whose careers were considered to be somehow "in the field of English." These people, presumably, would look out for one of their own and help me find a job. I was a little disappointed, after deliberately turning my back on my father and his connections, to be handed fifty pages of additional connections. But at least they were *my* connections, not his. The people on the list were teachers, technical writers, tutors, translators, and journalists. Loraine Best, class of '65, was one of the only ones with a library job, but this wasn't why I wrote to her. I simply started e-mailing every alum in alphabetical order, until it was time for midterms. I got from Aaronson to Chernack, and then I spent three weeks studying and drinking beer and breaking up with my boyfriend and waiting. Going alphabetically and without discrimination made it seem less like milking the connections and more like leaving it up to chance. We Russians have always been good at roulette.

I had no library science degree and no experience, but Loraine happened to need a children's librarian fast, after the old one was diagnosed with stage three breast cancer. She hadn't even had time yet to advertise the job, and so when my letter arrived she took it as an answer to her prayers and hired me over the phone.

I was offered the job while sitting on the top bunk of my dorm room, wearing underwear and a Violent Femmes T-shirt and wooly socks. Kate Phelps had died from the cancer by the time I rolled into town that June.

And of course Loraine threw it back in my face every few weeks: "I hired you sight unseen because I knew I was getting a Mount Holyoke graduate, and I thought that guaranteed a certain work ethic."

When I told my parents I'd be working the children's desk at a small library in a small town in Missouri, my father said, "This is because of some boyfriend? There are a million good boys in Chicago, and many of them are Russian. At some point you are wanting to be an *adult* librarian, no? I say this because you need a challenge. There are university libraries where I can pull on the strings."

My mother said, "At least you'll be in driving distance." When she didn't add anything else, I realized this was the kindest thing she could think to say.

Later that same fall, Ian entered the children's fiction contest. Five minutes before the deadline, he came downstairs alone to hand me his story, in a cover made of purple construction paper and decorated with a bright yellow hand cut from a Cheerios box. It was called "The Nothing Hand." He pushed his sweaty hair back and bounced up and down as if he expected me to read it right then.

"This looks great," I said, and thumbed through the typed pages for his benefit. I looked up at him leaning over my desk, at his hair that was now stuck straight back with sweat, and at the strange marks I'd never noticed before above his left eyebrow. There were four little pink indented dots, all in a straight row, evenly spaced a few millimeters apart. Could that have been from a fork? I'd heard that teachers had to keep files on any suspicious bruises or wounds, and I wondered if I should start doing the same. I was thinking also of Emily Alden, with that huge bruise on her neck last winter that she claimed was from her brother hitting her with a snowball.

"It's about this hand," Ian was saying, "that's totally invisible, and it's detached from any human body. It's kind of like a Greek myth, but there's a mortal at the end, and it's on its own separate page. So at the end of the story, you have to guess what the mortal is, and then you can turn the page and see if you were right."

"So there's a *moral*?"

"No, a mortal, because of how it's inspired by Greek myths. Get it? It's a joke. Also, I forgot page numbers."

"I'll bend the rules for you," I said. I already knew it would win first prize for the fifth grade, because the only other entry was about some kind of ninja battle. I read the beginning as soon as he left. He'd printed it out in dark blue:

THE NOTHING HAND
by Ian Alistair Drake
Grade 5

There once was a hand that was made of nothing. It was invisible to all of your senses but it could do whatever it would like. Here was its life:

Day 1: Steal doughnuts and hide.
Day 2: Eat the doughnuts it stole, through a special mouth that it had.

Day 3: Get revenge on bullies through using trickery.

Day 4: Hide under rocks in the forest, waiting for
trouble.

I flipped to the end to see the moral.

Mortal: Don't tell even the rabbits where you're hiding, because rabbits can't keep a secret.

I wondered why an invisible hand would need to hide. The
first year I ran the contest, a very fat little boy had handed in a
story about children who could shrink themselves to two inches
tall and ride around in toy cars. I remembered thinking that children's imaginary worlds were so closely connected with desire,
how that poor boy had so obviously wanted to shrink. So what
did *this* mean, coming from a child who was loud and omnipres-
ent and somewhat demanding—this wish for double invisibility?
Although, come to think of it, it wasn't a coincidence he spent all
his free time in a quiet room below ground, his face buried in biographies of Houdini. To the town of Hannibal, he was half-invisible
already.

I'd become friends with a woman named Sophie Bennett
who was my age and taught fourth grade at Hannibal Day, and I
decided to ask her about Ian the next time she came in. She poked
through nonfiction for an hour almost every weekend, checking
out whole armloads of books about Aztecs or mushrooms. That
Sunday afternoon she sank loudly into one of the child-sized computer chairs near my desk.

"I am so fucking sick," she said. She put her big canvas bag on
the floor beside her and looked around the room to see who was

there. She hated running into her students. A little girl who had come in by herself was coloring at a table, an older boy was playing computer games, and a couple of middle schoolers were working quietly with tutors. "I think I've had twelve healthy days since I started teaching. And now all my kids have lice. Seriously, don't touch anyone. Don't even touch their coats."

I laughed and walked in front of the desk so we could talk more quietly. "I have a question for you," I said, sitting next to her in one of the computer chairs. She took a big plastic hair clip out of her bag, put it in her mouth to hold it, and started gathering a ponytail.

"Hmm."

"Okay, Ian Drake. He's in fifth grade. Did you teach him last year?"

"No," she said, "I think Julie Leonard had him. But his family is legendary. Big nightmare."

"I actually had this whole confrontation with the mother. She comes down here, and she goes, 'My son needs to read holy books!' I've always had this whole speech prepared for that kind of occasion, where I single-handedly defend the First Amendment. And then she comes in here and the whole thing is just so *silly*, and I go totally blank."

"Yeah, no, they're fucking nuts." She looked around the room again, just in case. The little girl had her crayon lifted above her head and was apparently drawing in the air. "Very religious, which you might have gathered. The mother I think has had some psychiatric problems, and she's very definitely anorexic."

"I didn't notice," I said. I tried to think back. Her boniness had just seemed part of her personality.

"I mean, the good thing is Ian doesn't seem affected by it. He can be *very* moody and melodramatic, but that's just his big act. He's really the happiest kid in the world. He got up there last year in the spring musical and they have this cancan line, of all things, and he's the worst person in it, knocking everyone over, but he has this huge showbiz smile on his face. Totally into it. He'll do fine no matter what. Shit will hit the fan when he announces he's gay, but he'll get through it."

I laughed. "My God, people need to *stop* that."

Though to be honest, my indignant insistence that Ian wasn't anything-sexual wasn't entirely sincere. The question had crossed my mind plenty of times, particularly during his phase of reading books about furniture history, and I'd always imagined that some-day he'd come visit me with his partner and his adopted Chinese daughter, and I'd get to ask him what it was like growing up in Hannibal, and he'd tell me that reading had saved his life. And even if he wasn't gay, he'd come back and visit me anyway, with his cute wife and his twin boys who looked just like him, and then for some reason the "reading saved my life" part was still there.

Three girls came downstairs right then with backpacks and waved, giggling, at Sophie. She raised her eyebrows at me and bit her lip: we should stop talking.

"Okay," she said once the girls had settled in by the series shelf, "so what I need is books about lying. Picture books, folktales, whatever you got. We're having a little epidemic."

I found her some Abe Lincoln stories and a Chinese folktale called "The Empty Pot."

"Seriously, I think he's okay," she whispered as I was stamping the books. "You should see the dad, though. I think *he's* gay. That's why the mother's miserable. He's so far in the closet he's, like, back in fucking *Narnia*. Do I owe money?"

"Of course you do," I said, handing her the books and her receipt.

"Thanks, babe." She grinned and jingled her keys and headed upstairs.

My father called that night, quite worked up. "There are librarians on the Chicago news! They are yelling about this USA Patriot Act!" My father has a Russian accent that I don't register in person, but can catch the edges of over the phone or on my answering machine or when he tries to pepper his speech with strained American expressions like "I'm eating humble pie." It gives me something to do when I don't want to listen to what he's saying. To everyone else, apparently, his accent sounds fairly thick. "Lucy, tell me about this: does the George W. Bush government come and ask you questions?"

"I don't think the government is too interested in picture books."

"Let's say if a man with swarthy skin and a dark beard checks out a book about the making of bombs, does your boss telephone the FBI? Is the FBI already in the computer?"

I was sure that if the government contacted Loraine, she'd be one of the only librarians in the country who was thrilled to cooperate. "I wouldn't know. If they ask you for records, they simultaneously slap you with a lifetime gag order."

"Lucy, listen. This is Soviet-style tactics. If you have a head with your shoulders, you get out of this library business right away. This is how the trouble starts." I'd heard the KGB comparison a lot lately, most notably from Rocky, but hearing it in a Russian accent made it sound like an old Yakov Smirnoff routine. ("In Soviet Russia, library book checks *you* out!")

"I agree," I said. "But they really don't care who's borrowing the Dr. Seuss."

"These librarians on the news were shredding all their documents and erasing computer files. This is not a good idea, either. You trust me about this, as a victim of the Soviets. So you are damned if you help them and you are damned if you fight against them. This is not a good time to work in a library."

"Sure it is," I said. "Because of the enormous paycheck. I'll just keep my head down."

Although, sure, I'd have been happier if we still just used the borrower cards in their little paper pockets. Those could have been burned in an emergency, could have been tossed out the window as the Feds approached, or swapped with the card in the back of *Misty of Chincoteague*. I was all for catching terrorists, but not at the cost of turning the libraries from temples of information into mousetraps. Perhaps because I had no library science degree, I tended to overcompensate by taking the First Amendment a little more seriously than some other librarians. And of course I'd internalized my father's fear of Big Brother governments.

There was a nostalgia element for me, too, wishing for those borrower cards. Quite a few of my older books still had them, left behind when we went to computer in 1991. They chronicled all the children who read a book in the months or years or even decades before that time, but then they just stopped, as if civilization had come to an abrupt end. I always read the names as I re-shelved, and I'd discovered that certain ones popped up on hundreds of the lists. Allie Royston, for example, who must have been about ten years old in 1989, seemed to have read every horse book ever written. Another child checked out *Ellen Tebbits* six times in two years. These lists catalogued the best minds of each generation—the self-motivated, the literate, the curious, the insatiable. If we still used them, Ian's name would be in half the books. "Lucy, I tell you what you should do. First, you get out of this library job and you get a good new job. And then you write articles for all the newspapers. You are smarter than most of these librarian people, and you can write a good letter that explains what exactly is wrong with the USA Patriot Act. Freedom of the press!"

"Dad, people have already tried that. Thousands and thousands of people."

"Ah, but you have a personal experience of being a librarian, and you can say how this has affected you!"

"It really hasn't affected me at all."

"Lucy, you are twenty-six, okay? You have to ask, what have you done in these years? By the time I was twenty-six I have had an illegal capitalist business defying the Soviets, and then I have escaped the damned Soviets, at risk of life and limb, and I have started a new life in the home of the brave, okay? So if this is home of the brave, where are the brave?"

"They're getting ready for bed. They've had a long day checking out books to six-year-olds."

"Listen, my friend Shapko the Ukrainian is needing an assistant for his real estate selling. You would be good at this."

"Your friend Shapko who was arrested for mail fraud?"

"Not even indicted by grand jury! This American legal system is still good, until your George W. Bush gets his hands on it."

"I believe that's already happened, Dad."

"Exactly!"

As we hung up I wanted to shake my head and laugh, wanted to roll my eyes at someone, but at the same time I knew it must have been horrible for my father, having risked his life to leave Russia, having chosen America out of all the countries in the world, and then watching the government tighten its clench, chip away at the promised freedoms, haul young men off to Guantánamo with no charges, no lawyers, no warning. It didn't matter that it wasn't happening to him personally. The very fact that people's phones were being tapped was enough to remind him quite viscerally of pre-Yeltsin "state security."

In May of 2002, I'd been visiting my parents in their Chicago apartment when the phone rang during dinner. It was Magda Johnson, my mother's friend who'd grown up in Poland during World War II, and who now lived near Lincoln Park. I could hear her voice as my mother held the phone farther and farther from her own ear: "There are explosions in the street! Someone is shooting or bombing, and there is shouting all up and down the street!"

"It's Cinco de Mayo!" I'd called to my mother. "Tell her to turn on the news. It's just Cinco de Mayo!"

But Magda Johnson was still screaming, a five-year-old in a bomb shelter once again. For the past eight months, and maybe for the rest of her life.

And I had to remember that about my father, too: he hadn't bargained on this. He thought he'd left it behind.

I checked the clock to make sure rehearsal would be done in the theater downstairs, and then I blasted music and vacuumed. My blood pressure was up, and since it wasn't worth cursing an old Russian man for his idealism, I decided to take it out on my carpet. It never really did come clean, no matter what I did. Sections were oatmeal, sections were beige, and certain spots looked like details from crime scene photos. I had to angle the vacuum carefully around the stacks of books that served as a sort of second furniture, pedestals for coffee cups and mail and magazines. I refused to have bookshelves, horrified that I'd feel compelled to organize the books in some regimented system—Dewey or alphabetical or worse—and so the books lived in stacks, some as tall as me, in the most subjective order I could invent.

Thus Nabokov lived between Gogol and Hemingway, cradled between the Old World and the New; Willa Cather and Theodore Dreiser and Thomas Hardy were stacked together not for their chronological proximity but because they all reminded me in some way of dryness (though in Dreiser's case I think I was focused mostly on his name); George Eliot and Jane Austen shared a stack with Thackeray because all I had of his was *Vanity Fair*, and I thought that Becky Sharp would do best in the presence of ladies (and deep down I worried that if I put her next to David Copperfield, she might seduce him). Then there were various stacks of contemporary authors who I felt would get along together at cocktail parties, and there were at least three stacks of books I personally loathed but held on to just in case someone asked me to loan them a page-turner about a family of circus performers, or an experimental novel about a time-traveling nun. I'd hate to have to say that I knew the perfect book but I'd just given it away. Not that people often asked. But once in a while my landlord, Tim, or his partner, Lenny, would invite themselves in to peruse the stacks and ask the world's best question: "Hey, what do you think I should read?" It was nice to be prepared.

These stacks were my apartment's main decoration. I had some nice furniture from my parents, plus some standard-issue rectangular things from Ikea, but in the three years I'd lived there I'd never gotten around to hanging pictures. My bed was still a mattress on the floor. Maybe because of my father's family stories, the idea of having to run across a border had never been far from my mind. Excepting the books, I never liked to amass more possessions than could be moved in a cartop U-Haul. You never know when the Cossacks are going to invade.

A week later, a package arrived from my parents. It contained two issues of the Mount Holyoke alumnae magazine on which I'd never bothered changing my address, a box of Frango mints, and an editorial clipped from the *Trib* about the Patriot Act. I was flattered, really, that my father suddenly thought my job was dangerous, if not exciting. I almost wished it were true. My whole childhood, hearing stories of Russian revolutionaries and refugees, I'd been primed for a grand fight. And here I was with no one to rebel against but Loraine Best. And Janet Drake, who didn't even know my name.

I lay on my back on the floor and read in the magazine about a former classmate, one who'd lived on my freshman hall and used to burn incense and drink wine coolers, who had started a battered women's shelter in Maine and had recently spoken before Congress. On the next page was a girl who'd graduated just that spring and was measuring glacier melt when she wasn't busy collecting grant money. A woman from the class of '84 was lobbying for gay rights in California. There was a picture of her with her partner, in the nineteenth-century barn they'd restored together.

I imagined what they might write about me:

Lucy Hull, class of '02, courageously checked out *The Pushcart War* to a ten-year-old patron today, despite the preponderance therein of peashooters and the fact that the book does not in any way contain "the breath of God."

"It really wasn't a choice," said the 26-year-old Hull, who has done very little with her adult life besides stamping books, re-shelving books, and reading books aloud with funny voices. "It's basically illegal to deny a book to someone with a library card. I'm not quite sure why you're interviewing me."

Hull lives alone above a theater, frequently forgets to hydrate, and has recently developed a rash on the backs of her legs from the fabric of her desk chair.

That night, I dreamed about the borrower cards. Loraine showed me a plain red book and asked me who'd checked it out. I read her the list: Ian Drake, George W. Bush, and God Almighty.

4

The Ark

I had to give him credit: Ian was brilliant. He came one day in November with his babysitter, after several weeks of chaperoned checkouts in which he had halfheartedly borrowed various biographies and a collection of Native American myths and legends. ("They're all about crows," he said when he returned it. "My review is that this book is a little too crow-heavy.") The babysitter, Sonya, was a bedraggled Filipina woman with her own five-year-old daughter who sometimes silently accompanied them and then sat in the corner stroking the puppets. When Ian picked out chapter books, Sonya would flip them over in her hands, flick through the pages as if their appropriateness would thereby reveal itself, and then ask, "What your mother is going to say? I will show her this, okay?" Ian would invariably grab the book, shove it back on the shelf, and storm off to nonfiction.

That Saturday in November, he and Sonya came in without the five-year-old, and Ian immediately sat down at one of the computers opposite my desk—something he never did, not even to look up a book. He said, "Hey, Sonya, I'm going to play Noah's Mission online. Want to watch?"

"Your mom say no video games at the library."

Ian's voice became so shrill that I knew she'd agree to whatever he said, just to get him to stop. It was a voice like pepper spray. "This is the *one* game I'm allowed to play! And you've *seen* me play it at home! It's the one with Noah! You can *ask* her! You can call her right now and *ask* her, but she'll be really mad at you for calling because she's in the middle of her meeting, but you can call anyway!"

Sonya said, "Okay, okay, okay," and settled into the chair beside his.

It was the most inane and slow-paced computer game I'd ever seen, with graphics out of 1988. Noah had to run around collecting two of every animal, carrying them on his head back to the ark. Meanwhile, coconuts fell on him and eagles swooped down to carry off his loot. I had to cough to keep from laughing out loud when Noah died and fell off the bottom of the screen while the computer beeped away in a suddenly minor key. It normally drove me crazy when kids came in just to play games, but this one was perversely entertaining, if only for its awfulness, and I was secretly thrilled to see that Noah had nine more available lives. Sonya must have seen it too, because this was the point when she announced that she was heading upstairs to get a magazine.

Ian stared closely at the computer screen, balancing a goat on Noah's head, until Sonya had rounded the corner. Then he spun out of his chair and ran to my desk. "Mission accomplished! Wasn't that awesome? I bored her to death!" He took off the empty backpack that I realized just now he'd been wearing the whole time, and unzipped it. "Fill 'er up!"

I felt like I was on that old game show where you had three minutes to race around the supermarket finding all the things on your list. I practically trampled a roaming toddler to get at *A Wrinkle in Time*, and then I grabbed *The Westing Game* and *Haroun and the Sea of Stories* and *Five Children and It*. He followed me, holding the backpack open while I dumped things in. It was starting to look full, and I didn't want Sonya to be suspicious, but I couldn't resist adding *The Princess Bride*. I didn't know how long this load would have to last him. He zipped up and raced back to the computer, where Noah was still standing dumbly, goat on his head, unmarred by coconut or eagle. I went back to my own computer to enter all the books manually and check them out to my own account. I couldn't be sure that Loraine (or Sarah-Ann or Irene) wouldn't gladly rattle off Ian's list of checked-out books to his mother.

Sonya returned just a minute later, the latest John Grisham tucked under her arm. "God is flooding the world yet?"

"No, this game is stupid. Let's go."

"You no want to check out some books?"

"I'm just not that into reading anymore."

> (In a library in Missouri that was covered with vines
> Lived thousands of books in a hundred straight lines
> A boy came in at half past nine
> Every Saturday, rain or shine
> His book selections were clan-des-tine.)

5

Benefit

I saw Janet Drake again sooner than I wanted, though (thank God for the invisibility of the librarian) she didn't see me. Once a year all the librarians in the county wedged themselves into high heels, tried to pull the cat hair off their sweaters with masking tape, and smeared their lips with an awful tomato red that had gone stale in its tube, all to convince the benefit set of the greater Hannibal region that libraries do better with chairs and books and money. Late that November, as I walked into the Union League Club in a little black dress from college, what hit me was the smell of the people—dark and musty and masculine. It had been ages since I'd smelled cologne. I breathed it in and listened to the buzz of low voices.

Loraine wore a pale gold dress and waved her drink at me. I didn't see Rocky, but then he was easily lost in a thick, standing crowd. As I waited for my gin and tonic at the bar, I watched the professional benefit-goers warming up to their first sips of wine, and the clusters of librarians huddling in corners, their hair parted straight down the middle. This was what my father imagined I'd become. And there, just a few feet away, was Janet Drake. She looked nice, her shoulders wrapped in a shimmering green shawl, but she hugged it in close to her body and her jaw muscles pulsed tightly even as she smiled toward the half-drunk conversation around her. She said something and laughed at the same time, as if it were so funny she couldn't get it out with a straight face, but she didn't look terribly amused. I did that myself sometimes, what I called my Daisy Buchanan laugh. It was a light, airy laugh-talk that at its best sounded sparkling and witty and at its worst sounded like a choking cat. I had picked it up from a friend of my mother who pulled it off flawlessly every time, her silver jewelry jingling along in harmony. Watching Janet, I realized that I tended to do it when I was tremendously uncomfortable. I never did it consciously, and it was never genuine.

"You look like you need that," said someone beside me, and I realized I was still standing at the bar like a drunk, my gin and tonic half drained.

The man had curly hair the same color as his tuxedo. He was extremely overdressed.

"You found me out," I said. He had big shiny teeth. He held out his hand.

"I'm Glenn," he said. "I'm the penis."

"I'm sorry?"

"The pianist. For tonight." He nodded toward the empty grand piano in the corner.

"*Oh.*" Which explained the tuxedo. "I'm Lucy."

He glanced casually but not very subtly at my left hand. "Actually—I normally play percussion with the St. Louis Symphony.

I think this is called slumming it." He laughed, and the bartender handed him something brown with ice. "Are you a librarian?"

"We're easy to recognize."

"No, not at all—I mean, you just look younger. Than some of these people."

"Thank you," I said, and he finally exhaled. I told him where I worked and how little I enjoyed these events.

"I was a librarian once. At the music library at Oberlin, as an undergrad. My main job was to erase pencil marks from the last season's orchestra scores. And then as soon as I was done, they'd wrap up their next set of concerts, so I could never actually finish."

I laughed. "I spend much of my day erasing crayon marks."

"Hey, a lot of books would be improved by a little crayon!" Pretty lame, but I'd give it to him. He'd already finished his drink. "Usually I get to people-watch while I play, but I see they've turned the piano to the wall tonight." He glanced at a man in a cheap suit and apron who was jutting his chin toward the piano and tapping his watch. Glenn put down his glass and dried his hands on the cocktail napkin. "Damn. I always freeze my hands right before I have to play." He put them up to his mouth and breathed on them. He was attempting to lock me in some sort of twinkly, hypnotizing eye contact, and it was working. "Any requests?"

"Something to make them give money."

He laughed. "I'll work in 'Brother, Can You Spare a Dime?' Hey, listen." He took a deep breath, as if I didn't know what always came after the words "hey listen." "I'm rushed here, and like I said, I won't get time to mingle tonight, but I'm actually premiering a piece next weekend. Or, this orchestra is premiering *my* piece. It's jazz though, really, not at all boring. You should come." I raised my eyebrows and nodded. "I mean, I'll be up on stage and everything, but there's a party after that."

"I might be up for it," I said.

He took a business card out of his pocket, wrote a street address and "Starr Hall, 3:00, Sat., Dec. 3" and his number, and put it in my hand. He lifted my hand up toward his face and for a moment I thought he was going to kiss it. "Do you pray?"

"I'm sorry?"

"Do you play. Piano."

"Yes."

"I thought so. Good fingers." He grinned over his shoulder as he walked to the bench, his teeth white as his shirt.

I turned and saw Rocky staring at me from where he'd stationed himself by the olives. "The great thing," he'd said to me once, "is that since no one feels comfortable approaching me, no one feels awkward if I'm alone at a party. They think it's my natural state. So I don't have to worry what people think of me, and I get to sit there and observe."

"You do *not* mean that," I'd said. "And people *don't* think that, either." Watching him now, I realized they did. But there must have been a time, in grade school, at least, when it was the opposite, when children gave him all their attention, whether good or bad. I wondered when the switch happened.

My glass was empty, and as the bartender refilled it I vowed to slow down. I scratched quickly and ferociously at the backs of my thighs. My rash was worse, even though I hadn't worn shorts or a skirt for over a month. I knew it was that desk chair, though, because now my back was red, too, right up to my shoulder blades.

There were four men standing near Janet Drake, but the one straight across from her had to be her husband. He was a head

taller than everyone else, and his eyes seemed to follow a fran-
tic fly around the room. None of the other men, with their broad
shoulders and belly laughs and booming voices, could be described
as effeminate. Mr. Drake's face was scrunched into what he must
have thought was a wry smile, but it looked more like he was trying to condense his entire face into the space right between his
eyes. He appeared to be giving short answers or opinions every few
seconds, bobbing his head forward quickly like those plastic birds
that dip themselves into the water glass. He was as out of place in
the room as the librarians, despite his tan and his necktie full of
semaphore flags.

I wondered if Sonya would let Ian stay up to finish *Treasure
Island.*

Glenn started at the piano. He was good, not just the adequate
party player who can rip off a twelve-minute Andrew Lloyd Web-
ber medley. He sounded like he had at least forty fingers.

My second drink was half gone. I left the bar and headed
toward Rocky, but Loraine caught me by the shoulder. "I saw you
talking to people!" If I'd moved, she would have fallen down.

"Great party!"

"Yes, and you need to be ON. Tell them about the PROGRAMS."

"Okay," I said, and wiped her spittle off my cheek. I looked over
to check that Rocky was catching this, but he was suddenly busy
with the olives.

"And stay away from that angry woman. Don't make things
worse."

"Okay." I ducked out from under her hand, and the sudden
absence of my shoulder sent her lurching across the floor toward
a woman with an enormous sapphire necklace. Really, the more I
drank the more tempted I was to walk up and lecture Janet Drake

on the First Amendment. I loved the thought of her complaining to Loraine the next day that Sarah-Ann Drummond had accosted her at the party.

The rest of the night was a gin-flavored blur: dry tuna steak and soggy asparagus with a table of nine Hannibal socialites who couldn't stop talking about the Leukemia Ball, a slurred speech from Loraine about "gifting our precious resources to our local libraries," two hours of unexplained silent treatment from Rocky, and some superstealthy drunken spying on the Drakes. Halfway through dinner, Janet answered her phone, wrinkled her brow, said something to her husband, then laughed out a charming Daisy Buchanan explanation to the table and left the party, leading her husband by the hand. The one word I could make out with my superior lip-reading skills was "babysitter." As in, "Our son has whined the babysitter into calling us and making us come home."

I left a little early myself, and if Rocky wasn't going to talk to me, he could find someone else to help him into his van afterward. I wanted to ask him what was wrong, but underlying all my interactions with Rocky was the remote fear that he would suddenly tell me he loved me. I didn't know if it was true or not, and I had convinced myself that it probably wasn't. But the thought had occurred to me about a year back, and unlike most imaginary conversations I had with people in the mirror, I couldn't think of a good ending to that one.

On the way out, I put a dime on Glenn's piano along with my phone number.

When I parked back home, I could tell that the actors were still in rehearsal: no lights on upstairs, extra cars in the lot. The building (redbrick, two towns north of Hannibal) was home to the George Spelvin Memorial Theater, and I was neighbor to its five full-time company members, all of questionable mental health.

One of the original actors had owned the building and willed it to the troupe. So there was no official superintendent, just Tim the artistic director with his short blond ponytail. I'd seen him tacking up flyers for the open apartment on the lobby bulletin at the library one morning, after I'd lived for a year in an expensive apartment in Woodward that smelled like buttermilk. I didn't say anything to him then, but on my way out of work I tore off one of the little orange tags at the bottom of the paper. I'd seen him tearing off the first three himself that morning. I called the next day and he showed me the place that night.

"The walls are superthin," Tim had said as I followed him up the world's narrowest staircase. "But we're all in either rehearsal or performance every night, so it should be quiet when you get home. Of course," he said, turning around, scratching his head, smiling, "I don't know what performances sound like from up here." His teeth were yellow. His face was tan, but with thin untanned lines spreading from his eyes and mouth where wrinkles would later appear, as if he spent all day grinning into the sun. He started climbing again. "My own apartment is the one right next door," he said, "and my partner, Lenny, is usually up here in the evenings, but he's quiet. He's the only one who isn't an actor. Don't even ask me what he does, I don't even know what it's called. There are numbers involved."

"I really don't mind noise." I had made the mistake earlier of telling him I was a librarian. We came to what would be my door. "I work in the children's section. It's not like some great sanctuary of calm."

The apartment was tiny and ancient, with loud hinges, and

the kitchen was lined with heavy wooden cupboards. It smelled like cigarettes. The bathroom mirror was not a cabinet. I wrote him a check right there, holding it against the wall because there was nothing else to write on, and he was so happy that he picked me up and carried me out the door.

It was a good place to live. I could use the washing machine in the costume room, and I could get in free to the plays and even bring friends. I just couldn't run the dishwasher or flush the toilet between six and eleven, and I couldn't wear shoes in my kitchen, since it was right above the stage. Occasionally, I'd worry that Tim and Lenny were in the middle of some horrible domestic dispute, only to realize they were just running lines.

That night, though, as I collapsed onto my mattress still dressed, I could tell something was off. The rehearsal was so loud I could hear it from upstairs. I could sometimes hear plays when my windows were open to warm weather and the sound came through the wonky old vents and bounced off the bakery next door, but it was November. And late. And the play was *Uncle Vanya*—not usually a raucous affair, aside from the gunshots. Half an hour later, I was still awake and the noise was louder, coming up the stairs, and then someone was banging on my door.

When I opened it, Tim practically fell into the room. There were at least twelve people behind him—the actors and the sometimes-actors and the stage crew and Lenny—all laughing hysterically, but instinctively trying to keep the noise down, as if there were anyone left in the building to wake up. Tim said, "Oh my God, Lucy, were you asleep? We're so sorry!"

"No! I just got in!" I don't know why I was always so anxious to prove I wasn't one of *those* librarians, the ones who had left the benefit early to feed their cats.

"We need your help! You and only you! And you can't tell!" He lay down on my floor, limbs splayed like a starfish, and the others poured in behind him, one carrying a dingy wedding dress.

Apparently, Beth Hopkins, the red-haired actress who lived right above me, had left town right after rehearsal and needed to be revenged for some past prank involving the prop table. They had spent the past two hours replicating every photograph in her apartment with themselves as the subjects, taking on the same poses. So her brother shaking hands with Senator Glass would be replaced in its frame by Tim shaking hands with the assistant stage manager. Tim showed me that one on his digital camera—they'd both donned suits and were standing on the stage. "Lenny can change the background with his computer!" The woman who was currently playing Yelena cradled a baby doll in another shot. They had done fifteen photos already. They were hoping it would take Beth Hopkins several days to notice the changes.

Lenny showed me a framed photo he'd carried in with him. "This is you, okay?" It was a bride and groom, dancing in a ball-room. "You look *exactly* like this woman. Don't you think? You both have that sort of Audrey Hepburn tiny-person thing, but with the long hair, right?"

I didn't have much choice—and by now I was laughing too, caught up in the theatrics of it all—and so I ran to the bathroom to put on the dress, still musty from whatever production of *Much Ado About Nothing* it had last been washed for. When I came back out, feeling only slightly creepy and Miss Havisham-y, they had moved my coffee table and TV to make room for the crowd scene. I posed, dancing, with Lenny, whose complexion came closest to that of the Asian groom in the photo. Someone had put Ella Fitzgerald on my stereo. Tim held the camera and directed us all, telling the fake wedding guests to look happier, to cover their faces a little if they could, telling me to step more in front of Lenny and gaze into his eyes.

They got three or four good shots, then ran off to shoot some sort of night scene on the roof. I was strangely deflated when they left. It didn't feel quite right to invite myself along, and I had to work the next morning, but I still felt somehow that these were my people—these crazy, brave, and unapologetic souls—and yet, as useful as I'd been as a prop, they had failed to scoop me up and adopt me, to recognize me as one of their own.

They'd mistaken me for a librarian.

6

It's Only an Origami Moon

There are two possible explanations for the gift Ian gave me that December. One is that he knew only subconsciously what he was doing. The other is that he was making a conscious cry for help. But I don't believe it could have happened by chance. Was it Freud who said there's no such thing as a mistake?

It was December first ("The first day of Advent!" he announced), and he came clomping down the stairs, tracking ice chunks and salt to my desk. He reached into his coat pocket and handed me a complicated piece of origami, made of white paper and decorated in red and green marker around the edges. I held it up and tried to decide what it was, but I knew better than to guess out loud. The last origami he'd given me was supposed to represent Elvis's head.

"It's a Jesus!" he said. "In a manger!" Ian's glasses were covered in steam, so I couldn't even see his eyes, just his enormous grin.

I turned the paper so it looked like a small bundle lying on an upside-down trapezoid. "Oh, I get it," I said. "This is beautiful! Thank you!"

"Merry Christmas!" he shouted. He ran back up the stairs. His mother must have been waiting for him.

Baby Jesus sat on my desk until the next Saturday, when I was cleaning up. I unfolded the paper to put through the shredder for recycling, and saw that the inside was covered in typing. It was a printout of an e-mail from jmdrake68 to rita_mclaughlin. Of course I read it. After the heading, it said:

> Dear Rita, I hope this is the kind of testimonial you were looking for, feel free to post it!!!
>
> Friends,
>
> We are the parents of a beautiful ten-year-old son, who is the joy of our lives. Around his eighth birthday, we became deeply concerned because of his manner and behaviors, which weren't consistent with most boys his age. For awhile we were in deep denial. How could God's gift to us have been handed such a burden? We asked over and over what we might have done wrong. But after many prayers we came to realize God's greatest gifts can also be His greatest challenge for us.
>
> We enrolled Ian last month in Bob Lawson's GHM youth group, and Bob has been an inspiration. We drive over an hour to meetings, and we have so enjoyed our group time with other parents while the boys work with Pastor Bob. The veteran parents have given us such hope with their stories. One father said "Its like our son has been

reborn." And isn't that what Christ Jesus asks of each of us, to be reborn in Him?

Life is a journey, and we don't pretend there's an instant answer. We have much work to do ourselves, and we need to press on in our relationship with God and each other, before our own healing can start.

We ask for your prayers in the coming months, and offer ours up for you.

In His Grip,

Janet and Larry D.

I ran upstairs and showed Rocky the letter. "Is this about what I think it's about? And what is 'In His Grip'?"

Rocky read it, laughing and shaking his head. "What are they, Pentecostal?"

"Fundamentalist, I think, of some variety. I get the impression it's one of those big evangelical churches with a rock band."

He read it again. "This is profoundly messed up," he said, and I was impressed that I got that much of a reaction. The day before, I'd told him about an independent bookstore in Hannibal going under, and he'd said, "What do you expect? I've seen you use Amazon. It's just the way things are now." He was always willing to express anger, but surprise was usually beneath him.

"What should I do?"

He laughed. "Absolutely nothing. What, you're going to call the police? I'd love to hear that phone call. 'So I have this piece of

origami . . .' Nobody broke any laws. Except maybe you, by reading a private e-mail."

"That's not what I mean. I love how you pretend I overreact
even when I don't. But I could tell his school, right? His teachers
would want to know if this is going on."

"Don't do it, Lucy. Don't get involved. And you're so big on pri-
vacy and the First Amendment, yeah? You weren't meant to see
this." He folded the paper in quarters and held it out over the recycling. "Can I toss it? So you don't do anything rash?"

"Sure. Of course."

But yes, of course, I dug it out later and kept it.

It was easy to research, as there was a disturbing bounty of information on the Internet. Bob Lawson was the balding, red-faced
founder of Glad Heart Ministries, an organization "dedicated to the
rehabilitation of sexually confused brothers and sisters in Christ."
In the course of a five-hundred-dollar weekend seminar, "backslidden adults" could be returned to a natural and healthy state of het-
erosexuality, but would need additional weekly counseling to keep
from slipping back into sin. Only five years after its founding, there
were branches in six states, but Pastor Bob himself still ran the St.
Louis branch. Ian was apparently enrolled in the youth group, in
which children ages ten through thirteen whose parents suspected
they were "headed down the wrong path" could learn, through
prayer and workbook exercises, to lead "healthy, Godly lives" and
to understand that "sexuality is a choice, not an identity." The
older teenagers were sent to "Reboot Camp," but the stated point
of the youth group was to "speak to our children before the secular
media has reached them with its political agenda."

"Pastor Bob Lawson," read the biography page, "lived for seventeen years as a homosexual before coming to Christ, and learning that His abiding love could fill the vacuum he had felt for so long. Bob has been married since 1994 to DeLinda Reese-Lawson, a former lesbian, and the couple have three children. Bob and DeLinda's marriage is a testament to the fact that it is Christ's love that keeps a marriage and a family together, and that earthly love is only a manifestation of that higher love. When our relationship with God is pure, our relation with His other earthly servants shall be pure as well."

Elsewhere online I found testimonials, renunciations, and articles from the Christian and secular presses. Eight months earlier, Pastor Bob had been photographed leaving a gay nightclub, after which he stated that he had been "ministering to the sick."

My blood pressure rose just looking at his fat-faced picture. If I weren't at work, I might have actually yelled at the computer. I wondered if Ian even understood why he was going to the meetings—did they explain it all, or did they try to keep the kids in the dark, hoping the options would never occur to them?

What would happen to Ian, hanging on Pastor Bob's every word? He was an only child, like me—he would latch on to any adult within fifty feet. No Chinese baby, no "reading saved my life." He could turn into Pastor Bob himself.

I took Rocky's advice and resisted the urge to tell Sophie Bennett, or anyone else at Hannibal Day, or anyone else at all. But I wanted to tell everyone I saw on the street, to write in to advice columns, to document it in my hypothetical file of weird bruises. Like a good Russian, I wanted to break into Pastor Bob's house and poison him. Like a good American, I wanted to sue somebody. But like a good librarian, I just sat at my desk and waited.

7

Drummer Boy

That same afternoon, Glenn the pianist called and talked me into making the drive the next day to Starr Hall, which turned out to be the theater of a community college. It was an afternoon performance—probably not a good sign for a premiere—and I'd told Loraine my father was in town so I could take off work. ("You remember about this afternoon, right?" I'd said as I headed out the door. "I reminded you at the benefit?" I was banking, as I often did, on her tendency to pretend full knowledge of any conversation she might have been drunk for. Rocky claimed he once got a raise this way.)

They were holding a ticket for me at the counter just under "Lucy," and I found an isolated seat toward the back and started reading my computer printout program. Glenn was born in upstate New York, it said, and started composing at the age of nine. He was proficient on over twenty-five percussion instruments. I wondered what it took to be proficient on the triangle.

I was surprised when Glenn came out to conduct. I hadn't read my program carefully enough. At least he didn't look ridiculous up there, the way some conductors wave their arms around as if they're trying to fly. He stood straight in his tux, the same tux I'd seen him in before, moving his arms in stiff little lines. The music was modern and mercifully jazzy. The main theme sounded familiar, but I couldn't place it. I leaned back and closed my eyes.

Ian had told me a few weeks earlier about his idea for The Ultimate Symphony. "At the beginning, they bring this enormous grandfather clock on stage, and it would look normal, but really someone's hiding inside. So then the clock plays Big Ben, and then the whole orchestra starts playing, and the main part of their song is the same as Big Ben. Do you know the Big Ben song?"

"Yes," I'd said, and hummed it to convince him. He was leaning over my desk at the time, out of breath from the heap of science books he'd lugged all the way downstairs to return instead of shoving in the drop slot. Sonya was on the floor reading her daughter an Arthur book, glancing up occasionally to make sure Ian was still accounted for.

"And then they play for fifteen minutes, but if they take the wrong amount of time, the guy in the clock can speed up the gears. So just as they finish that movement, the clock strikes the fifteen minutes thing, where it plays just the very first part of Big Ben. Then they play again, and each movement is timed just right so the clock strikes, and then at the very end it's been a whole hour, and this time when the clock plays the song, they play it right along with it, very loudly. But it would be *ritardando*, and that's why you need the guy in the clock, to slow it down. It would be a very sad symphony, and it would be about World War II."

"That's great!" I'd said. "You should start composing that."

He made a face. "I can't. I have soccer on Tuesdays, and French on Mondays and Wednesdays, and this religion class thing every weekend, and science camp on Mondays after French, and piano on Thursday, and then even when I practice piano I can't work on my symphony, because my piano teacher says the important thing is to work on left hand."

"That's absolutely tragic."

"That's the other thing about my symphony. All the piano parts would just be for your right hand."

I opened my eyes and tried to concentrate on Glenn's music. I scratched a leg with my right hand, and my back with my left. The more I scratched, the more I itched. The xylophone was taking a turn at the theme, echoed by the woodwinds, and suddenly I recognized it. It was almost exactly the jingle from the Mr. Clean ads, the one you know by heart if you've ever stayed home sick on the couch and watched daytime talk shows: "Mister CLEAN, Mister CLEAN, da da DA da, da da DA da . . ." I leaned my face on my hands to keep from laughing, as if anyone were watching me.

Afterward, I wandered into a hallway that looked like it might lead backstage, and after three steps, Glenn was in front of me beaming. The front of his tuxedo jacket was covered in white lint.

"Trying to escape," he said, "or coming to find me?"

"Looking for the booze," said Daisy Buchanan.

He stuck by me at the party and laughed at himself and told me a story about trying to build the world's longest golf ball racecourse when he was eight. I found him very charming, although that might have had something to do with the fact that I couldn't remember my last date that didn't involve Rocky and a Hitchcock revival.

Leaning in a corner, where the other guests had abandoned us to each other, I told him the story of my truncated last name, and

I told him about my apartment, and I tried to explain about the late-night photo shoot. "I don't get it," he said.

After my fourth glass of wine, I told him how I could hear the plays with the window open, and he said he didn't believe me, that he'd have to hear it himself. And even though I recognized it as an excuse, a fairly lame one, I told him sure, he could come hear for himself. It was only just after seven, and *Vanya* started at eight. In my building, he insisted we take the ancient elevator because he thought it looked fun, with its iron gate and its "last inspected on" sheet deftly covered by Tim with an "I Brake for Corgis" sticker. He laughed at my piles of books, and we pulled chairs over to the open window to watch the crowd trickle in from the little restaurants across the street. We wore our coats and shared a blanket. The buzz of voices in the lobby came straight up, and then we could actually hear all the people move slowly from under my living room to under my kitchen and bedroom as they found their seats, the chairs creaking open, the audience dropping their post-dinner bodies onto the ancient springs.

One night that previous summer, as they drifted in, I was sure I heard Ian's voice from down below. I'd had a long day with him—it was Saturday, and he camped out from nine to four—and I must have had his voice stuck in my head. It was just some woman, I realized, calling out to her friends and talking about the Indian place across the street. I remember wishing—even then, before things started to happen—that Ian could have been there, front row or backstage, watching Shakespeare and falling in love and seeing the universe open up for him. I could put a book in his hands, but I couldn't take him by the ankles and dip him headfirst in another world. And for some reason, I knew even then that he needed it.

Glenn and I sat there through most of the first act, just listening to the warped but mostly intelligible voices. He smoked three cigarettes and kept grinning at me. I put my head on his shoulder, sleepy from the wine.

When Glenn got up to use the bathroom, I had to stop him. "This is embarrassing," I said, "but you can't flush during the show." He laughed and kept walking. "No, I'm serious. The pipes go right above the stage. You can *go*, if you have to, but you can't flush. They're done by eleven most nights."

"You're kidding."

"No, there's a schedule in the bathroom. Tim prints one up for me, and one for his partner, Lenny."

"Is that legal, for them to make you do that?"

"I don't know, but my rent is three hundred dollars, so I don't really care."

"But I can flush it in the morning, right?" he said.

"That's very presumptuous."

But it wasn't really, and he had good breath and beautiful eyelashes, and later he showed me how his forearms were stronger than his biceps from playing the piano, and truth be told, Mr. Clean is a little dirty.

8

Exhibit D: The Cots
(or, If You Give a Librarian a Closet)

I*f you give a librarian a closet, she will probably fill it with junk.*

If she fills it with junk, some of the junk will be books in need of repair.

If some of the junk is books, and the closet is off of a back room anyway, she will hide more books there, books that she thinks are crap like the Stormy Sisters series, but which her boss thinks the library should keep.

If she hides crappy books there, she will be in no rush to clean the closet, since she would then be out a hiding place.

If she goes ten months without cleaning it, she will go to great lengths to hide the mess from her alcoholic and temperamental boss.

If she wants to hide the mess from her boss, she will stuff the front of the closet with cots that were once used for nap hour of the short-lived library day care, circa 1996.

If she stuffs the closet with cots, they will remain there until removed by a certain boy on a certain fateful night—but until that night, the closet will fester unopened for months.

If the closet festers unopened for months, the librarian will probably decorate the closet door with cartoons and posters in an effort to distract her fellow librarians from the thought of ever opening the closet.

If a librarian decorates a closet door, she will use such items as a Conan the Librarian cartoon, a large sticker that says "The world is quiet here," a poster of If You Give a Mouse a Cookie, *a CPR chart, and a bookstore café napkin signed by Michael Chabon.*

If she uses these items, her boss will ask, "What the hell does this mean, 'The world is quiet here'? Is it political?" and her boss will also ask, "You're not filing Michael Chabon in the children's section, are you?" but her boss, distracted by these items, will never think to open the door.

If her boss never opens the door, she will forget that she has given the librarian a closet and will, by the end of the year, offer the librarian a second closet.

If she gives the librarian a second closet, the librarian will probably fill it with junk.

9

The Predecessor

"It kills me," I said.

Rocky and I had gone to a showing of It's a Wonderful Life, as if we couldn't catch it on TV, and now we were at Pasta Palace, at a corner table. Rocky was twining his fettuccini Alfredo into a big yarn ball of grease around his fork. "It's not your problem," he said. "There's no abuse, and he hasn't asked you for help, and you don't even know them. You need to think about something else."

"Do you know what they call it, on these Web sites? They say 'SSAD,' for Same-Sex Attraction Disorder, like it's a condition you have, but if you don't give in to it, you're not gay. They'll talk about 'having' SSAD. Like having dyslexia or something."

"That is fucked up, but it's not your responsibility."

"I might be the only person who knows about it," I said. I thought about mentioning the fork mark on Ian's head, but I knew Rocky would just roll his eyes.

He talked, as he often did, with his mouth full: "You're not even his teacher."

"Sorry. I'll shut up." But I wouldn't stop thinking about it. "I can see your fettuccini when you talk."

Rocky wiped his mouth and smiled. "*I Can See Your Fettuccini. By Dr. Seuss.*" For some reason this was very funny to us, the way he'd twist things I said into the titles of picture books. *Too Much Tequila,* by Margaret Wise Brown. *The Very Obvious Nose Job,* by Eric Carle. He announced them in the voice of a father introducing his daughter to a childhood classic.

"So what are we supposed to talk about?" I said. Usually we discussed the movie, but *It's a Wonderful Life* alternately annoyed me and made me cry, and we'd both seen it a hundred times.

(George Bailey, in despair: "Tell me where my wife is!"

Clarence the angel, paroxysms of horror and grief: "You're not going to like it, George. She's just about to close up the *library*!"

And there she runs in thick glasses, clutching books to her useless breasts. This nightmare Mary Bailey has ruined her eyesight from long hours reading alone in the dark.

How strange, that this one profession should be so associated with loneliness, virginity, female desperation. The librarian with her turtleneck sweater. She's never left her hometown. She sits at the circulation desk and dreams of love.)

"Actually, I have a favor to ask."

"What?" I took a big bite of pizza so I'd have time to stall if necessary.

"My cousin's wedding, in Kansas City. It's March twenty-fifth, I think. A Saturday."

I had to swallow now, to make sure I was answering the right question. "You need a ride, or a date?"

"I wouldn't mind the ride, actually, but I was thinking of the date."

I took another bite of pizza. Three things I wouldn't find fun: a wedding where I didn't know anyone; driving all the way to Kansas City; worrying what Rocky would think this meant.

"You can say no. I don't *need* a date. It would just be fun."

"I'm not good at those things. You saw me at the benefit, talking to the piano player and the bartender instead of the donors." I don't know why I felt compelled to imply that I hadn't seen any more of Glenn—we'd had two dates since the concert.

"These people aren't intimidating. My cousin's the host at a pancake house, very down to earth. But don't sweat it. Whatever."

"I'll check," I said. "But actually, March twenty-fifth—I think I'm in Chicago that weekend. I'll check, though." I could always make that true, if I needed to. Right then a baby at the next table drowned us out with his screaming. Beautiful, merciful screaming.

I said before that I'd never met anyone like Ian. It was only a half-truth, one of my specialties. So here it comes, the big, repressed memory. And I'm not even paying to lie on your couch.

Senior year of high school, my friend Darren invited me up to the projection room for a smoke. He wasn't really my friend, not yet, too cool for me with his baggy green corduroys and his blond hair dyed pink with Kool-Aid, but we had APs and honors classes together, which meant we could act like friends without going through the whole preliminary stage. I'd never been up to the booth before—of all the kinds of geek I was, audiovisual geek was not among them—but it was exactly what I thought: lots of switches and lights, an old paint can half-full of cigarette butts. I knew Darren was gay, or I would have thought it was a low-budget date. He lit our cigarettes and we stared out the little window, down at the seats in the auditorium, like something was about to happen out there.

He asked how I was doing—I'd been dumped a couple of weeks earlier, three days before Homecoming—and I pretended to be recovering. I said, "I'd pay good money to be gay."

Darren looked shocked, confused, horribly wounded. I said, "I'm sorry, I mean I know it's really hard . . ."

"You know I'm gay?" Of course I did. The entire school knew. People talked about how brave he was to be out of the closet. Gossip about his love life would win you a rapt audience in the cafeteria. "Because I've only told, like, two people. Ever."

So I lied. I said, "I have exceptional gaydar. It's a talent. Seriously, if college doesn't work out, it could be my *career*."

"Oh." He tapped his ashes onto some kind of control panel. "I mean, I guess maybe it's obvious. Like my dad has always been worried about it, from the time I was, like, three. He took away all my coloring books."

"Why?"

"I guess I was a little too into them. And then he wouldn't let me play with girls, but then my mom was like, it's worse for him to always play with boys, so then I wasn't allowed to play with anyone but my cousins. They're Catholic. My parents. Well, so are my cousins, but you know what I mean."

We talked through enough cigarettes to make my throat sore, and I suppose he was impressed that I hadn't flipped out on him, that I was talking with him about this like it didn't shock me. I'd guess 80 percent of the kids at school would have had the same reaction, would have been thrilled just to get a private audience with Darren Alquist, but Darren didn't seem to know that, and I couldn't tell him without letting on how far out of the closet he inadvertently was. Besides, if I pretended I was one of the only ones who could understand him, it might lead to his friendship, and he was far more interesting, more popular, than my other friends. I had some vague vision of our sitting together in the cafeteria and checking out boys.

Deep into the conversation he said, "It's like from the time I was born, they've been taking away pieces of me and plugging in these fake parts. Like my dad took away my coloring books and gave me Legos, and then all the guys in middle school made fun of the way I walked until I got this fake walk I have to think about every second. And then *this* school, God, it's like they took away my heart and gave me a chunk of lead."

I said, "It's like the Tin Woodman." He raised one eyebrow—effortlessly, as if he raised one eyebrow all the time. "In the book, not the movie. How he started off real, then he chopped his arm off and got a tin arm, and finally everything was tin."

He nodded and laughed and I knew it would happen, our friendship. And it did—we smoked and watched track practice from the roof of the arts building, we partnered up for a film project for English, he drew a picture of a giraffe inside my locker. In my yearbook, he signed in green Sharpie: "Dearest Lucy, if ever I'm bound and tortured as a hostage of the Bolivian National Guard, the memory of our time together will get me through the pain."

I wrote him a few times from college but didn't hear back. Someone told me he'd dropped out of Pomona.

And here's what's sick: you already know what happened next, because it's a cliché. And it's a cliché for a reason, because these stories always end this way, with the kid's poor mom trying to clean the shit out of his pants before the paramedics arrive, and that's the part that gets repeated between your former classmates on breaks home from college—not the part about how he got the gun or even why he did it or how many times he'd tried it before, but the part about the shit in his pants and how his mother was scrubbing at him with a towel like it would make a difference, like she didn't want her family embarrassed in front of the coroner.

Back at college after the funeral, I made a big deal about it to my friends, about how I could have stopped it if I'd said the right thing, how I'd had so many opportunities but never taken them. But I was caught up in the cliché of it, the scripts you choose from when someone dies, and I didn't really mean it at all. I might as well have said, "He was so young, he had his whole life ahead of him!" or "It should have been me!" or "How could a kind God let such a terrible thing happen?" I wouldn't have felt any of them, just somehow enjoyed the recitation.

Only about five years later did it hit me, heavy and hard as Darren's chunk-of-lead heart: it *had* been my fault, as much as anybody's, and there *were* things I could have said, and when Brian Willis made a joke in Calculus about how Darren was late because somebody dropped their soap in the locker room shower, I could have stood up and punched him in his swollen, freckled face.

So there it is, my deep-seated motivation, what I was projecting onto Ian, my heart-tugging excuse. I'd have a hard time convincing a jury that this alone could justify what I did. But I do think it made me an angrier person. You have to accept that, at least: beneath everything, despite a privileged life and a sense of humor, I was an angry person. I enjoyed blaming people. When I heard about idiots like Pastor Bob, I seethed with rage. I actually *seethed*. For weeks afterward, driving in my car, I'd rant at the Pastor Bobs

of the world in a monologue that must have looked, in the rearview mirrors of those driving ahead of me, like an impassioned
tirade at a former lover.

Every morning on my way to work, my rant was interrupted by the
sight of Janet Drake running down Waxwing Avenue, even when
the sidewalks were coated with ice. I'd probably seen her every day
for two years but never realized it was always the same person, the
same pink jogging suit, the same pointy elbows, until I'd talked to
her. She was always running north, back toward home from wherever she'd been. They lived somewhere within walking distance of
the library, but I'd pass her about ten minutes before I got to work.
How many miles was that? How many miles had she already run
before I saw her? And she was very often in the rec center fitness
room too—there when I arrived after work at 6:15 and still there
at 7:00 when I darted out past her elliptical machine, hoping she
wouldn't recognize me. How then did she have all this time to be
overbearing?

"Miss Hull?"

"Yes, Ian."

He leaned forward on my desk so he was supporting himself
with his chest. Sonya was upstairs, where she'd been staying more
and more frequently on their library visits. I wondered if she really
trusted Ian, or if she just didn't care about Janet Drake's instructions. She was under the continued impression that he was down
here playing Noah's Mission. Now that it was always cold out, he'd
developed a system of stuffing one book in the front of his pants

and one in the back, his parka covering them both. "Will you be open on Christmas?"

"On Christmas? No. We're closed from the twenty-fourth to the twenty-sixth. So this is the last day to check stuff out."

He dropped down to the floor so I couldn't see him. "You mean you're closed *on* both those days too? So you're closed for *three* days?"

"Yep."

He stood up again, his face pink and crumpled like a two-year-old's. Dramatically, deliberately, he buried his head in his arms and turned away from me.

"Ian, it's only three days."

His breathing was fast and loud, his shoulders pumping up and down.

"Ian?"

"THAT'S NOT FAIR!" he shouted, and the mother reading with her toddler on the floor turned to see what had happened.

"Ian." I came out from behind the desk and put my hands on his shoulders. He jerked his body away from me. I had seen him be melodramatic with Sonya, and Sophie Bennett told me recently that his teachers were finding him incredibly annoying this year, but he'd never done it to *me* before. I bent down to peek through his arms and see his face. He wasn't actually crying, just heaving and sighing loudly.

"You know, Ian," I said, "you can check out a lot of stuff right before we close and bring it back after."

"That's not true. Because then we're out of *town*. For almost a whole week, until New Year's, and my mom will check my suitcase. So I'd have to get stupid books, like Hardy Boys, and then I could only get ten books anyway, because I'm only allowed to check out

how old I am." A lot of families had that rule: a five-year-old could
borrow five books, and so on. He leaned back against the big pot-
ted tree by the wall and almost sent it crashing down.

"I think ten books should be plenty, don't you? You don't want
your suitcase to get much heavier than that."

"And my mom would never let me bring extra books because
she *never* lets me do *anything*."

"Sounds tough," I said. I went back behind my desk. He looked
between his arms to see if I was still watching him, which I was.
He picked at the leaves of the plant for a minute, breathing loudly,
then stomped over to the mythology shelf.

He ended up checking out the first ten Bobbsey Twins books.
"Are these as stupid as they look?"

"Pretty much," I said.

"Awesome."

At the end of the day, Glenn appeared at my desk with the library
copy of *1,000 Great Date Nights*. "Pick one," he said.

I hadn't invited him to come see me at work, and the presumption bothered me. We'd seen each other quite a few times since
the night of the concert, and he'd been e-mailing me constantly,
but lately I'd been keeping my replies short. There was something
a little too slick about him, the way he'd ask me questions straight
out of GQ's date guide, like "What's your favorite childhood memory?" And the way he would just show up like this, flashing his
piano-key teeth.

I was glad there was no one around. I'd had a few desperate
and fruitless requests that afternoon for *The Polar Express* and *The
Night Before Christmas*, but right now the basement was empty.

"Let's be spontaneous," he said. He was saying this a lot lately, like it was some great virtue. For a jazz musician, I suppose it is—four bars to fill, and a horn in your hands—but it doesn't do a librarian a hell of a lot of good.

I started flipping through the book. "Don't take me to feed the ducks."

"Hey," he said. He leaned over the desk. "I'll take ya to the moon, baby." Cheesy Sinatra voice and wiggling eyebrows.

I could hear Loraine's heels clunking unevenly on the stairs. "Okay," I whispered. "Pretend to browse, fast." I stood up and yanked the white bed sheet off my desk chair and tossed it under the desk. I'd been using it all week, hoping it would protect my skin from the chair fabric, but if anything, my rash had gotten worse. I was considering switching to one of the beanbag chairs, propping it up on a wide stack of books like a giant orange beanbag throne.

Loraine leaned over the desk to hand me a sealed envelope, which I knew from experience probably contained a twenty-dollar gift card to one of the chain restaurants by the highway. "Merry Christmas!" she said. "And Hanukkah too, of course. Make sure you get some sleep. You could really use it." Glenn stood there pretending to be fascinated by the Junie B. Jones books. When she left I closed up, and Glenn and I walked upstairs together. We passed Rocky at the main desk, and I thought of introducing Glenn as an old friend, but of course Rocky had seen him at the benefit. So instead I just said, "Merry Christmas! I'll call you for a movie!" and Rocky gave a look like he was trying not to laugh. No: more like he was trying hard to look like he was trying not to laugh, but couldn't get it quite right.

Glenn and I went to Trattoria del Norte and drank a lot of wine, and I struggled to make conversation. We didn't have much in common, I was discovering. And the more I thought about it, I wasn't sure I wanted to date someone whose magnum opus was inadvertently based on a tile cleaner jingle. Nor did I want to be around when someone pointed this out to him. He didn't seem even slightly aware of my ambivalence, though, and he just kept grinning at me from across the table, trying to stare into my eyes. I'd watched *The Music Man* enough times as a child to be wary of smiling musicians. The way they waltz into your library singing, swinging that con man briefcase and telling you to be spontaneous. They tell you this whole damn town could be saved with a little luck and a good marching band.

To fill the silence I almost started telling Glenn about Ian's temper tantrum, but thought better of it. If I was already bothering Rocky, who knew the kid and worked with me, how much would I annoy someone who *really* didn't care? And amid the five hundred stupid decisions I made that winter—decisions that pointed straight to jail or worse—this drunken, half-arbitrary choice was probably the one that saved my life.

10

Stupid

I tried to be objective in the way I watched Ian that winter, after
I read the origami e-mail. I don't think I was imagining the way
his eyes had gone dull or how he tended to shifted his weight heavily back and forth between his feet now, as if he were angrily waiting for a bathroom. He had always been moody, but before there
had been good moods, and slightly manic moods, and now there
weren't. I gave him *The Search for Delicious* in early January, and
he returned it the next day.

"It was too boring," he said. "I stopped." I was shocked. *The
Search for Delicious*, which my best readers will finish in a day, skipping dinner if necessary.

"Well, what do you want now?"

"Something else stupid."

"You want something stupid?"

"Well, it's all stupid, so I guess I don't care. I'll read a baby
book." He squeezed himself into one of the plastic chairs built

for three-year-old rear ends and picked *Blueberries for Sal* without looking. He flipped the pages so fast I worried he'd rip them. "This book is the smartest book ever. This book is a genius. This book is too hard for me. Yay." He shoved it back horizontally on top of the other picture books.

Another day, he came bolting down the stairs, his coat still zipped. "Don't tell her I'm down here!" he whispered, and ran past my desk and into the aisles. In the brief second I saw his face, it didn't look scared, but it didn't look exactly like a child playing a game, either. It looked like he was trying to be bad.

A minute later, Mrs. Drake came down the stairs as fast as she could in her stacked heels and jeans and gray cashmere. "I'm sorry, Sarah-Ann, have you seen my son, Ian?" My God, she was thin. Her elbows were the widest part of her arms.

Ian couldn't see me from where he was, so I pointed silently down the biography aisle. She disappeared where he had, and after I heard Ian's high screech, I watched her drag him back to the stairs, pink fingernails around his shoulder. Ian's voice echoed down the steps: "But Mom, you can't be mad at me, because—*ow!*—because when I was hiding, I already repented! Mom, I already repented, you're not allowed to get mad!"

I should have paid more attention, then, to his sneakiness, his slipperiness, his tendency to hide. I also should have noticed, the next week, when he started asking about the janitor. He stood in front of my desk, his face studiedly bored, his voice a monotone.

"Who cleans this stupid library?"

"I'm sorry, Ian, I didn't understand that."

"I said, who cleans the library."

"A very nice lady named Mrs. Macready comes and vacuums. She has white hair."

"Does she clean it every day?"

"I have no idea. Probably not. More like every other."

"Does she clean it before you get here, or after you leave?"

"Okay, I have some work to do."

"I thought your work was answering questions for kids."

"Yes, questions about books. Do you have a question about a book?"

He picked up *Carry On, Mr. Bowditch* from the edge of my desk. "Yes. If I dropped this, and we waited for the janitor to clean it up, would she clean it up before the library opened, or after it closed?"

"The answer is *you* would clean it up, because you made the mess."

He dropped the book on the floor and ran upstairs.

I didn't see him for ten days after that, which might have been a record. The next time he came in he brought me a plate of cookies, each covered in bright blue frosting with a splotch of green in the middle. He looked almost like his old self, walking on tiptoes to where I stood by the return cart. I had decided not to sit down in my desk chair for a week, to see if the rash would clear up. Sonya waved at me, pointed her daughter toward the puppets, and headed back upstairs.

"Even though it's still January, I made cookies for St. Patrick's Day, because it's the next good holiday! The blue is to represent the ocean, and the green is to represent Ireland! I food-colored the frosting, and my hands are still blue." He put the cellophane-covered paper plate on the return cart and showed me his pale blue palms.

"You look like a Smurf."

"A what? And also, I'm sorry about throwing your book. *And*, the reason I haven't been here is I had my baptism, and we had a party, and I got about five thousand books."

I peeled back the cellophane and took out a cookie. "What did you get?"

"I got some origami books, and then these five books from this series called Towards the Light. It's about these kids at the end of the earth, and most people have risen to heaven, but these kids stay behind to try to get everyone else saved. They're really for teenagers, but they're easy."

"Huh. Are they any good?"

"Yeah, they're really fun. There's a movie of them, too, but my mom thinks it might be too scary. She has to watch it first, to see. Do you have any here?"

I was trying to swallow the cookie, which was somehow both dry and sticky at the same time. "You know, we don't have a lot of kids' fiction that's religious. But we do have nonfiction books about religion."

"Oh, yeah. There's the ones like the stupid Eyewitness book with the dumb India gods with all the arms. I already read them all. You should get Towards the Light."

I knew the kind of series Ian was talking about. One week when I was twelve and staying with a born-again neighbor, I read three books off her daughter's bookshelf and found them tremendous fun, the closest thing I'd ever read to a romance novel or a crime thriller. The only one I can still remember started on a charter plane flying over Africa, with a "backslidden" Christian noticing that the pilot prayed before he ate his sandwich. He asked him about it and they talked, but before long the plane crashed, leaving them all lost in the Sahara, et cetera, et cetera, until every-one found Jesus or died. But I hadn't actually thought those books were *good*. How could Ian, the child who'd read *The Wind in the Willows* seven times, fall for it?

"Anyway, it was pretty cool because I got to have friends from church come to my open house after, and that's all I get this year because I'm too old for a birthday party."

His birthday was in April, I knew from his computer account. "What, eleven? That's not too old at all," I said. "Is no one in your grade having a party this year?"

He sighed, peeled back the cellophane, and rearranged the cookies to fill the gap from the one I'd taken. "It's not exactly that. It's more that, okay, last year? I had my party and all the people I wanted to invite were girls, and we had this very fantastic party that was mostly just a treasure hunt outside. But my dad said this year it has to be either all boys or exactly half and half. And no one even does a half and half party anymore. Everyone does a sleepover, and I just really don't want to. So my dad said I can't have a party at all, and then I said okay, could I have my friends from this religion class thing instead, and he said definitely not, but I don't even get why. So then he said I was too old for birthdays anyway, and I should just save up my allowance and buy myself something."

Ian seemed sad—devastated, really—but I got the impression the wound wasn't fresh. His birthday was still four months away, but he'd already been stewing on this one awhile. I had tried, all along, to be noncommittal, the neutral and friendly librarian—kind of like the therapist who just sits and nods. But in this case, I couldn't help taking sides. I said, "Ian, that really doesn't sound fair. I don't think that's fair at all."

He smiled at me, looked over his shoulder to make sure Sonya wasn't coming down the stairs, and helped himself to an Ireland cookie. I took a second myself, although the first was still mostly lodged in my throat.

What I needed right then was the perfect novel to put in his hands, the one that would fly him fifty thousand miles away from his mother and Pastor Bob Lawson and Hannibal, Missouri. Instead I said, "These cookies are fantastic."

11

Pumpkin Head

I found Tim the artistic director leaning against the wall outside his apartment, his eyes wet and happy. I was back early from Glenn's, having made an excuse about work in the morning.

"Lucy the librarian!" He kissed me on the cheek. "I'm completely drunk! We're having a State of the Union party! I'm getting the costumes! Come help me!" He sat on the floor to tie his shoe. Inside his apartment people were laughing, and it sounded like plates were breaking.

"Tim, here's a question for you," I said as we headed down to the costume shop.

Tim unlocked the door and pulled the chain on the overhead lightbulb. This was the room where I came to do my laundry and had once shrieked at what I thought was an animal on the table but turned out to be a wig. It was a carefully organized space, with rows of labeled plastic bins: "Sparklies," "Hats," "Military," "Tights," "Women's Shoes, 7–9," "Elastics." The walls were decorated with old show posters and an enormous buck's head with a straw hat hanging off one antler.

"Yes!" he shouted. "A question! Ask!" He pulled a cardboard box from under the table in the middle of the room and started pawing through it.

"Okay," I said. "What books would you suggest for a ten-year-old boy who needs some indirect support on some sexuality issues he might or might not have?"

"Oh." He picked a red bathrobe out of the box and tossed it across the ancient avocado green sewing machine in the corner. "There's tons of good stuff out there now, but it's mainly for older kids. Is he a good reader? Pick out some costumes. Pretty much anything. We have, like, sixty-five people, I swear to God. I didn't know Lenny had friends."

I pulled the Hats bin from its shelf. There was an Abe Lincoln near the top, which I figured was as good as anything. I took it out and put it on the table. "The thing is, it has to be innocuous. His parents would have a fit if I gave him, like, *Come On Out of the Closet, Bobby.*"

"An excellent piece of literature, if I recall." He was draping both his shoulders with piles of what looked like housedresses. "Seriously, I can answer this question." He pointed his finger at me and squinted. "'The Ugly Duckling.' That's what you want."

"No," I said. "This kid is ten. And *smart*. He'd laugh at me."

"Okay. Then what you want is definitely the Oz series. The whole thing, not just the first one." I started to agree, but he kept talking. "*Because*, here's the thing about Oz." He emptied the whole Sparklies bin onto the table, then scooped it all back in again. He put the bin in my arms and set the Lincoln hat on top of it. "Because you know there's this whole rabid gay cult following, right? Which is only partly due to Judy Garland." He grabbed two shiny Elizabethan-looking tunics off the clothes rack, picked up the red bathrobe, and opened the door. "Two things: in the whole series, no real love stories. Can you grab the light? There's only these really farcical ones. So it's like this realm free from hetero love. And there's even a boy who turns into a girl. Just, poof."

"Right. Ozma," I said.

"And second, everyone is so *weird*, but they're all completely accepted. It's like, okay, you have a pumpkin head, and that guy's made of tin, and you're a talking chicken, but what the hell, let's do a road trip."

Lenny met us in the upstairs hall, looking as drunk as Tim. He grabbed the dresses off Tim's shoulders, shouted "Costumes!" and flung them into the apartment. People were already putting them on over their clothes as we came through the door. Beth Hopkins, the red-haired actress whose photos I'd helped desecrate, ran and grabbed the Sparklies bin from my arms and started tossing the glittery headbands and scarves and earrings around the room.

"Everybody, you know Lucy!" Tim shouted. "We love Lucy! She puts up with everything!"

Beth wheeled around and grabbed my shoulder. "You were a fantastic bride! A beautiful bride!"

I laughed. "How long did it take you to figure it all out?"

"Oh my God, like, two weeks! Literally!"

I ended up watching the party more than participating in it. The Lincoln hat was placed on my head at one point, and I settled into the love seat with a beer Lenny got me. Most of the men put on dresses to become Republican housewives, some of the women lounged around as prostitutes, others were various Shakespearean characters, and Tim slouched in a big chair with the bathrobe and shouted racial slurs across the room. Lenny turned up the TV as the president stepped to the podium and the white-haired men behind him stood to applaud. The point of the party seemed to be to react to the address in a manner appropriate to your assumed character. Lenny, in one of the Elizabethan tunics, would scream and cross himself whenever the space program was mentioned. For the most part, Tim and the Republican housewives shouted encouragement at any hint of bigotry. Whenever the president said "nucular," everyone was obliged to take a drink.

I leaned my head back and stared at my president, his satellite-dish ears and stern eyes. He spoke into the camera about preserving civilization. "We are all ambassadors," he said, "spreading the good news of America abroad. American values, American freedoms. And we will fight for those values. And we will *preserve* those values."

"Yeah, hegemony!" shouted Tim, tossing his empty beer bottle towards the bookcase.

"Hail Caesar!" shouted a prostitute.

Someone started singing "O Canada."

I wondered, as I sat there, if there were ever moments of unadulterated reality in Tim's life. Every time I saw him he was either drunk or wearing a costume or both.

I watched him now undoing his ponytail and pulling his blond hair straight down around his face. "I'm John Lennon!" he shouted in a British accent. "I'm bloody confused by all this shit. Who the bloody hell is this large-eared bloke? Hey! Abraham Lincoln! You're bloody silent! What do you make of this president?"

I tried to think of something Lincolnesque to say. Parts of the

Gettysburg Address went through my head, but that wasn't exactly funny.

"Give him a break!" the stage manager shouted for me. "He's *dead*, for chrissake!"

"Well so am I!" wailed Lennon. "We're two bloody *victims*, we are!"

The president told a man in the front row to stand up. This man had been laid off two years ago, and now because of business growth he enjoyed a new job managing an assembly line. He could feed his six children now. The man looked left and right like a nervous squirrel. He didn't seem sure when to sit down again. I always hated the presidential speeches even when I liked the president, hated their upbeat transparency. Our national actor, hired to tell us it would all be fine.

"You are lucky," my father would often say, "that you can make fun of your president this way. You know what happened if you made jokes about Stalin? If someone wanted to tell you a joke about Stalin, he took you first in a dark closet and checked for wires. People died all the time because of jokes. Most men who were dragged away in the night, it was because someone overheard their stupid joke. Have I told you the one about the cat and the mustard?"

Around midnight, Tim came over suddenly and sat beside me, his hand on my shoulder. "There's another thing," he said. "About Oz." He looked very drunk, but he didn't sound it. "I think part of the appeal is that there's this guy who can *fix* everything for you. They all go to the wizard to be *normal*, you know? That's what draws some kids in. But then it doesn't work out, and the book totally sucker punches them with the humbug thing. And that's

what *resonates*, because it's what they knew all along in their gut."
And then he belched and laughed at himself.

I fell asleep fast that night with beer sloshing in my stomach,
and slept like I always do, with my right arm straight up under my
head like I'm the Statue of Liberty, like clueless me is trying to
light someone's way.

12

The Week Before

Anyone who's heard this kind of story before, the kind where someone does something rash and throws away everything she has, will be looking for what I was running away from. Because surely I was running away from something, too. Surely I must have been deeply dissatisfied with my life. Or I had a failed and embarrassing affair, or I didn't want to face that I was subconsciously in love with Rocky, or I felt like a fake because I was, believe it or not, illiterate. Yes, there you go. I was an illiterate librarian, who needed to run away because I'd stolen money from Rocky after he broke my heart by having an affair with Loraine.

No. There was nothing. I wasn't at a boiling point; I'd just been simmering along. Granted, I wasn't particularly thrilled with my job. I'd always thought that by twenty-six I'd be doing something a little more glamorous with my life. Hannibal was a little stifling. I was fairly bored. None of those qualifies as a reason, an excuse, or even a motivation for doing what I did. If that makes me seem somehow selfless, like everything I did was for Ian, it shouldn't. I was more hapless than selfless, and dumb luck had a lot to do with it.

Hapless, clueless, directionless. Selfless only by default. A Hull, through and through.

So there it is: I had no particular reason to leave, no particular reason to throw my life away. But I didn't have much holding me there, either.

The rash on my legs and back had turned to thick red scabs. After the fifth prescription lotion failed to work, Dr. Chen told me to get more sleep. "And drink more water," she said. "Sometimes our bodies are just trying to tell us something."

The snow was a crust on the grass that March, but the parking lots were brown slush. Every morning, I thought of calling in sick.

Rocky and I hadn't been to a movie in two months. When I asked how things were going, he'd say something like "Lots of Nora Roberts."

"Yeah, but how are *you?*"

"Superb."

Ian came downstairs one afternoon, his eyes red around the rims like he'd either been crying or rubbing his face on a cat. He called hello on his way to the new science fiction display that I'd decorated with tinfoil aliens, and then said, "Mr. Walters says to send up staples." Mr. Walters was Rocky, and I wondered why he hadn't phoned down or e-mailed. When Ian checked out *The Little Grey Men* ten minutes later (or rather, when I checked it out for him under my own name and watched as he shoved it halfway down his pants), I handed him a box of staples and asked him to take it up. Ian hadn't been staying long, lately. His fingernails were half gone from biting.

"Is Mr. Walters your boyfriend?" he asked. He balanced the staple box on top of his head, and stuck both arms out for balance.

"No. I have a different boyfriend." I didn't like that it felt so urgent to set the record straight.

"You should have Mr. Walters be your boyfriend. He has a red cross."

"A what?"

Ian turned and the staples fell onto the floor. He put them back on his head and held them there with one hand as he walked to the stairs. "I forget what it is," he called back. "A red something. I'm a Nigerian woman, and I'm crossing the Sahara."

"Good luck with that."

When I went up to get lunch across the street, I thought I'd ask Rocky if he knew what Ian meant about the red cross, but both when I left and when I returned, Rocky was back in the office. I got the feeling he wanted me to ask what was wrong, but I didn't feel like playing that game.

And this is where the story should end, and sometimes, sitting here, pressing the top of my knee against the bottom of the table, listening to the shallow keystrokes of the graduate students at their laptops, waiting for the sun to sink into the window frame and blind me with red light, sometimes I think this *is* where it ended, that everything that followed was a dream. That maybe I'm looking back now, imagining what might have happened if only I'd done something. When really I did nothing. When I spent the next five years sitting peacefully in Hannibal, watching Ian turn

eleven and then twelve, then realizing he hadn't been in to see
me for a while, then seeing him only a couple of times a year as
I drove past him on the sidewalk and wondered how his life was
going, not wanting to embarrass him by rolling down my window
and calling out.

But no, it did happen. The only thing up for debate is whether
it happened *to* me, or whether I made it happen.

13

Out of the Hobbit-Hole

"MEE, MAY, MAH, MO, MOO!" sang Tim's wall at six o'clock on Monday morning.

"TEE-TEE-TEE-TEE-TEE-TEE-TEE-TEE-TEE-TEE-TEE-TEE-TEE!

"To sit in solemn silence in a dull dark dock, in a pestilential prison with a life-long lock, awaiting the sensation of a short sharp shock, from a cheap and chippy chopper on a big black block!

"eeeeeeeeeeeEEEEEEEEEEEEEEeeeeeeeeee!"

"Oh my God," I said to Tim's wall through my pillow at six o'clock on Monday morning. "Oh my God, shut up."

"Eaaaaiiiiouwah, eyoe, ae," said the wall, which was Tim practicing his lines minus all the consonants.

Outside, a dark midwestern storm was barreling in, the first of the year, and the growing thunder sounded something like Dumpsters scraping on gravel or God chewing rocks. The wind was almost as loud as the thunder, and I wasn't always confident that my windows wouldn't crash out of their rotted frames. I thought of turning on music to go back to sleep, but couldn't bear adding to the noise level.

I let myself put on old jeans and hiking boots and spent three minutes scratching my back against the corner of my dresser like a psychotic cat. It was only a matter of time before I really broke the skin, before someone approached me on the street and asked why the back of my shirt was soaked in blood. I headed to work early to get the summer reading flyers finished, and to see what damage Sarah-Ann had done yesterday, closing up by herself. It was pouring rain by the time I got there at seven, and branches were down all over the neighborhood. I shook myself off in the lobby and wiped my feet and locked the door again behind me. I'd have two hours alone.

Maybe because of the quiet, I was more tuned in to details that morning—always a problem for me, since in stories and movies, a focus on little details tends to indicate imminent disaster. Someone in a movie unlocks his door, checks his mail, turns on his light, and you know he's got about thirty seconds to live. So I was irrationally filled with dread that morning, as I often was when I entered the library early and alone and the only sounds I could hear were my fingers on paper or my purse sliding into the desk drawer.

I sat in the darkness for a moment, then got up to turn on the downstairs lights, all six light switches, one after the other, different walls and display cases dramatically announcing themselves. I was still soaking wet and cold from the rain. I probably made some noise, as I tend to do in silence—humming or whistling or popping my lips. I went behind my desk and sank again into the soft, spinning chair, when a sound like crumpling paper came from the end of one of the fiction aisles. My stomach turned liquid and I pulled my feet up on the chair. I'd only ever had one mouse in my apartment, but it bothered me so much, the idea of some little thing invading like that, that I'd stayed late at work every night for a week until I was sure it was poisoned and gone. Now I banged my fist hard on the desk to scare this one away. I lowered my foot and kicked the drawers and listened for more scampering.

"Miss Hull?" said Ian's voice. I was so used to him saying my name just like that, that I looked for him right in front of the desk and not where the sounds had come from. And then I was reminding myself not to swear as I stumbled down the aisle.

Ian was squatting on the floor by the big plant stand with books and T-shirts and blankets spread around him.

He was giggling. He looked terrified. He took his glasses off and wiped his eyes.

"Don't tell. Please," he said. "I mean my parents, or the police. I'm veryveryveryvery sorry."

I sat beside him on the carpet, attempting a placid smile and not processing much of anything. "OK." I waited. He was biting the knee of his jeans and rocking back and forth, but he wasn't crying, not really.

"Look!" he said suddenly, and way too loudly, and reached behind himself. "I made a real knapsack!" He held out a long, thick twig with what looked like a balled-up flannel shirt tied to the end. He handed it to me. It was heavy.

"What's in here?" I felt the lumps in the shirt, then carefully laid the stick on the ground. Ian untied it.

He was suddenly breathing normally and smiling, sitting cross-legged and leaning back against the shelf. "Number one: dental floss." He picked it out of the pile. "Shampoo. PowerBars. Don't you think that's good, that I brought PowerBars? They have pretty much every vitamin."

He held out a small plastic cup. "For water. And toothbrushing. Here's my medicine." He held up an asthma inhaler and a bottle of pills. "Toothbrush, toothpaste, pool pass, socks."

Calm, normal voice: "Are you going swimming?"

"No." He almost laughed. "It's my ID. In case I need one for something."

"Well, that's very thorough, Ian."

The morning sun reflecting off his glasses gave him yellow moon-eyes.

"Do you know why I didn't bring anything to do?"

"No, I don't."

"Because I was coming *here*. There are books, and I can write things, and I've been doing origami. I'm sorry I robbed the craft cupboard. Look!" He reached into the plant behind him and pulled out a paper crane. All the pots were filled with folded pieces of notebook and construction paper. In the biggest one he'd set up a village with houses and people and trees. Other pots had families and animals, small and large, and many of my plants had bright paper flowers stuck in their leaves. "Here's my plane-wreck one." In one pot was a crumpled paper airplane with its nose in the dirt, surrounded by red and orange triangles. "Those are the flames." He perched the crane in the leaves of a spider plant.

"Wow," I said. "So you must've been here a long time."

He looked at his watch. "Fourteen hours."

No swearing. "You slept here overnight?"

"Here's what I did. My parents were really busy with hosting this Bible study thing at our house, and so I just walked here. And that other lady didn't even really look around when she left, even though I was ready to hide behind all the different shelves, wherever she walked. And then I got a cot from the closet in that other room, and blankets, and brought it all here. But I put it back when I woke up. I watered your plants."

"Thank you."

"So you wouldn't have to do it later and get the origami wet."

He tied the edges of his knapsack back up, using the sleeves to make knots around the stick. I got up off the floor and brought over the rolling stool to sit on.

"Okay," I said. "Your mom and dad have been scared for a really long time now. We're going to call them."

Ian pulled a book off the shelf and held it open, right in front of his face. He mumbled into it. "I don't think that's so good an idea."

I tried to pull the book down, but he was strong. "Do you want to call them, or should I?" He didn't say anything. "So I should do it?" I was expecting a tantrum like the one before Christmas, expecting him to throw the book down and scream, but nothing happened. I stood and walked to my desk. "What's your phone number?" His head appeared at the near end of the aisle, but still down by the floor. He must have crawled there. He told me the number, loudly and slowly, and I dialed.

"*You have reached the Human Resources Department of Missouri Electric,*" said the phone. "*Our operating hours are nine to five thirty, Monday through Friday.*"

"Ian," I said, hanging up, "do you live at the power company?" His face was gone from the aisle. "Ian, what's your real number?"

"I forget," he said from right behind me. I jumped and hit my knee on the desk.

I pulled the phone book out from underneath the phone and flipped to the D section. "Okay. Then let's just look you up."

"We're unlisted," he said, smiling. It was true. No Drakes in Hannibal. I flopped the phone book closed and watched the utter relief settle on his face. He was playing with the bottom button on his shirt, practically ripping it off, but he was taking deep, slow breaths, doing a good job of holding himself together. He must have been planning this for weeks. Did he think he was going to live in the library? Fourteen hours was longer than the normal punish-your-parents runaway scenario.

"Well," I said, "I'm happy you came to visit me, Ian, but the library opens pretty soon, and you can't live in my plants." He giggled, but it turned into a choke. "We can either call the police, or I can drive you home."

He turned and kicked my file cabinet, once, hard, and walked toward his aisle crying silently, his face a violent red. He came back with his coat on, carrying his knapsack and a large blue backpack I hadn't seen before. It looked stuffed, probably with clothes. He nodded at me and then started up the stairs. I left the lights on but locked everything up, and met him in the parking lot. I was surprised that he was waiting for me, that he hadn't run off. Maybe, on some level, I really had wanted him to make a run for it. But he was still here, standing in the rain by my little pale-blue car. He wanted to go home.

I got in my driver's seat and unlocked the passenger door from inside before I realized he was waiting for the back door. It hit me as it hadn't yet that he was ten, that he rode in the backseat, that he probably still took baths, that he might have a night-light. He got in and had to dig around between the seats for the seat belt, and I tried to remember if anyone had ever sat back there before. I started the car, and NPR blasted from the radio, something about a shuttle launch. I turned it off and we started driving down Waxwing Avenue. I didn't ask him for his address, because I didn't know the residential parts of town well enough. But he gave me directions, announcing each one straight into my ear over the back of my seat.

"Turn left at the next stop sign!" he shouted. "Keep going for one mile!" "Turn left and then immediately right!"

"Ian," I said after a while, "I think you're sending me in a big circle." Really I wasn't sure, but it was taking a long time and I knew he usually walked to the library.

"No, no!" he shouted. "I'm not, and in fact if you look right up here it's going to be exactly the last house on your left!"

I watched along the left side until I saw a tall yellow house with perfectly conical little cedar trees along the fence. We stopped by the curb. The newspaper was still at the end of the driveway in its orange plastic, and a short old man was running from his car to the house with a magazine held between his head and the rain.

"Ian, that's not your dad."

He looked out the window. "Yeah, you're right."

"Is this your house, though?"

"I'm not sure."

"You're not *sure?*"

"Well, they painted our house very recently, and it sort of looks different, so it's not familiar to me."

I closed my eyes. "Okay, we're going to the police station."

There was complete silence in the backseat. I looked in the rearview mirror and he wasn't there. I turned off the car and opened my door to jump out and catch him, wherever he was running, but then I saw him crumpled up on the floor of the backseat, his arms up on his head like in a bomb drill. His whole body

heaved with crying or vomiting, I couldn't see. He'd left his glasses
and coat up on the seat.

I opened the back door and squatted down on the curb and put
my hand on his back. His shirt was hot and wet, and it stuck to
him. He said something I couldn't understand.

"What?"

He lifted his head enough to wipe his nose on his sleeve.
"*Please*, you're supposed to just keep driving for a while."

There was a thickening fog around my head like alcohol or a
dream, and I knew I would do it, if only because I didn't want to
take him to the police against his will and lose his trust forever,
and I didn't want to take him home, and I didn't want to drop
him in the middle of the road. It was only a few hours later that
I realized I could have taken him back to the library and waited
for Rocky. It was several days later that I remembered what was
even more obvious: his address and phone number would have
been in the computer file, right there below his name and above
his twelve-dollar fine. But I couldn't think over the sound of his
sobbing. Or maybe I couldn't think of anything *but* his sobbing.
Or maybe on some level, this was what I'd wanted all along: to get
him out of Hannibal, if only for a few minutes. I just hadn't wished
it so literally.

"Drive where?" I asked.

"*Some*where," he said. "My grandmother's house."

I knew he didn't have a grandmother.

"Okay," I said.

14

Down the Rabbit Hole

A nd so they set off, our comrades the librarian and the bright-
cheeked lad, as the sudden winds bent the grass in the fields and
raged against the car, seeming almost to lift it from beneath and carry
it down the street. When the clouds finally parted and the winds died
down, the still-rising sun slid beams of red light through the windows,
shining on their hair so it looked for all the world as if they were on fire.
There were several roads nearby, but it did not take them long to find
the one painted with yellow lines and dotted with weathered billboards.
Within a short time they were driving briskly toward the west, the boy
navigating with directions that came from no place but the lovely magic
of his imagination. The sun shone brightly and the birds sang sweetly
and the Library Lady hummed as she drove on the black and sparkling
road, and although (truth be told) her face betrayed some anxiety about
the journey ahead, she did not feel nearly so bad as you might think.

———

Really, we were a little lost. I let him go on with the game of navigating a bit too long, until we were on some kind of rural route, and the sky was still so overcast that I couldn't tell what direction we were heading in. I didn't have one of those dashboard compasses, and I've never had much of an internal compass, either. Nor, I reflected, did I seem to have much of a moral compass. My cell phone was two feet away, in my purse. I could call the police now, and the car was going fast enough that Ian wouldn't jump out. Then again, how would I explain that a child who had been missing overnight was now in my car, miles from home, although actually, officer, I didn't know exactly where in the hell we were?

About twenty minutes in, Ian stopped trying to navigate and instead launched an incessant babble about robots that could do your homework and how long it would take to eat an entire tree, if you blended it up into milkshakes. If he was trying to make me lose track of time, he did a decent job. I felt hungry, and when I looked at the clock it was 10:22. I hadn't even eaten breakfast—I had planned to run across the street and grab a bagel before the library opened.

I turned onto what looked like a busier road, hoping to find a gas station.

"I didn't tell you to turn here!"

I lied. "The other way would have been circling back. I thought you weren't taking me in a circle."

"You're getting us lost!" He seemed genuinely angry, so panicked that for a second I wondered if he'd actually been directing me to his grandmother. But no, he was worried I was heading back home.

"We need gas," I said. When he leaned over my seat, he saw the needle on empty. It had been there for the past two years, actually, so that I had to count the miles between fill-ups, but come to think of it we probably *were* running low. We stopped at a Texaco, and as I ran the pump I realized that if I pretended I had to go inside to pay, I could take my phone and call someone without Ian hearing. Rocky, maybe, to tell him what was going on. But he was hardly friendly lately, and he thought I was obsessed with Ian. I wasn't sure he'd believe the details of the story. I didn't know how to call the Drakes. I could call the police and make something up, tell them Ian had just now shown up at the door of my apartment, and it would take a while to calm him down, but I'd drive him to the station in an hour or two. And then I'd buy a map or ask directions, and speed the entire way back.

I opened my door to talk to him. "I'm going inside to get food. Do you want anything?"

He patted his backpack. "I have peanut butter, and jelly, and saltines, which is enough for about one hundred sandwiches, even though they're small. Plus my PowerBars."

"You want a Snickers?" Now I was even talking like a kidnapper.

"I don't think you should go inside there," he said. His face was turning red again. Didn't this normally work the other way around? Kidnapper stops at gas station, threatens victim not to leave the car, victim makes mad dash to highway.

"Ian, I at least have to *pay*. The machine won't read my card."

He undid his seat belt and hopped out onto the pavement. "Okay, then I'm coming with you, and I want a 3 Musketeers."

Inside the Quik Stop, I waited till he was absorbed in the candy rack, then told him I was using the bathroom. He thought for a second. "Give me your phone first."

"Do you want to make a call?" I put it in his palm.

"No."

I bought chips and a soda for myself, and on our way out I got two hundred dollars from the ATM. I hated to be this far from home without a safe amount of cash, and I figured two hundred would cover us for roadside emergencies and dinner, if need be. I imagined we might stop somewhere, a nicer chain restaurant maybe, and talk things over before I dropped him at home or the police station.

Back in the car I asked for my phone back, and I was relieved when he handed it over. It had occurred to me that he might have thrown it away or flushed it down the men's toilet. I said, "I think this is getting silly, and in the next two minutes you need to choose who we're going to call. We can call your parents, or the police, or someone you're related to." He didn't answer. "Or maybe the mom of one of your friends."

He was grinning into the rearview. "Guess why not."

"Because you don't want to."

"No. Because if you call them, I'll say you kidnapped me from the library last night, and you wouldn't let me go."

The grin could have meant he was joking, but he also looked about to cry.

"I just don't think you would do that," I said. (It was the way I'd always imagined talking down an armed madman: "But you're a *good person*. You don't *want* to hurt me.")

He thought for a second. "Yes, I would *definitely* do that. And I would tell them everything about the inside of your car, and that would be the evidence."

"How would you explain your backpack?" I had pulled back out onto the road, heading in the direction that I hoped was toward Hannibal. I also hoped he was too preoccupied to notice.

"I'd throw it away. And if I didn't have time to throw it away, I'd say you told me to pack my bag for an exciting sleepover at the library, only when I got there you took out this knife and told me I should get in the car, because you always wanted a child and now you could have one." I wondered if he'd thought this up just now, or late at night in the library, or months ago.

I won't lie: in a small way, it was a relief to have my mind made up for me, to know that calling for help was off the table. I felt, for a moment, like I wasn't the guilty one.

And then he started to cry again, and I couldn't even be mad at him. He was desperate and ten years old.

He wasn't navigating anymore, and it seemed like the wisest thing would be to keep heading back east toward Hannibal, if only to have more options.

The two travelers did not converse much that afternoon, as both were tired and bewildered, though they stopped along the way for food and drink and played many games concerning road signs and the alphabet and the license plates of passing cars. Once, after a silence of many minutes, the boy sat up straight and began to sing out loud in a high voice like a floating balloon:

> *"Speed, bonnie boat,*
> *Like a bird on the wi-hing,*
> *Onward! the sailors cry,*
> *Carry the lad*
> *That's born to be Ki-hing*
> *Over the sea to Skye-hye-hye-hye-hye-hye!"*

The Library Lady smiled. "Where did you learn that?" she queried.
"School," replied the golden-faced lad. "You got any gum?"

*The Library Lady replied that she did not, and the boy commenced
chewing on his tongue.*

"*You know, you look like a cow when you do that,*" *remarked the
librarian, and the two laughed heartily as they crossed the border into
the next state.*

I thought we were heading in the right direction, and if there were
any signs pointing the way to the nearest big city, I either didn't
see them or couldn't summon the focus to read them. I knew we
were going east for quite a while, and since we'd started off going
west, I figured that was good. We crossed a long bridge, one I didn't
pay much attention to until I was faced with "Cairo, Illinois Wel-
comes You!" *That* I could read. We had crossed the entire Mississippi Goddamn River without my noticing.

On the other side of the road, the side leading back to the
bridge, traffic was backed up behind three state trooper cars. In a
moment of near cardiac arrest, I thought they were looking for *us*,
until I realized we were headed the other way. They were checking for drunks or fugitives or both, but not for us. At least not yet.

It was 1:16. If we'd been meandering for six hours, it would be
at least four or five hours straight back. More than that, because
I'd have to find a different bridge back to Missouri. By then Ian
would have been missing for twenty-four hours, long enough for
the police to pull out all the stops. If they saw my car approaching
Hannibal with Ian in the backseat, I wouldn't even have time to
explain before they hauled me off and let Ian tell his story.

My best bet was to drive till Ian got tired of the whole thing,
till he missed his family, till he agreed not to turn me in. Most
kids gave up the runaway thing after—what, one day? Two? (I was

thinking of those kids who hide in their own garages, with a jar of pickles and a teddy bear, and their parents know exactly where they are.) And in the meantime, he'd get a nice vacation from his mother and Pastor Bob. I could somehow introduce him to stellar gay role models. I could let him read *The Egypt Game*. We could find the wizard.

I was finally thinking clearly enough to realize I had to call the library, and now, or the Hannibal police would have two missing persons cases on their hands, and it wouldn't be long before they linked them together. And come to think of it, this coming Saturday was the very one I'd lied about when I told Rocky I couldn't make it to his cousin's wedding—I'd mentally stored the date, reminding myself to take at least Saturday off and then say something about having visited the Field Museum—and I might be able to work with that. (How lovely, in the midst of what felt eerily like the first act of a Greek tragedy, to discover this one piece of luck.) I could send Ian back as soon as he was ready, then stay away myself for the rest of the week and pretend it was a planned vacation. It might be nice to have a little recovery time.

If I called Rocky now, before the police came knocking, before he had any reason to think I was lying, he might get it in his head that he'd known about this vacation all along. And if I hadn't told him the details, it was only because he'd been ignoring me lately. By the time I called Loraine and she asked Rocky for verification, he'd gladly back me up. We all did that for each other instinctively anyway, not so much out of teamwork but from the assumption that if it was Loraine's memory versus someone else's word, you'd do best to believe the one that hadn't been steeped in vodka.

I pulled over to the side of the road and said, "You can listen to me make this call. If I don't call the library right now, they're

going to wonder where I am, and they'll send the police out looking for me. Then the police will track my car, and then our little
adventure will be over anyway." The idea that the police would
spend energy looking for a twenty-six-year-old woman who was
four hours late for work when they had a missing child to worry
about, and the idea that they could somehow electronically track
a car that didn't even have a CD player, somehow both skated by.
He nodded slowly.

"You should say you're very sick. Do you know a good trick?"

"I don't need a trick. I do need you to be completely silent."

I knew Rocky's cell wouldn't be on, as long as he was still inside
the library. "Rocky!" I said to his voice mail, an octave too high.
"Just calling to make sure Sarah-Ann and Irene haven't burned
down the basement yet. Please tell me Loraine remembered this
trip and didn't make a complete mess of things. She said she'd
worked everything out with Sarah-Ann, but Lord knows what that
really means." I took a breath and willed myself to slow down. "So
Chicago is freezing, I got here this morning, but everything's good.
Have a great time at the wedding this weekend, if I don't talk to
you before then! Sorry again that I couldn't make it, believe me,
I'd rather be there! Oh, and I'm wondering if I left my sunglasses
on the upstairs desk yesterday! Call me later!"

Then I turned my own phone off. I wasn't ready for the return
call, and I wasn't prepared to improvise more lies.

Ian said, "That was really good! About the sunglasses!"

"Thanks, I guess."

And here I need to plead that despite all evidence to the con-
trary, I do have a conscience. I could picture the Drakes crying

and praying and not being able to eat, even to swallow water. They were imagining he was dead or raped or lost in the woods. But I was also in shock, and going on adrenaline, and I knew that if I focused on the Drakes for more than two seconds, I'd drive straight into the median. It wasn't so much that I did not think of them, but that I *could* not think of them.

Ian was very quiet that afternoon, and I was thankful for the peace. He slept a little, then woke up and steered me north. "This way looks very familiar," he said, as we passed a mile marker and a Video Palace. "I know we're going the right way." I stayed in the right-hand lane. It wasn't as if we were in a hurry. I was still looking, ostensibly, for a place to cross back west, over the river. But at the same time, circling back toward Hannibal felt like a worse and worse idea. Wasn't that the biggest mistake a criminal could make? To return to the scene of the crime? Besides which, the farther north we got, the closer we were to Chicago, where I knew my way around, and where no one would think to look, and where we had a place to stay. My parents were in Argentina, vacationing and visiting a "cousin" who wasn't really anyone's cousin, and they wouldn't be back till Friday. We couldn't get there tonight, but if I hadn't been jailed by this time tomorrow, it might be a nice option.

He slept quite a lot, the deep sleep of someone who's just suffered an asthma attack or a seizure. I doubted he'd even closed his eyes much the night before. He was relaxing finally, and I wondered why. Every mile we drove, I felt worse. Last night his parents would have called the police, and the police, although they'd have been very solicitous, very thorough, probably wouldn't have gone into full code red. Ten-year-old boys run off to live in the woods all the time, and they come home when they're hungry. But by now they had to be seriously alarmed. The earnest people of Hannibal were probably voting what color ribbon to tie on their car antennas and mailboxes. I wondered if Rocky had called me back to tell me all about it, but I still didn't dare turn on my phone.

By ten o'clock that night, I was worried I'd fall asleep on the road. We got off the highway at a promising exit, and Ian spotted a budget hotel that looked not entirely horrifying. I paid with cash from the gas station ATM, and we checked in as Charlie Bucket and Veruca Salt, and got two rooms. (This seemed important, despite my limited funds. I hated to think of the way it would look to anyone—judge, jury, Ian's parents, the media—if it ever came out that we'd stayed together at night. When my only defense would be "No! No! He's probably gay!") As we climbed the stairs, I said, "You didn't leave your parents a note, did you?" I don't know why it hadn't occurred to me before.

"Yeah," he said. I stopped on the landing. He was wearing his backpack across his chest, dragging his feet. "I just said don't worry, and I left them directions for tuna."

"For what?"

"My guinea pig. Her name is Tuna, and she's a white crested. She's named after tuna fish."

"What did the note say?"

"It said basically, like, 'One scoop of food every day, change the chips once a week, fresh water.' I left it on her cage."

"Nothing else?"

"No. Definitely no."

I started climbing again, and wondered what else he hadn't told me.

"Oh, wait," he said. "There was one other thing."

I stopped and put my forehead against the brick wall and felt the blood pound in my ears. "Yes?"

"It was just about her vitamin. You need to relax a little bit." He turned and climbed the rest of the stairs backward.

The rest of the night felt like a hangover. I fell asleep easily and deeply, as if my subconscious couldn't wait for the chance to work things out in dream logic. But I was awake by 3:11, staring at the red clock numbers and wondering if Ian was still in the next room. Beside the clock, I could just make out the biggest letters on a little folded sign:

OOPS! FORGET SOMETHING?

It must have been about sewing kits and razors available at the front desk. I tried not to look at it. I closed my eyes. The comforter was scratchy, but of course that was the tradeoff for the hotel being cheap enough that I could pay cash. I had used my bank card that one time, but I wasn't going to risk a paper trail again.

I felt like Alice, who jumped down after the rabbit never once considering how in the world she was to get out again. If Glenn were there, he would tell me to go with the flow, improvise, be spontaneous. Though actually, if Glenn were there, he might be too busy contacting the FBI to give inspirational advice.

Ian had given me a finger of toothpaste before bed, but I had no brush, and my mouth felt disgusting now. I could get a toothbrush from the desk. Which didn't matter, because I was going to jail. And I was going to hell, for worrying about myself instead of his poor parents. Maybe some human rights group would come to my defense, and everyone would see how I'd rescued this child from a terrible fate. I'd escape to Mexico while awaiting trial. Ian would at least remember that someone tried to save him, once. Until the sun came up, I lay there running through various half-dreamed scenarios, most of them about jail, some heroic, some where everyone was yelling at me in Russian. I stumbled to the moldy shower with a horrible dryness in my throat.

(I make it sound as if I had no choice. I wanted to think I had no choice. Of course I had a million of them. The hot water of the shower made that clear. Maybe it came down to this: beneath all the justification, all the panic, I believed we were in the right. I believed this was the home of the brave. And here we were. Here were the brave.)

As I thought things through, I found that I was deeply, almost physically, relieved that Ian had left the note for his parents. The police would be alarmed, certainly, and the good folks of Hannibal would be out with their flashlights, but there was a profound difference, let's face it, between a runaway and a kid who just vanished in the night. Among other things, the search would be local. They'd look in the shed behind his school, in the woods, at the Starbucks—and all over the library, certainly—but ten-year-old runaways didn't tend to get themselves across state lines. They didn't leave in cars. They didn't have money. It would be a few days, at least, before they started looking into adult accomplices. Janet Drake didn't even know my name. In a truly ideal world, suspicion would alight on Pastor Bob. They'd give him a hard time, check out his basement. If you'd asked me a week ago who would flee Hannibal with Ian, my money would have been on Pastor Sicko Bobbo.

At 7:00 I sat cross-legged on the bed and called the main library number. After that first pit stop, Ian had stopped demanding I surrender my phone—either because he trusted me now, or because he knew I was too deep in this mess to get out with a single phone call. I got Loraine's voice mail, which I hoped she remembered how to check. She asked Rocky at least once a week to help her "get the messages out from in there." "Loraine!" I said. "It's Lucy, just checking in. Sorry we didn't talk before I left, but thank you so much for taking care of everything. I assume Sarah-Ann is the one covering my hours this week, and of course she knows exactly what to do, but you could remind her that read-aloud is Friday at 4:30, and we're on *The Borrowers*, which I think is in my desk. If she can't find it, it's by Mary Norton, N-O-R. And then the craft lady comes Wednesday, but I think that's it. So . . . as I said when we talked, I'll be back by Monday morning. I have my phone with me, and thanks for taking care of all this! Bye!"

If Loraine stayed true to form, in an hour or two she'd be yelling at Sarah-Ann for not remembering my vacation, which had clearly been scheduled weeks ago. "Even Rocky knew about this," she'd say, "and he doesn't even work under her!"

As I hung up, I looked at my phone and saw I had no messages at all. Four recent calls, though, all from the library yesterday

morning, all before I called Rocky's cell. They would have been
worried, of course, especially if someone noticed all the lights I'd
left on. But they hadn't been worried enough to leave panicked
messages, and that was a good sign. I imagined a couple of calm
ones sitting on my home phone: "Lucy, we're just wondering where
you are," et cetera.

Ian knocked on my door (fast and loud, a lot of knocks) and I
opened it. He stood there fully dressed, hair combed, holding out
his tube of toothpaste. His eyes looked red, but he was grinning
and bouncing on his toes.

"I thought you could use some fresh breath," he said.

15

Anthem

That day I let him sit in the passenger seat. He was probably tall enough, and I felt I'd be a safer driver without someone shouting things from behind me.

I'd bought him a packet of six little powdered donuts from the hotel vending machine, and now he was wearing them like rings, taking tiny bites from the outside edges. He had on a Cardinals cap, but it was big and boxy, like he'd never worn it before. I wondered if he'd dug it out from under his bed just because it seemed like something good to run away in.

I got back on the interstate. "So, where are we going, buddy?"

He looked surprised, like he'd forgotten he was the navigator. "Oh, you stay on this road quite a while, still."

"We're going toward Chicago," I said. "Does your grandmother happen to live in Chicago? Because I know a place we could stay that's a lot nicer than a hotel. It would take us a pretty long time to get there, but there's lots of food, and books."

"WE DEF-IN-ITE-LY HAVE TO PASS THROUGH CHI-CA-GO." He was a robot now, apparently. "BUT SHE DOES NOT LIVE THERE."

"Great."

For one last time, I considered turning around and driving back to Hannibal without telling him. I could have distracted him from the road signs if I really wanted, and we'd be back by nightfall and I could drop him on a street corner and head out of town. But I could picture him so clearly dry-sobbing into his arm, saying "She came in on Sunday when the library was closing, and she made me get in her car, and she said she was taking me to get some candy! And I love candy, and I didn't know better, because she wasn't a stranger! And she started asking all about how much money my dad makes!" There would be a national search, and the newscasters would give the story its own theme music. I wouldn't stand a chance, even in Mexico. And come to think of it, I didn't even have my passport with me. No, he really had to want to go home. And judging from the blissful expression on his face as he stuck his head out the passenger window like a golden retriever, that wasn't quite yet.

Thirty miles later, thirty miles farther away from yesterday morning, when I hadn't yet thrown my life away and ruined his parents': "Miss Hull, do you have any CDs?"

"My car only plays tapes. But I don't have either."

Ian stuck his finger in the tape flap, then pulled it out and pressed eject. A tape popped out, one I'd never seen before.

"It's not mine," I said.

I realized that I actually hadn't used the tape deck since I'd bought the car two years before. I listened to NPR on my way to work and needed silence to navigate traffic on the way home. I'd bought the car from a guy in Kenton who handed it over caked in McDonald's wrappers and golf tees and cigarette butts.

"Maybe it's karaoke!" He pushed the tape back in and pressed Rewind. The player churned backward, and I was momentarily surprised that it was capable of this.

"AND NOW!" screamed the tape. Ian lunged and turned down the volume. "Our national anthem, as sung by. . . . Miss Gina Arena!" A stadium-sized crowd made happy noises, like they knew who she was. Ian suddenly popped upright in the seat, pulled off his baseball cap, and slapped it over his heart.

"*Australians all let us rejoice, for we are young and free,*" sang a woman's voice, ringing and angelic. Behind her, the crowd sang along.

"What *is* this?" Ian kept his hat hovering above his breastbone, unsure of the protocol.

"*We've golden soil and wealth for toil, our home is girt by sea!*"

"That would be the national anthem of *Australia*." I hadn't even noticed the announcer's accent, I was so focused on the road, on the million images of doom flashing across the windshield. "*Our land abounds in nature's gifts of beauty rich and rare! In history's page let every stage advance Australia fair!*" We both laughed through the rest of the song, but Ian never put his hat down. When the song finished and some ancient World Cup game started, he rewound it.

"Let's learn it!" he said, and so we spent the next hour singing along and trying to understand all the words. We got pretty good, and when we tried without the tape we weren't perfect, but "we had gusto!" as Ian put it.

Watching him with his hat on his heart, singing the anthem of another country, I imagined an Ian born somewhere else, Finland or San Francisco or one hundred years in the future, in a world without Pastor Bobs. Most of America was like Hannibal, Missouri, no matter what was in the news about East Coast cities, no matter what was in the movies, no matter how many prime-time sitcoms featured spunky gay sidekicks. To be fair, maybe most of the planet was like Hannibal, Missouri.

To get "Advance Australia Fair" out of our heads, I turned on the radio and flipped around. Ian wasn't interested in anything until we got to what must have been a Christian station.

"Turn this up! I love this song!" he said, and started singing along:

> *When Jesus walked oh-oh!*
> *On the mountain tops oh-oh!*
> *He didn't stop no-oh!*
> *No He didn't stop!*

It sounded almost like a Seattle band from the nineties, but with Jesus lyrics. "Where did you learn that?" I asked.

"Oh, I go to this thing. This class, with these kids. It's okay. And we listen to music, and sometimes this one leader guy brings his guitar."

I didn't want to push the subject, but I thought it would be good for him to talk about it. "What else do you do?"

"Some stuff. We do, like, workbooks and we read stuff. And then we always play sports. We mostly play football, but it's not tackle."

I looked out my left window so he wouldn't see me biting my laugh. It was partly the image of Ian playing football. I remembered one Family Fun Day when I tried to toss him a balloon, and he ducked. And it was partly the fact that they wouldn't let them tackle.

"Do they teach you things?"

"Yeah, it's kind of like Sunday school. Only it's probably more fun, because you can wear jeans."

"Is it all good stuff? Do you believe everything they tell you?"

He pulled down the passenger-side sunshield, and looked in the mirror while he stretched his cheeks back in a fish face. "Well, it's all from the Bible, so it's definitely true."

Hard to argue with, since I wasn't about to assail his entire religion. Sadly, my primary motivation for silence was not empathy but strategy—the second he got mad at me, he might decide to use the next phone he saw to turn me in.

So instead, in my most neutral voice, I said, "I know about that kind of class." It was an invitation to skip the awkward part of the conversation and tell me more.

But he didn't say anything, just sat there looking out the window.

16

Head on a Pike

When Ian did talk again, it was to ask about the Russian flag sticker on my rear window. My father had stuck it there the previous summer, in a sudden fit of national pride. It was around the same time he started asking if I wouldn't like to change my name back to Hulkinov. He never volunteered to do it himself—too many business contacts would be confused—but for me, he said, it wouldn't matter.

My father had a complete narrative for every link in the Hulkinov ancestry, from the scholar-warrior of the notoriously impaled head on down. He wore the family crest on a gold ring, on the pointer finger of his right hand, as only someone European with a portfolio of shady business dealings can.

"This young fellow," he would say over the long Saturday breakfasts of my childhood, loosening the ring so it slid down his bent finger like a single brass knuckle, "was a swashbuckler. He took the bulls by their horns. Next Hulkinov is his son, who hides in the wheat fields when the enemy comes for revenge, trying to kill the only son of the great warrior. They think they will find him home, but off he goes to make his fortune, does not come home to roost for twenty-three years. Next Hulkinov, he charges to the battle on his horse, kills forty men in one day. Becomes a favorite of the czar."

By the time he got to the Bolshevik revolution I was usually catatonic, but next came the best parts—his father and himself. His father, a man who peered half-starved out of photographs, his face stretched between giant round ears, had weaseled his way into the good graces of Stalin, only to perpetrate against Uncle Joe some unforgivable offense about which my father was always exasperatingly vague. I entertained various theories for years— Had he filched a left-behind Romanov Fabergé egg? Stolen Stalin's mistress?—before I realized that if it were anything half that interesting, my father the fabulist would long ago have woven it into a cloth of finest hyperbole. It probably had to do with taxation laws or Party infighting. My grandfather, in any event, left his wife and eight-year-old son, took a box of cigars, a bottle of vodka, and a change of clothes, and told them he was off to Siberia before Stalin had the chance to ship him there. That was it, and all through my childhood I fantasized he'd come knocking on the door of our Chicago apartment, snow still crusted to his coat, beard thick with icicles. My father insisted he died only a few years later in Novosibirsk, but I knew better.

My father's older brother, Ilya, died trying to cross the border into Romania, but that was all I knew. There was one photograph of my father and his brother, and every time it was shown, my father would say, "This is my brother Ilya, who died crossing the border to Romania." Period.

And my father himself, the summer he turned twenty, a week
after his underground chocolate company had been discovered by
his neighbor, looked out the window of his mother's house one
night to see two men in thin brown coats bent over the back of
his car. Ilya had built the car himself from scraps, and he and my
father shared it. When my father dared to go outside an hour later,
he found a fat potato crammed tight into the tailpipe. Who these
men had been, and why they'd tried killing him with vegetables
rather than just hauling him away at daybreak like everyone else,
I could never quite get straight. In any event, my father removed
the potato with kitchen tongs, packed a bag of clothes, kissed his
mother's cigarette-wrinkled mouth, and drove to the Volga, where
he jumped from the dock to a shipping boat, clung for two minutes to a rope on the boat's outer wall, and then plunged into the
river, breaking his leg on the way. He lost his bag swimming, then
filled his belly with air and lay flat like a floating log, letting the
current carry him downstream. "I did the dead man's float to stay
alive," he'd say, relishing the irony. For two hours he floated in the
cold August water until two brothers in a little fishing boat pulled
him up, waterlogged and half drowned, and laid him to dry on the
boat floor like a prize catch. By the time he made it over the border, through Romania and Yugoslavia and into the Italian refugee
camp, he'd lost twenty pounds and grown a beard.

In third grade, when we studied Ellis Island, I imagined him
sailing on a steamer past Lady Liberty with a blanket over his
shoulders, getting chalked and checked for lice, sleeping in quar-
antine. I even raised my hand and said it, until Mrs. Herman's
puzzled look cut me short. Really, my father flew into Idlewild in
mismatched refugee clothes. It was 1959 and he had yellow pants
and a chest-length Rasputin beard and bulging eyes. The way he

told it later was that as he gripped the cold railing and stumbled down the airplane steps to the tarmac, the Pan Am ground crew turned from their luggage carts to stare and laugh. Sometimes I wonder if he took that as permission to rip off every American he met, to cast himself as the scholar-warrior and everyone else as the head on the pike. He had very little with him—the clothes from the Italian camp, one hundred American dollars, and his papers—but he did have that ring and its four hundred years of warrior lore.

In his Saturday litanies he billed the Hulkinovs as a line of adventurers charging bareheaded into battle, but I realized now that half of them were only runaways. And which was I, heading deeper into trouble with every mile I fled from home?

We stopped at a burger place for lunch, our third fast food meal in two days. Because we were sick of grease, we both ordered anemic little salads in clear boxes, and after Ian bowed his head and sat in silence for about ten seconds, he drowned his iceberg lettuce in ranch dressing. I picked at mine with the plastic fork, not eating much. My God, I was turning into Janet Drake. Ian started recounting for me every shocking injury received by everyone he'd ever known. A girl's teeth that got stuck in another girl's forehead, a woman whose nose was bloodied by flying Mardi Gras beads, a classmate who caught his own ear with a fishing hook.

"How did you get the scars above your eyebrow?" I asked.

"I went like this." He stood his plastic fork on end on the table, and pretended to ram his head down onto the prongs. So at least I'd been partly right. "I was mad at myself, I think. I forget."

It did sound like something he'd do, inflicting pain on himself for sheer dramatic impact. I believed him. But I realized now that the only vague evidence I'd had of any kind of physical abuse had just vanished. Ian popped a little tomato in his mouth and swallowed it whole.

Back in the car, I checked my messages. Still nothing from the library, which was starting to seem a little eerie, but one from Glenn saying "We need to talk about the weekend." We had been planning on Mexican and Blockbuster that Friday. When Ian fell asleep, his forehead on the window and his glasses in his lap, I called Glenn back. "Hey, I'm calling from the road," I said. There was no point pretending I was still in Hannibal—for one thing, he might show up again at the library. "I'm actually on my way to Chicago."

"*Chicago?*"

"I didn't tell you?" I said. "I was sure I told you. I have this old friend from high school who's been sick, and I was planning to come up just for a couple days, but it looks like it might be longer."

"*Chicago,*" he said. "That's so funny." His tone was odd, as if he didn't believe me. I wondered, briefly, if the police were listening in. He might be sitting in a detective's office, sweating all over the table, trying to sound calm, hoping to keep me on the line as long as he could. But of course he wasn't. This wasn't a movie. Things didn't work that fast in Hannibal.

"Yeah. I'm staying with my parents."

We couldn't stay any longer than the one night, though—even if Glenn wasn't bugged now, the more time that passed the more likelihood there was of people reading the papers and pooling information. As soon as they suspected me, Glenn and Rocky would tell them where to look.

"Hey, is your friend okay?"

By friend, I thought he meant Ian. I recovered in time. "She will be, I'm sure. I'm just helping out a little."

"Just don't donate any major organs, okay? That's not what you're doing, is it?"

I laughed. "I'll tell you all about it when we get back. When *I* get back."

"Can't wait."

I was becoming a fabulous liar. I'd always excelled at embellishment, white lies, covers for unfinished homework, but I hadn't had practice with something so serious, so consequential. And I wasn't even sweating. I lifted my hands off the wheel to check. Not a drop of moisture. It was like I'd been born to the outlaw life. If I lost my library job, I could go pro.

Submitted for the record, the entire history of my criminal career, up to that point in time:

> **Age 4:** Standing in line at the post office with my mother, I have a lollipop from the bank drive-thru. The boy behind me is maybe three, and I see him staring at my lollipop, on the verge of tears. I turn so he can see it better, and I take a huge, purple-tongued lick. He begins to scream, and his mother can't figure out why. I'm the only one who knows. It's the first deliberately cruel thing I remember doing. It might also be the

model for all my future relationships with men, but this is beside the point.

Age 5: My father begins sending me into the halls of our apartment building to steal various things left by the doorman outside our neighbors' doors. Dry cleaning, UPS boxes, even milk in glass bottles that a family downstairs has delivered from a farm in Wisconsin as late as 1986. Note that we are far from poor. My father later says that he simply couldn't help himself: in Russia, if someone had been so foolish as to leave unguarded milk outside the door, you would take it and then brag about it all over town, letting everyone at the bar laugh at the people who thought they were so rich they could leave their milk on the stoop. At the time, he simply tells me these are things our neighbors don't want anymore, so they've put them in the hall for someone to take. He tries on the freshly pressed oxford shirts and sends me back with the ones that don't fit, to hang back over the doorknobs in their plastic shrouds.

Age 8: My father fills my coat pockets with nine little jars of caviar at Dominick's. This I know is stealing, but I am too busy pretending I am a mother fish to care. I am a fish, and these are the millions of tiny eggs I'm carrying upstream.

Age 15: I cheat on my sophomore Advanced Algebra final. It's surprisingly easy, and no one finds out. I expect to feel guilty but don't.

Ages 17 through 20: Significant but unextraordinary underage drinking, etc. Nothing a presidential candidate would even bother denying.

Ages 23-26: Theft from Hannibal Public Library of over one hundred books I deemed inferior, one stapler, one ten-year-old child, and several reams of computer paper.

I reflected now that aside from the drinking, all these things involved stealing on some level—math answers, caviar, lightly starched shirts. Even the lollipop incident had felt like a kind of theft, like I was reaching out and grabbing that little boy right by his sucker-craving eyes. Perhaps we're all hardwired for our crimes. Liars are always liars and thieves are always thieves, and killers are born violent. The form our sins take just depends on circumstance: how far we sink in the world, how badly we're raised. Who walks into our little library and upsets the universe.

17

Debussy's Horns

After we fueled up and bought chocolate to stay awake, we were completely out of cash. "Count the change," I said, and handed Ian my Tupperware of coins. He poured it all onto his lap and started building little stacks.

"Guess how many dollars we have," he said finally.

"About two."

"No, one. Plus twenty cents. But you could also say that we have one to the millionth power. Then you could say we're millionaires."

Time passed more quickly that afternoon with a specific destination in mind, and the scenery certainly improved as we passed through the Chicago suburbs. My parents live on Lake Shore Drive, in an apartment worth more than I'd make in fifty years. I don't tend to tell people this. And I certainly don't take my parents' money, partly because I'm sure my father made most of it illegally, not on real estate. The Russian Mafia in Chicago is bigger than you'd think.

I doubt my father has ever hurt anyone, not physically, but he does some funny things with numbers. Zeros are conjured out of thin air, decimal points moved, entire bank accounts erased or invented. His friend the travel agent went to jail in the eighties for printing false ticket receipts for his friends. His friend the restaurant owner vanished forever a few years back.

"Wow, it's all carved!" Ian said as we pulled up. He meant the building, with its elaborate scrollwork above the front door. I still had the sticker on my car, so we got waved right into the garage, and I parked in my parents' empty space.

"Have you ever been to Chicago before?" I asked him. I'd been too lost in my own thoughts as we entered the city to ask. And he'd been busy sticking his head out the window into the freezing air so he could see the tops of buildings.

"No, but I've been to St. Louis a lot. But not even the fun parts."

We rode the shiny new elevator up to the fourteenth floor, and I opened the door onto the living room—its white leather furniture and glass coffee table and the row of windows overlooking the half-frozen lake.

"Cool!" he said, and he leaned over the back of the couch to press his hands and face against the glass. "Can we eat on the balcony?" It was almost dinnertime.

"Too cold. Windy City."

I showed Ian how to work the TV, regretted it for one horrible instant when it occurred to me that he might see himself on the news, then relaxed when he managed to find Nickelodeon. I left him there and took a shower and changed into my mother's

white blouse and blue wool cardigan and khakis. She was a couple of sizes bigger than me, but it was so nice to feel clean that I
didn't mind. I shoved my dirty clothes into the washer in the big
bathroom closet. Ian wanted to do his laundry separately, and
himself.

We found spinach ravioli in the freezer and an unopened jar of
marinara in the pantry. For myself, I opened a bottle of what was
probably a very expensive Syrah.

"Are you an alcoholic?" Ian asked.

"Not yet," I said.

We sat at the long, glass dining table, and Ian was unduly
excited to see his feet through it. He pretended to kick the plates
from underneath.

"Did you grow up here?" he asked.

"Yep. Since I was two. Same apartment."

"Where's your bedroom?"

"They turned it into a library. Isn't that funny? I'll show you
later."

It was dark out now, and I loved how the night turned the windows to black mirrors. There were sirens every few minutes—a
sound I'd always associated with home, rather than tragedy, even
now when I kept thinking they were coming for me. On the highway that afternoon, an ambulance had passed us with sirens blar-
ing, and I'd very nearly stopped breathing. From up here, though,
the sounds of the distant emergency vehicles were just the constant and reassuring accents of the city noise below, the reminder
that life was going on without us, and so was death, and most people in the world had other things to think about than a hapless
librarian and the boy she had inadvertently kidnapped. I loved
standing there, fourteen stories above the streets. I thought of

Robert Frost: "I'd like to get away from earth awhile." Skyscrapers, birch trees, a nice big glass of wine.

"I have a question," Ian said. "If you grew up here, how did you ever play sports?"

"I played them at school," I said. "And there's a workout room on the top floor."

"But what about on weekends?"

"Nope. Except sometimes my father and I would move the barstools to make goals, and we'd play soccer with a beach ball. Soccer is a very big deal in Russia." I'd been telling him earlier about my father's escape.

"Can we try it?" I was surprised this was so important to him. I remembered what Sophie Bennett had said about his lack of coordination in the cancan line. Then again, he was a ten-year-old boy who hadn't run around much in the last two days, except up and down the sidewalks of highway rest areas.

"Sure," I said. "But I don't think they have beach balls here anymore."

"We could definitely make a ball out of clothes."

Once we'd cleared the dishes, I helped Ian find a drawer of my father's white undershirts, and he worked to tie them into a ball with kitchen twine. We moved the four barstools to make goals at either end of the living room, and we each stood in one. We kicked the ball of shirts back and forth, one shot each, trying to block and score. He wasn't that good, but neither was I. The ball started to unravel every fifth or sixth shot, and Ian would stop to fix it.

"Do you play soccer at home?" I asked.

"Well, I'm on a team, but it's pretty stupid, and mostly I'm just in charge of handing out orange slices. At recess I usually play something called Ian Ball, but I can't show you here because there's no Dumpster."

There was the sound of a key in the door, and Ian froze where he was bending over the ball to retie the string. "It's the cleaning lady," I said, but even before I heard my father's loud voice I realized it was too late for Krystyna.

"Dad!" I said before he could find us and have a heart attack. "Dad, we're in here." My mother came around the corner first, her eyes big and white. She had her leather travel bag over her shoulder, and her hair looked slept on from the plane.

"Lucy!" she said, walking toward me with her arms open, the bag falling, "Sweetheart, what's wrong? We saw your car. My God, you look terrible."

"I'm fine, I'm okay," I said.

"We came home early, your father's stomach is a mess, don't even ask." As she was hugging me, my father came into the room, that big Russian grin, yellow and crooked, already spread across his face. "Great God," he said, "and who is this new boyfriend?"

Before Ian could say something ridiculous, I said, "Oh, do you remember my friend Janna Glass, from high school?"

Janna Glass *was* someone who'd been at Chicago Latin with me, a girl who once stole French fries off my plate, a name I'd pulled at random, but no one my parents would know. They shook their heads.

"This is her son, Ian." Why had I said Ian? Why not any other name in the world?

Ian held out his hand to my father. "Ian Glass," he said. "Ian Bartholomew Glass."

"She's in the hospital, so I drove up to help out. We came over here for a change of pace."

"Well what's wrong with her?" said my tactful mother. She took off her heavy green coat, and I could feel the cold fly off it as she did.

"My mother tried to kill herself," Ian said. He was a decent liar, I realized, a calm one. "My father ran off with a floozy, so she tried to kill herself with pills. But now she's going to put her life back together." He must have watched a hell of a lot of TV in addition to reading.

"Oh, you poor *lamb*. You should both stay the night. We have the couch and the air mattress." After they put their bags away, my mother gave us piles of blankets and blew up the mattress with a hair dryer. "Where shall we put it?"

"Definitely the library," Ian said. "I love to sleep in a library." I watched down the hall as my mother made up the bed with pillows and sheets and one of my old teddy bears that she pulled out of a closet. My father clapped me on the back, and Ian too, and said, "Who will have a beer?"

Ian looked horrified. "No, thank you," he said. "I'm cool." He looked at me to see if he'd done the right thing, and I tried not to laugh. It was clearly something he'd been coached to say during a school assembly on peer pressure.

"You are 'cool'? You are a 'cool cat'?" My father grinned down.

"Ian, you're welcome to ignore my father."

My father got himself a tall glass of beer, then sat on the couch and pointed to a chair for Ian. "Come sit and I show you something you will not believe with your own two eyes."

Ian sat, probably relieved that the conversation had not progressed to an offer of crack.

My father pulled back the light hair combed across his balding head, revealing his forehead. "Now you look closely here under the lamp, and you tell me what it is you see."

Ian leaned toward him. "Did you fall down?"

My father was thrilled. "No! This I was born with! Two bumps, one per side!" He touched one, then the other. "Now," he said to me, "you show yours." I reluctantly pulled my hair back from where it normally sweeps down to hide the two knobs of bone. They aren't terribly prominent, but about one out of twenty times that I have my hair back, someone will ask if I've hit my head. "Horns!" my father proclaimed. "You have heard of the French composer Debussy." Ian nodded as if he had. "Debussy had this also, these two horns. And so it is proof that this is the sign of great genius. Extra room for the brain!"

Ian clapped in appreciation. "That's awesome!"

"Awesome," my father repeated, laughing. "Lucy, it turns out your dad is awesome."

18

Chocolate Factory, Leningrad

My father then started in on the Great Hulkinov Lineage, and I leaned my head back and closed my eyes. It was a relief, after three days, that someone else was engaging Ian in conversation. I tried to clear my mind, although of course that was impossible.

I had a silent film reel of the Drakes playing continuously in my head. Their minister would be sitting in their living room with them. Or maybe it would be Pastor Bob. Or three studious police detectives. I would like to think that I worried more for them than for myself. But if that were true, I'd have turned the car around, hand-delivered Ian to their door, and let the consequences rain down on me. The horns didn't lie. My father and I were alike, wagging our forked tails and stealing what we wanted. The devil only thinks of himself.

But no. The one I worried about most was *Ian*. Otherwise, why had I thrown my life away for him?

"Okay," my father was saying, "so I will tell you about my chocolate factory."

Ian sat straight up, tired as he obviously was. This was about the most intriguing thing you could possibly say to a Roald Dahl fan. I'd heard the story many times, and over the years it had mutated from a straightforward account of adolescent rebellion into something akin to the later works of García Márquez, and then into the key event of twentieth-century Russian history.

"Now in Russia," he said, "when I grew up, it was USSR. You have heard of this?" Ian nodded. "Very strict, very boring. And we had *no good chocolate*. And chocolate, it is my one true love."

"So now look at him, he's diabetic!" my mother called from the library.

"We had instead light brown chocolate that tasted like chalk. You could hold it in your hand five hours, and still it wouldn't melt. But when I was seventeen years old, my uncle was allowed to travel to Switzerland, and he sneaked me back beautiful real chocolate. This is almost black, and it smells like a forest. Not like this Hershey nonsense. You are a fan of chocolate, yes?"

For his answer, Ian panted like a dog.

"So you are catching my drift. And I hogged my chocolate, but I described it to my friends. And they did not believe me! So I have the idea that I'm going to sell real chocolate to all the town. And do you know what the problem is?"

Ian shook his head.

"You could not start your own business in USSR! I have to do this in secret. So I go to my friend Sergei, and he could get what he wanted on the black market, and this included chocolate. He was the only one who could get jazz records."

"What's a black market?"

"Black market is where I sell you something, but in secret because it is against the law."

"Like drugs?"

"No, like jazz records. Okay. So Sergei and I start a chocolate factory in the basement of my house. We realize it is cheaper to buy big blocks, and so we buy *bricks* of chocolate, each one as big as an encyclopedia set. We have to wheel them into my basement on a cart. And we take a hammer and a wedge of wood, and we hammer the chocolate into pieces, and then over the furnace we melt this into chocolate soup."

Ian rubbed his belly in appreciation.

"Then we pour the soup into a mold Sergei has made, and we have 250 chocolate bars the size of my finger." He held up his crooked pointer finger. "I will tell you, this is not a good idea. The chocolate turns gray colored if you melt it like this, but still it is better than whatever else. So we wrap these in paper that says 'Chocolate Company, Leningrad.' Now we were not in Leningrad, but this was to cover up. And we sold the chocolate bars to other boys. Girls we could not trust. Some boys gave us money, and some would trade us things like toilet paper."

Ian wasn't going to let that one slip by. "Toilet paper?"

"The bad kind was like a cactus. The good kind was worth more than gold. So we sell so much chocolate that at the stores, no one will buy any more of the disgusting old chocolate. Once they had one little taste of ours, one sniff, they knew they could never eat the horrible chalk again. And before long, the mayor gets the wind of this, that the stores could not sell chocolate bars, and he sends a letter to Joseph Stalin himself, saying, 'In my town, the people are so happy, they no longer need to eat sweets!' And this encouraged Stalin! He thought, 'Aha! It has worked! My plan for a better Russia has worked!' So without my chocolate bars, who knows, the world could be different." But he said it with such a smirk, even Ian couldn't take him seriously.

"Did you ever get caught?"

He laughed. "Very soon I was busy with school, and so I closed the chocolate factory down. But I was always on the black market. I could get for people good vodka, beer, cigarettes, gum, magazines of naked ladies. I was a very rich boy."

I was shocked—not that he told a ten-year-old about the naked ladies, but that he'd alter his story this much. His exaggerations normally accrued little by little, but he'd never changed the substance of the story like this before. It must have been for Ian's benefit, to give the tale a happier ending than a potato in a tailpipe. Or maybe he'd intuited that we didn't need a story right then about getting caught.

"Why did you leave Russia if you were very rich?" Ian asked.

"No one was really rich in the USSR. Because what would you buy with your money? Not a Mercedes."

I tuned out again as my mother came back in the room. She rolled her eyes at me and took my father's empty beer glass into the kitchen. Come to think of it, I had no idea if even the basics of the story were accurate. Sometimes, he said that Stalin gave a famous speech on the radio about the town that needed no chocolate. Other times, he and Sergei were originally caught by the town mayor, but bribed him with one hundred chocolate bars, and he kept his silence, until two years later, when the mailman caught them. Sometimes they made a fortune, and sometimes the chocolate was given away free, as a gesture of political resistance. But it really hadn't occurred to me till then that the entire thing might be a lie, that the whole idea of an underground chocolate factory was just a little too good to be true. It bothered me more than I would have expected.

Even now, five years later, I know that my whole Russia, the one in my mind, is still a lie. My mental map of the motherland is dotted with fictions, the way old Atlantic maps showed mermaids, sea monsters: here, north of Moscow, is my father's chocolate factory; here is Raskolnikov, pausing on his staircase; here is Ivan Ilyich, hanging curtains; here flows the Volga, polluted with refugees; there trots Gogol's nose; here the brave citizens throw rocks at Stalin's statue; there flee the Romanov children into the night, their pockets stuffed with gold; and up there lies Siberia, my grandfather crunching his way back home. Through it all, a thin line of truth: the road my college choir bus took from Perm to Yekaterinburg to Chelyabinsk, from concert hall to cathedral, past graffiti-covered concrete walls, past cottages with clotheslines.

But then, the America of my father and his friends had been a lie, too, before they landed on the tarmac: toilets that never clogged, children singing in the streets, a movie star on every corner, Marlboro cigarettes for free. Maybe in some ways they all still lived in a dream America. The land of milk and honey, after all—so why not free milk from the hallway? Why not free honey from the store?

It makes me wonder what kinds of fiction I'm capable of, by nature and nurture. I wonder, looking back at that time in Hannibal, how much I projected onto Ian. And I wonder how truthfully I remember our drive, and what he said, and whether I might have seen him crying in the rearview but blocked it out.

And I wonder if any of this happened at all. Occasionally when

I wake up, and before I open my eyes, I'll try remembering that I never left Hannibal, to see if I can shake myself out of this dream. Or I'll try remembering that I'm in jail. But when I do open my eyes, I see the wall of my new apartment, and there's nothing I can do about it. Maybe that's why I prefer this new library to my own bedroom: looking at the million book spines, I can imagine a million alternate endings. It turned out the butler did it all, or I ended up marrying Mr. Darcy, or we went and watched a girl ride the merry-go-round in Central Park, or we beat on against the current in our little boats, or Atticus Finch was there when we woke up in the morning.

Or better still, I can imagine it's a story that hasn't been written yet, that there's still time to change everything.

Ian went to bed early, excited by the room and the air mattress, and my parents made coffee and plied me with questions about Janna Glass. We moved to the table, and I tried mightily to sit up straight, to appear awake and unpanicked. "Which one was she?" asked my mother. I was glad I'd taken my yearbooks to Hannibal a year before, so she couldn't look Janna up and see her frizzy black hair and huge eyes. She could never be Ian's mother any more than I could.

"So finally you have an adventure," my father said.

"Not really. Just helping out."

He gave me a conspiratorial look, a look that said, *Listen, we used to steal dry cleaning together. You got your first cashmere sweater this way.* "Okay," he said. "Okay." He drank his coffee while my mother asked about Janna Glass's suicide attempt.

"Did he find her like that?" she asked. I had said she took a bottle of pills, that I didn't know what kind, that she'd called 911 for help just in time.

"No," I said. "He was in school."

"Does he go to Latin?"

"No, somewhere else."

"Where's the father?"

"No one knows."

My whole childhood was like this, having to reenact every moment of my day at the dinner table. I got excellent grades in science because my mother made me explain to her again and again every experiment we did in lab. She finally went to bed, and I was about to go too when my father leaned across the table.

"You could use some money, yes?" He asked it almost triumphantly, knowing I hadn't accepted his money in four years, knowing I'd have to say yes this time. He pushed money on people the way my mother's family pushed food, and he was equally offended when anyone turned him down.

I let my head rest on my arm, on top of the cold table. "Actually, I could. It's just that I'm up here on short notice, and I don't know how long I'm staying. But of course I'll pay you back."

He walked into the library where Ian was asleep and came back a minute later with a business envelope full of fifties and hundreds. One thousand dollars, I would count later.

"This is emergency fund," he said. "You keep it. Now do you want the Mercedes? It's a good car. Your car is going to fall apart in the middle of the road. This is how they call a lemon."

"It's okay." Aside from the fact that I didn't plan to stay in Chicago, I was certain his car would raise more red flags for the police than my own. For one thing, he'd bought it from a man named Uncle Nicolai, who was not my actual uncle and who had no discernible job other than doing favors for other Russians. Plus, my father had lost his Illinois driver's license the year before and was driving on one he had somehow obtained from Colorado, where he owned property.

"Where are you going after this?" he asked.

"Home," I said. "Missouri."

He gave me the stolen dry cleaning look again. "Where are you going really?"

I must have turned red, and I couldn't think of what to say. But it didn't matter, I realized. He couldn't have guessed everything, and even if he had, he seemed strangely proud of me. "It depends how long this thing takes. I might head out east to visit some college people."

"Ah. This is perfect, then. Will you go near Pittsburgh?" The way my father pronounced the names of American cities, it made them sound like islands in the Black Sea.

I wasn't thinking fast enough. "Maybe." He knew it was where my college roommate lived, so I could hardly have said no, even if I'd been more awake.

"Okay, so you can take some things for me. I have some things for my friend Leo that I don't want to send through the mail. You can drop these at his house, and I'll give you the address. I tell him you're coming."

"Wait, no," I said. "What kind of stuff?"

He laughed. "Papers. What, you think drugs? You think your father is a drug seller? I'm sending uranium? Your father the Russian arms dealer, this is what you think?"

"I'm just wondering if this could possibly get me arrested." Law-abiding me.

He went into the study again and came back with a shoebox.

"Look," he said, opening the lid. It looked like mostly receipts and some other papers, folded in half. "This is small potatoes, okay?"

I said, "I don't really want to mess with this."

He closed the lid of the box and put his fingers to his temples. "Lucy, you are translucent," he said. "You are not okay. So all right, you go to Pittsburgh and do this, maybe everything turns out just fine. The apple does not fall off the tree." Whether he was implying that I was my father's daughter, or that he wasn't going to let go of me, I wasn't sure. Either way, he didn't know what he was talking about.

I shook my head and said, "Fine, okay." I wanted to go to bed. I knew, on some level, that as soon as I agreed, I was obligated to go as far as Pittsburgh, even if Ian suddenly decided to go home. If I didn't deliver the box, it might be a minor inconvenience, or someone might get killed. I'd rather not have a murder on my conscience, even if it meant extending the kidnapping a few more days. I shouldn't have agreed at all. But I was tired, to the point where my blinks were longer than the spaces in between.

"You're a good Russian girl," he said. He disappeared with the box, and when he came back he'd secured the lid with a wide strip of packing tape that ran all the way around. He wrote down the address on the back of an envelope. He said, "I tell them you're coming."

19

Courage, Heart, Brain

T his is the mess that Lucy made.

This is the boy who lived in the mess that Lucy made.

This is the man who told tales to the boy who lived in the mess that Lucy made.

This is the chocolate that flavored the tales that were told to the boy who lived in the mess that Lucy made.

This is the mayor, all forlorn, who was bribed by the chocolate that flavored the tales that were told to the boy who lived in the mess that Lucy made.

This is the Russia that might be a myth that cradled the mayor, all *forlorn, who was bribed by the chocolate that flavored the tales that were told to the boy who lived in the mess that Lucy made.*

This is Lucy, all forlorn, on her parents' couch on Wednesday morn, considering the compulsion that prompted the abduction of the traumatized boy who read the books that lived on the shelves that lined the walls of the little brick building that brewed up the mess that Lucy made.

Ian and I slept in that morning, but my father slept later. "You don't want to know about his stomach," my mother said as she scrambled some eggs. "The hotel should make us pay for the damage."

Ian just poked at his eggs, but drank five glasses of orange juice. I wanted to tell him to stop so we wouldn't have to pull over all morning for him to pee, but my mother thought I was just driving him back to the hospital.

Before we left, I went into the library and stepped over the air mattress to get my passport out of my mother's file cabinet. It was something I should have had anyway, but a passport was the kind of thing she insisted on keeping for me, lest I lose it. I wondered if she pictured my apartment floor carpeted in dolls and sticker books and glitter, if she thought I'd lose it under my bed behind my fourth grade math book. It was right there in my document file, in front of my birth certificate and my SAT scores and a lot of early report cards that said ominous things about my inability to sit still at a desk. I was twenty years old in the passport photo, bright-faced and ready to fly to Italy with my parents. I put it in my purse. I took it not because I planned to flee the country, but because it was mine, and because I wanted to be prepared. It was like Ian and his ridiculous pool pass. (And maybe, for some reason, we were both just desperate to identify ourselves: Yes, this is me, this smiling, over-lit person. Not the refugee you see before you.) My father's laptop was on, and I realized I was going to look online whether I wanted to or not. When I first decided to stay here, it crossed my mind that I wouldn't be able to log on to the computer, and I'd been surprisingly relieved. I didn't want to know what was out there. I still didn't want to, but now the computer was up and running, and here I was searching Ian's name. It seemed there were a few news articles in regional papers ("Local Youth Missing," "Hannibal Boy Missing Since Sunday"), but when I tried to follow the links they all wanted my password. I'd have to pay a monthly fee for access and give them my name. I looked up the home page of Hannibal Day and found nothing but a photo of bright-hatted children smiling in the snow, and an outdated reminder of the Winter Break schedule. Finally I looked up Pastor Bob, and found that in the past couple of months he'd started a sort of prayer blog—essentially one press release per week, disguised as a prayer.

That week's entry was called "And Off We Go! Spreading God's Love Across America!" It was hard to read: calligraphic font on a pale blue background. It came back to me suddenly, my friend Darren Alquist at the mall that last year of high school, as we walked by the window display of Good Pastures Christian Books, the framed, flowered poems, the paperbacks with sunset covers: "How do they know God likes calligraphy so much? What if God *hates* calligraphy?" We'd say it again, for weeks afterward. I'd write it in his yearbook: "God hates calligraphy!" It looked appropriately Christian here on Pastor Bob's site, but it was maybe not the best move for someone trying desperately not to seem gay.

Halfway down the page, after the announcement of his depar-

ture for an East Coast tour with DeLinda "in the BobMobile!" was
the following:

> *Please pray for Ian D., a young sheep in our St. Louis*
> *fold that the Lord has allowed to let wander. We pray for his*
> *return, and for his loving parents who have been my loyal*
> *supporters. "Put on his finger a ring, and on his feet put san-*
> *dals. Bring forth and slaughter the fatted calf. We shall feast*
> *and celebrate, for this is my son who was dead and is now*
> *alive; he was lost and now is found." Luke 15:22–24.*

I'd like to say it was hard to hate Pastor Bob when he was (or
seemed) so sincere. It wasn't. I stared at the blurry photo of Bob
and DeLinda on the steps of the BobMobile (disappointingly, just
a large blue bus), at the way his arm flopped pudgy and pale out
of the sleeve of his yellow polo and around her shoulders, at her
drugged-politician's-wife smile, and it was all I could do not to stab
a pencil through the screen of my father's laptop.

I quickly logged onto my own e-mail account, where there were
eighteen new messages, but none that looked relevant right now. I
wrote to Rocky: "Saw Loraine's identical twin today on the street!
You would've died! Don't know if I told you, the reason I'm here is
to take my shift helping out a sick friend from high school . . . So
my phone's off when I'm at the hospital, but please leave me a message and let me know the library still stands!" I felt marginally better,
now that the two stories kind of matched. There were probably too
many exclamation points, but I couldn't bear to erase them. I wanted
to take shelter behind their manic enthusiasm, their idiotic sparkle.

———

When I reemerged, Ian had gotten his clothes from the dryer, and my mother was folding up the big white undershirt of my father's that Ian had slept in. I went into the bedroom to say good-bye to my father. He was sleeping with an ice pack on his head, like always. It wasn't that he had headaches—he simply couldn't sleep unless he felt the cold of a Russian night. The blankets were only for my mother. I woke him up and kissed him on the cheek, and he said, "Stay out of trouble."

"I will," I said. My father, God bless him, pretended to believe me. He can believe anything he wants.

It was almost ten by the time we got into the elevator, gleefully sniffing the sleeves of our freshly washed clothes. The envelope of money was folded into my jeans pocket, a huge lump I kept checking. Ian had his backpack, and I had my purse and plastic superstore bag and the shoebox. It was an old Hush Puppies box, the trademark basset hound gazing from the lid with those awful eyes.

"Can we see the lobby?" Ian asked. Yesterday we'd come up through the garage. I pressed the "L" button.

"It's not much to see. It's not like a hotel."

"Is there a doorman?"

"No, it's not the kind of building people come to on foot. But there's a security guard."

But when the elevator opened and we stepped out, the desk by the front door was vacant. "Is he arresting that guy?" Ian pointed out through the glass front doors, to where the security guard was talking to a man. The man was wearing black jeans and holding a duffel bag and a huge bouquet of red roses.

The man was Glenn.

———

Before I could drag Ian back into the elevator and escape to the car, Glenn saw me through the window and waved and pointed at me and held up the flowers and said something to the guard. I couldn't run now that he'd spotted me, especially since he must have seen Ian, too. The guard looked at me for approval, and I apparently nodded. Glenn came through the door in a blast of cold air and walked with the flowers held aloft.

"Surprise!"

"Yes, it is!"

"I tracked down the building, but they wouldn't let me in without an apartment number!" He handed me the roses and was moving in with his arms open when he noticed Ian standing beside me, staring up.

"Who's the dude?" Ian said. The word *dude* sounded as strange in his mouth as the word *Pittsburgh* in my father's.

"I was wondering the same thing." Glenn plastered a grin on his face, determined to look like a guy who thought kids were absolutely great.

Before Ian could introduce himself, I said, "This is Joey." Because who knew what was on the St. Louis news about a missing boy named Ian. Plus, even though I'd refrained from telling Glenn about the origami e-mail, I must have mentioned Ian before. He was the center of most of my library stories. "Joey is the son of the friend I was telling you about. Janna Glass. I'm taking care of him for a while. Actually, I'm driving him to his grandmother's house in Cleveland, to stay there while his mother recovers."

Ian stuck out his hand. "Joseph Michael Glass."

Glenn shook Ian's hand, grinning less and less convincingly.

Ian said, "I guess I'll just keep calling you Dude."

"So here's what happened." Glenn turned back to me, apparently satisfied that he'd paid sufficient attention to the kid. "You know yesterday, when we talked? I was calling to say we'd have to put off the date because I was going to be, guess where—"

"Chicago?" Ian said.

Glenn ignored him. "I told you how sometimes I sub with the CSO, and I got a call Monday morning, so I caught a ride up here and did the concert last night—which was mind-blowing, by the way—and I spent the morning trying to find your place. Not easy! I remembered you said Lake Shore Drive, though, so I did some detective work, and long story short, I'm at your deposal!"

"My what?"

"I said, I'm at your disposal, milady." He bowed at the waist.

I remembered right then that there were security cameras in the lobby. Every second we stood there, we were being videotaped. If police came on my trail my father would cover for me, but the security guard would certainly remember us after this spectacle, and the tapes would be Exhibit F in court.

"That's so sweet," I said. "The problem is that we're leaving. We need to get Joey to his grandma's."

"This is tragic!" Glenn said, but he was laughing. His feelings weren't going to be terribly hurt, not until I was thrown in jail and he realized he'd been dating a madwoman.

Meanwhile Ian was turning in circles, holding his backpack out as ballast. "Guess what, though!" he shouted. "We have two more seats in the car! You can come with us!"

I couldn't talk or breathe, and Glenn chose this moment to finally acknowledge Ian. "Now that's a great idea. I love Cleveland!" He turned to me. "Is that okay? I have a couple days off, because they're doing the string quartet series. I mean, I've got all my stuff right here." He meant the duffel bag lying at his feet. Had he been planning to stay on my parents' floor?

Since no good lie came to me, I found myself nodding. I considered breaking up with him right there, but on what grounds? How? And if he went back to Missouri, he might watch the news. He obviously hadn't yet, or he would have recognized Ian. Whereas if he went home in a couple of days, at least maybe the story would be dying down.

We rode the elevator down to the garage. I balanced the roses on top of the shoebox and tried to keep from throwing up.

While Glenn put his bag in the trunk, I got in the front and Ian got in the backseat next to the shoebox and the roses. I turned and whispered to him. *"What were you thinking?"*

"I felt sorry for him. Roses are extremely expensive."

Glenn got in and squeezed my knee, and we were off.

"Hey," Ian said when we were out on Lake Shore Drive again, the sun glaring onto the water and the midday joggers. "If you're Dorothy and I'm the Scarecrow, then Dude is the Cowardly Lion! And this box of stuff is the Tin Woodman!"

"Maybe you're Toto," I said. He laughed and started barking. It was true, the Scarecrow didn't fit him. He didn't need more brains. Courage, he would need lots of. A strong heart. I tried to remember what vital organ Dorothy lacked. Oh, yes. She wanted to go home.

20

Fugitive

Over the next three hours, Ian serenaded Glenn almost continuously with the Australian national anthem, which he said he'd learned in school. I couldn't see straight for fear Ian would slip and say something about our ride so far.

"I woke up so late yesterday," he said at one point. "Because my uncle forgot to get me up. My uncle Jose. Then he made me huevos rancheros, which are a specialty of his native land."

"Which is?" said Glenn. He laughed and glanced over at me.

"Venezuela," said Ian. "And the capital is Caracas, in case you were wondering."

"I was."

Ian started singing again, mercifully precluding any conversation. We passed a sign for the Hobart, Indiana, Outlet Mall, and I took the exit. I almost said, "The airline lost my luggage," before I realized Glenn knew I'd driven. Instead I said, "When I drove up I didn't think I'd need many clothes. Everything was kind of sudden." I parked outside what turned out to be just a large strip mall, and told Ian to come with me. I knew Glenn would stay outside to smoke, and I didn't want to leave the two of them alone, lest Ian invent additional exotic relatives.

Glenn sat on the hood of the car to catch up on his nicotine while Ian and I went into a crunchy outdoorsy store, one of those ones based in Maine, since it would be the most likely to sell coats. The farther north we drove, the more inadequate my green fleece grew against the March cold.

"Why did you say my name was Joey?" he asked. He was touching every single piece of clothing we passed. I was happy that he thought to bring his backpack inside with him rather than leave it with Glenn, and I was happy that the lethargic, teenaged salespeople didn't seem to mind his trudging through their store with an overloaded pack, knocking into all the displays.

"Because I think I've talked about you before."

"Really?" He looked amazed and ecstatic. He stuck his hand up the wrong end of a sweater sleeve. "What did you say?"

I was about to make up something silly, something about how the library was going to start charging him rent, when I realized this might be an opportunity. I said, "I told him you have very good instincts about who you are and what you like, and that I hope you won't let other people ever change your mind."

"It sounds like you were giving one of those really boring speeches from assembly. You should have told him I was good at computer solitaire, which is true, because I'm the absolute master."

"Help me find some warm shirts," I said.

I'd found four of them and a puffy orange coat when Ian came skipping back up to me holding a red cotton dress, the scoop-necked, short-sleeved variety of awkward length that belongs on a third grade teacher. Or a librarian. It was probably the only dress they sold here. "You should get this, in case we go to a fancy restaurant."

"Like McDonald's?" I said, but I took the hanger anyway. He threw his backpack onto the floor of my dressing room, and I told him I'd meet him back out there in ten minutes.

I tried on the shirts, long-sleeved and almost identical in red and blue and black and green. I noticed in the mirror that my rash was clearing up. I felt the backs of my legs, and they were a lot better too, less crusty and hot. So it had been the desk chair all along, and if I got back to Hannibal in one piece, I'd tell Dr. Chen. I'd buy a new chair myself, or one of those huge yoga balls.

My face, on the other hand, was a mess now—stress acne and dark circles and dry, peeling lips—and perhaps that's why the orange coat made me look like such a convict. I stared at myself in the mirror and tried to get used to it. I imagined handcuffs and ankle weights. By the time I took the coat off it felt like my own, so I decided I'd buy it even though I didn't particularly care for it. This was my usual approach to purchasing clothes. If something felt right, like I'd owned it all along, I had to get it. I realized this was also my approach to kidnapping.

I felt dizzy suddenly, from the fluorescent lights and the cramped dressing room, and I sat down with my head between my knees. Ian's backpack was there on the floor, crammed impossibly full with his runaway gear. The twig from his now disassembled knapsack was sticking out, preventing the zipper from closing all the way. As I waited for the blood to return to my head, I unzipped it and poked around the top layer. A flannel shirt, three pairs of folded socks, his retainer case. With his phone number on both sides, in purple marker.

I think I took action so quickly right then in part because I wanted to prove to myself that I always would have, if only I'd had the Drakes' number. It had been part of the story I'd been telling myself in order to sleep at night. I stuck my head out the door to make sure Ian wasn't standing right there, then whipped out my phone and dialed as fast as I could. But before I even heard a ring, I had managed to think through the fact that this was my own cell phone, traceable and registered, and that I had absolutely no idea what I'd say to the Drakes that wouldn't make things worse or upset them tremendously or lead to our being swarmed by police on the highway within the next fifteen minutes. I pushed the hang-up button so hard I hurt my thumb.

I found a pen in my purse and copied the number onto the back of my checkbook. I knew that if I had a few hours to think, and if there were any pay phones left in America, I could work something out.

I stuffed the retainer case back in the backpack and stood to look at the red dress in the mirror. I slowed my breathing, and tried to slow my pulse. I pivoted my hips, and the skirt flew out around me.

I bought it, along with the other things. Maybe I was feeling rich. Walking to the register, I almost joked aloud to Ian that the dress was useful in case I needed to prostitute myself. Then I remembered he was ten.

When we got back to the car, there was Glenn, smoking what was probably his third cigarette.

"Isn't that illegal?" Ian asked me.

"What, smoking? No."

He waved one hand rapidly in front of his face as he approached the car. He was holding his breath.

I hadn't smoked since college, but right then, the smoke smelled sweet and light and a little like oranges, and I had the urge to put my mouth right onto the other end of Glenn's cigarette and inhale the flame and leaves and everything.

Instead, I got into the car with Ian and waited for Glenn to finish. How responsible of me, I thought. It occurred to me that if I never got rid of Ian, this would be my life for the next eight years, that of the responsible single mother sacrificing so her boy could have a decent life. I wanted a cigarette now even more.

In the car, Glenn told me a story about the guest conductor he'd worked with in Chicago, how he was ninety years old and they had the defibrillator kit ready backstage just in case, how Glenn had been terrified that every time he hit the bass drum the man was going to keel over. "I mean, it was fucking *terrifying*," he said.

I gave him a look.

"Oh, the kid's heard the word before, right, Joey? What are you, seven? Eight?"

"Seven," Ian said. I checked the rearview. He had the best poker face I'd ever seen on a child.

"No kidding. You're a big guy. When I was seven I liked cheeseburgers. You like cheeseburgers?"

"Yummy!"

"So anyway, I'm hitting this drum, and I look up, and the guy is covered in flop sweat, and so I look over at the timpanist, and he starts *mouthing* something to me."

I tuned Glenn out and listened to Ian's singing instead. He had left off the Australian anthem and begun "Hava Nagila," which he probably *had* learned in school. At this rate, at least Glenn's testimony might ultimately confuse a jury. "I swear, your honor, he was a Jewish kid, no more than seven years old. His uncle was from Venezuela."

We stopped for gas near the Ohio border, and although there was a pay phone, it was right out there in front, and I couldn't use it without Ian knowing. Instead, in a fit of immaturity, I decided to buy a pack of Camels, just to have on hand. It felt good to stick them, with a new green plastic lighter, into the pocket of my purse, right next to my passport—like a little nicotine lifejacket. Ian was in the bathroom, and Glenn was filling three cups with Slushees.

Ian drank most of his just on the walk back to the car. He was skipping ahead of us. "I dig your little friend," Glenn said.

"He's a riot, isn't he?"

"Yeah. I mean, I hope we can grab some alone time in Cleveland. Have you been to the art museum?"

I had spent much of our time in the car frantically thinking of ways to ditch Glenn before we got that far. If this were a movie, I'd have to kill him. This would lead, inevitably, to a series of three more murders of escalating desperation, and finally it would be some stupid detail—the lights I'd left on in the library, for instance—that would do me in. But I hadn't come up with a real plan yet. The breakup seemed wisest, and even better would be getting him to break up with me, leaving of his own volition. Kick him out, and I'd make him suspicious or vindictive.

"Yeah, I'm not really into art museums," I lied. I was going to hell for that one. Among other things. "I don't really see the point."

"Something else, then."

I stopped walking in the middle of the parking lot. "Listen, I've been meaning to say. Your premiere. That I went to. Which was great."

"Yeah."

"Okay, it's funny—do you know those Mr. Clean ads? That they've had forever?"

"What?"

"Okay, it's 'Mr. Clean, Mr. Clean, *da da DA da, da da DA da* . . .' You know what I'm talking about, right?"

"No." He laughed and shook his head, as if this were something cute and not me telling him his career was a travesty.

"Yeah, it's the same tune as your song. Your piece, I mean. The same melody."

"Okay."

"No, you don't get it."

"I get it. Same tune." He was trying to kiss me.

"No, listen: '*da da DA da, da da DA da* . . .' Don't you recognize that?"

He stared into space like he was trying to remember something. "*Shit*," he said.

I'd given Ian the keys, so he was already waiting for us in the backseat, holding up the shoebox and shaking it around. He put it down when we got in.

"So, Dude," Ian said as we merged back on the highway. "Tell us about your new movie, Dude." He shoved a fistful of invisible microphone between the two front seats. "I hear you're in love with Julia Roberts."

Glenn wasn't amused. He looked like he was still lost in his head, reaching back through time to the commercials of his youth, thinking through his piece. He stretched his neck and rubbed his chin. He hadn't shaved, and the stubble was coming in whitish gray, like the hair just above his temples and brow.

"Miss Hull, how did you first meet Dude, and why doesn't he ever say anything?"

Glenn snapped out of his trance and looked at me. "Did he just call you 'Miss Hull'?" he said.

Before Ian could make something up, I said, "His mother is big on respect for adults."

Glenn laughed and looked back at Ian. "I see," he said. "Very respectful, dude."

Ian said, "I only respect ladies." That was the end of it, and even when we stopped for dinner at a sit-down chain just outside Cleveland, Glenn didn't say anything except to order his turkey burger and curly fries.

The relish with which Ian guzzled his chocolate milk suggested he wasn't normally allowed to have it. "So, Mr. Dude, did you know that Miss Hull's dad ran a chocolate factory?" Glenn didn't even seem aware that Ian was talking to him. "But Miss Hull, that wasn't a true story, was it? It didn't make any sense. I think he was kidding."

"I think you might be right." I'd put it out of my mind, but really, some of the dizziness and fuzzy-headedness I'd been feeling all day had to do with that realization, the idea that the rug of my family history might have just been yanked out from under me.

"But he really is Russian, right? Because he had a really good accent."

In my state of mind, it actually took me a second while I made sure I could recall him speaking fluent Russian on many specific occasions to other, legitimate Russians before I could answer confidently.

As soon as the food came and Ian started in on his BLT, I excused myself to go to the bathroom. As I'd hoped, there was a pay phone in the back hallway. I stuffed in a bunch of coins and took out my checkbook and punched in the number. I knew it was a huge risk to call from the place where we were stopping, but we would drive a few miles farther after dinner, and they couldn't comb the whole area by eight in the morning. Regardless of whether it was Mr. or Mrs. Drake who answered, or even the police themselves, I would say the same thing I'd practiced.

In the car that afternoon, I had considered calling to tell them that Ian was at the Cleveland Museum of Art, then leaving him there on the steps and speeding off to the airport with Glenn, getting the first flight to Puerto Rico, or the farthest point for which Glenn wouldn't need a passport. I'd tell Glenn I was being spontaneous. And then I'd either run away even farther or sit tight and wait to be arrested. But to be honest, it wasn't a serious scenario. I wasn't ready to face jail, I wasn't ready to leave behind my entire country, and I didn't want Glenn to be blamed for anything. And if I were just going to toss Ian back, without his being ready, without his gaining some kind of magical strength to face the next eight years of his life, then what had all this been for? As accidental as it all had been, surely there must have been some kind of *point.*

And so I'd settled on two carefully worded sentences of reassurance. I was prepared even for Pastor Bob himself to answer the phone. What I wasn't prepared for was Ian answering. There was his voice, distinctive and adenoidal, after four rings. "Hello?" I almost slammed the phone down but managed to hold onto it. "Hello, this is the Drakes? Please leave a message for the Drakes." I did hang up the phone then, but softly, and my arm was actually shaking, all the way up to the shoulder. I had logical reasons for hanging up—top among them, not wanting my voice to be played back and analyzed, broadcast on the news—but more than that, I felt that leaving a message with Ian himself (which is somehow what it felt like) would be a worse betrayal than simply saying quickly to Mr. Drake, "I've seen your son. He's in good hands, and he'll be home soon." And it was a betrayal I hadn't prepared myself for.

Walking back to the table, I felt irrationally angry at the Drakes for not being home. Had they gone out to dinner? They were probably at a prayer meeting. A candlelight vigil. But still. What if that had been Ian himself calling, and they'd missed their chance? Or maybe they were screening their calls, tired of well-wishers and people offering casseroles. But it helped to have a reason to be angry with them. (Another one, on top of the Pastor Bob issue.) I was looking for all the justification I could find.

Ian had stuck all four frilly toothpicks into one quarter of his BLT, and he was telling Glenn about his Ultimate Symphony. Glenn looked like he was in pain. "And then what would be even cooler, would be that you rent out this huge room, or like a stadium or something, and you have a hundred Big Ben clocks all the way around, and then they all play it at once. Only it would have to be computerized, right? Because otherwise if just one guy messed up, it would sound very awkward. Would that be illegal, to use the Big Ben theme song? Do you think they would sue me?"

Instead of answering, Glenn flagged down the waitress and ordered a martini.

I made a valiant effort to change the subject. "There was a girl in my high school orchestra who fell asleep once in the middle of a concert. She was a flute player, and she just fell asleep with her head on the music stand." She had been on drugs, of course, but I figured it made the story less interesting. Ian spent the rest of dinner pretending to be narcoleptic.

On the way out, he grabbed two handfuls of red and white mints from the counter and shoved them into his pockets. I wondered if we could live on them in an emergency.

Glenn was under the impression that we were dropping Ian at his grandmother's that night, but I explained that he would stay with us in the hotel, because she wouldn't be ready for him until the morning. At the front desk I asked for three separate rooms, and Glenn didn't stop me. Presuming that I accomplished the break tonight, he'd need a place to sleep away from me. I went to my room to brush my teeth and plan the attack, but before I could even spit out my toothpaste Glenn was knocking on the door.

"What?" I said.

He walked right by me and sat down on the edge of the bed, on the peach-flowered bedspread, and said, "Lucy, what the hell is going on?"

I turned the desk chair to face the room and sat down. "The mother is very sick," I said. "What do you mean?"

He shook his head like he was trying to get water out of his ears. "I was sitting there in my room thinking, and the more I think, the weirder it gets. For starters, you come to Chicago and don't pack a single change of clothes? And the kid is going to live with his grandmother, right, but all he brings is one backpack."

"He's just staying with her," I said. "For a week or two."

"No schoolbooks? And why isn't he calling his mom?"

I stood up. "You think this is a detective novel? It's really not all that fascinating. And I'm sure he'll call from the room."

"*Then*," he said, like a prosecuting attorney with a cornered witness, "at dinner, you say 'this girl at my high school.' I thought you said his mom went to Latin. So you'd say '*our* high school,' or you'd just say 'Latin.'"

"Are you trying to make a citizen's arrest? You're being ridiculous."

He lay back on the bed like he owned it and looked up at the ceiling. "I mean, is he your kid or something?"

I practically shouted, but more out of relief than anger. I was almost laughing. "You think he's my *son*?"

"It would make sense. Maybe he lives with your parents, you went to pick him up, you're taking him to see his dad, I don't know."

I really was laughing now. I was laughing so hard that I wanted to flop on the bed, but not beside Glenn, so I sat back on the chair. "You think my sixty-year-old parents are raising my son while I live in Hannibal, of all places? And then you think I dated you and kept him a secret. And he calls me Miss Hull."

He propped himself up on his elbows. His face was scrunched into an angry-little-boy expression. God, he was *jealous*. "Then what the hell is the deal?"

I said, "You're not in a thriller movie, Glenn. His mother is very sick, but that's as far as the drama goes. Look, if you're really this worked up, maybe we just need some breathing room. Maybe you should let us do our own thing tomorrow. You could go to the art museum by yourself while I drop him off."

"Yeah," he said. "Yeah, that's probably best. I mean, I'll ride with you into the city, and then I need some time to clear my head." I'd still have to figure out how to ditch him for good tomorrow, but this was a decent start. He stood up and walked out of my room without saying good night. I wasn't worried about him grilling Ian tomorrow, because I knew he'd just sit there sulking, more of a ten-year-old than the actual ten-year-old.

I tried to open my window and couldn't. It was a smoking room, though, so I lit the first cigarette of the pack and sat on the chair, as far from the flammable bedspread as I could get. I'd forgotten how the smoke can almost burn your throat, how you really are inhaling something hot. The room turned clear and smooth and vibrant, and my fingers and feet buzzed. I turned on the TV and found, of all things, the movie version of *The Fugitive*. I watched the second half and imagined what would have happened if Ian and I had decided not to take Glenn with us, if we had run instead all over Chicago, across the green-dyed river, hiding in skyscrapers. I fell asleep and dreamed the same thing.

21

Choose Your Own Fiasco

Y ou are alone in a strange hotel. Next door is Ian, a child you've inadvertently abducted. Down the hall is Glenn, who is starting to get suspicious. Under your bed is a shoebox filled with Lord knows what. You are expected in Pittsburgh. If you choose to run away in the night, go to number 1. If you choose to stay put, go to number 2.

1. You flee on foot, leaving your car behind so Glenn can more conveniently turn Ian in to the authorities. After hitching a ride to the Cleveland airport, you face the ticket agent with your father's cash in hand. If you decide to fly to Alaska, go to number 3. If you choose St. Louis, Missouri, go to number 4.

2. You wake in the morning to Glenn pounding at your door, accompanied by two police detectives and a reporter from the local NBC affiliate. You are trapped. If you choose to seduce the NBC reporter and elope with him to Alaska, go

to number 3. If you decide to let yourself be handcuffed, go
to number 5.

3. Alaska turns out to be quite cold in March. You are reminded
of your grandfather, vanishing into the Siberian wilderness.
Suddenly, you become aware of a man staggering toward you
across the tundra. It is your grandfather, calling to you in Russian. If you choose to embrace him, go to number 6. If you
panic and get on a plane back to Missouri, go to number 4.

4. There are cops all over the St. Louis airport, and your photo is
on every wall. In your absence, Ian has been reunited with his
family, and is being interviewed on the Today show. A man in
livery is holding a sign that reads HULL. If you go with him,
skip to number 7. If you throw up your hands and surrender,
go to number 5.

5. You receive a reduced sentence in exchange for turning in your
father and his shoebox full of plutonium. Your years in prison
aren't pleasant, but you do get a lot of reading done, and
Loraine isn't around to ask why your shirt is wrinkled. You
could do worse. The end.

6. Your grandfather is dead, and so are you. You have crossed
over to the other side, which looks and feels remarkably like
a large, snowy field. Fortunately, you are wearing your puffy
orange coat. The end.

7. Your chauffeur whisks you away. When he takes off his cap,
you realize he is the most handsome man in the universe. He

*invites you to his vacation home in Alaska. If you accept, go
to number 3. If you order him to take you to Ian's house, go
to number 8.*

8. *Ian is not as pleased to see you as you hoped. Tuna the guinea
pig bares her fangs, and Larry Drake has you in his rifle cross-
hairs. After your arrest, Janet Drake displays her Christian
mercy to the world by convincing the judge that instead of jail
time, you be sentenced to five years of rehabilitative therapy
with Pastor Bob. The five years start tomorrow. The end.*

9. *Your hard work has paid off. The treasure you collected in
Florida is worth millions, and the noise in the street turns
out to be your ticker-tape parade. Ian's adoption by Tim and
Lenny is now official, and the Hull Library will soon be complete. Congratulations!*

22

I Could Not Have a Tongue

The next morning, we all piled into the car with doughnuts and coffee and orange juice from the table in the lobby. I was wearing my new red shirt, and it felt like a clean, soft cocoon. Glenn just stared out the window, and Ian seemed to be asleep in the back. A few miles onto the highway, though, he said, "I can't wait till Dude leaves, because then I can sit in the front."

"No you can't," I said, although I'd let him before. I hoped he wouldn't bring this up right now.

"You're too short," Glenn said. "Look what would happen." He pulled the shoulder strap higher up on his own body and mimed falling forward into it with his neck. He made a choking noise and stuck his tongue out.

Ian said, "My mom lets me if I put the belt behind my head. And also I'm in a very high percentile for height. Look, this is from last summer and I was already four foot six."

I wondered what on earth he could be handing to Glenn that

was from last summer when I remembered the pool pass, the one with his name on it and "Hannibal Public Pool" across the top, and an orange-tinted photo of Ian with wet hair and steamed-up glasses, droplets of water still clinging to his shoulders. He was holding it there between the seats, waiting as Glenn reached for it.

I jerked the car half a lane to the right. It wasn't intentional, just what happened when I tried to yank my hand back to swat the pass away from Glenn without letting go of the wheel. We didn't hit anyone, but we barely missed a Jeep lagging a few feet behind us in the right lane, and by the time we got straightened out we were all hyperventilating and Ian was screaming. The angry honks escorted us down the road for the next five seconds, like the other drivers were building walls of sound to control us, to keep us in line.

"What in the hell was that?" Glenn said.

I said, "*Please* don't swear in front of Joey."

Glenn grabbed a napkin and scrubbed at the coffee that had run down his white oxford. When I looked in the rearview, Ian was zipping his backpack. He grimaced into the mirror to let me know he realized what he'd done and had put the pass away.

After that, I put on the radio as loud as seemed natural for that early in the morning. I was already sick of every song on frequent DJ rotation. When I'm ninety years old, if someone asks me what songs were popular that March, I'll still be able to rattle them off.

We pulled up to the art museum at about 11:30, and Glenn ripped his bag out of the trunk like I'd stolen it from him. I'd gotten out to help him, and Ian stayed in the backseat doing a book of invisible ink puzzles.

I still didn't quite know how to get rid of Glenn. My throat was burning from last night's cigarettes. I said, "Look, I'm not sure how long this is going to take."

"Right."

"I mean, I might need to stay there with them. And then, honestly, if I go back to Chicago, it'll be to help my friend. She might need a bone marrow donation, and I've been thinking about seeing if I'm a match." Glenn had never asked what was specifically wrong with Janna Glass, and Ian hadn't given him the movie-of-the-week version.

He sighed and stared over my shoulder. "Let's make this easy. I have friends here I can probably crash with. I'm in a weird head space right now. How about we do the romantic weekend sometime when you're not babysitting."

"That's good. You'll call me?" I couldn't have engineered it better—he was staying away from Missouri for now, and he didn't completely hate me.

"Yeah." He slung his bag strap over his shoulder and kissed me on the cheek. "Stay out of trouble. Don't drive crazy." He disappeared through the museum doors.

When I got back in, Ian said, "Can't I sit up front again? I seriously am tall enough," and I was too exhausted to say no. I was actually relieved not to have him next to my father's shoebox, which this morning I'd tucked back under the driver's seat, after sleeping with it under my bed. Ian had been using it as a lap desk for his invisible ink book all morning, though, and now it was just sitting on the middle of the backseat. Maybe it looked less suspicious there. I wasn't so much concerned for the safety of the contents as terrified that someone would see that sad old basset hound, intuit what was in the box, and slap the cuffs on me—not for the crime I'd actually committed, but the ones my father had.

An hour later, and an hour closer to Pittsburgh, Ian was loudly composing a song called "States You Can Say Without Closing Your Mouth."

"*Oh, Iowa, Ohio, Oahu, Hawaii!*" he sang. "*Ooh, yeah! Uh-huh! Hi! Woah, Hawaii, wow!*"

He took his feet off the dashboard and looked at me. "Do you think I could use *R*s? You don't really close your mouth—your tongue doesn't touch anything. Especially if you had an English accent."

"Sure," I said. "Definitely."

"*Where are you, Ohio?*" he sang with a British accent. "*Oh, here! Oh, Iowa, Ohio, Oahu, Hawaii!*"

I took one hand off the steering wheel to hit it on my jeans in applause.

"This is great!" he said. "I could not have a tongue and I'd be fine!" It reminded me of what Sophie Bennett had said about him, that he was the kind of kid who would turn out all right no matter what. But I couldn't *really* believe that, or else what was I doing out here?

Now that Glenn was out of the car, now that the monotony of the drive had dulled my adrenaline to the point where I could almost think linearly, I felt I had to try to talk seriously with him. I wanted to say something helpful and profound that he could remember after I'd been locked away. If I ran the risk of his getting so angry that he turned me in—so be it. Better than this all being for nothing.

I said, for some inane, incomprehensible reason, "You know, the first real librarians were monks and nuns. They copied books by hand, and they kept them safe in the monastery."

"Oh." He put his foot back up on the dashboard. The great thing about ten-year-olds is they don't balk at non sequiturs. "Is that why libraries are so quiet? Because the monks couldn't talk?"

"Maybe. I never thought of that before."

"Why do monks stop talking?"

"For religious reasons. I'm not exactly sure."

"But the Bible never says not to talk. I know that *definitely*."

"I think they partly just liked it that way. They liked living in the mountains in a quiet place." I was being ridiculously cautious— trying just to crack the lid on the can of worms, not bust it open on the sidewalk. "I mean, none of them ever got married. They chose just to live with other monks. Or other nuns. People have been doing that for a long time, just choosing not to get married and to live with their friends instead. You used to have to be a monk or a nun to do it, but that's a really hard life. Now a lot of people just do it to be happy."

He leaned the passenger seat back as far as it would go. "If people visited the library, did they have to not talk at all?"

"I don't think people really visited. The monks just *kept* the books. Sometimes they chained them down to the shelves, so they wouldn't be stolen."

"Because they were so valuable?"

"Right. They had all those illuminated letters, and each one took months to copy. "

"If I were copying a book, I would always put in some of my own words, or a secret message. About some really huge secret. Do you think they ever did that?"

"Maybe. Sure. What kind of secret?"

"About treasure. I think I'd like to be a monk."

"I think you'd talk too much."

I tried to come up with another angle of approach, but a few minutes later he was asleep on the leaned-back seat.

23

One Light, Two Light,
Red Light, Blue Light

As I drove, I made a list in my head of all the people who could link me to Ian's disappearance. If the authorities got the slightest hint, one anonymous phone tip, they'd have their pick of witnesses now. My father would know to lie for me, but my mother would make a mess of it, and who knew what Glenn would do. Loraine, of course, would recognize Ian's name on posters or in the papers, but she didn't know quite how much time he spent with me. Tim the landlord would notice I was gone, but he wouldn't know about Ian. I realized I should call and tell him I was out of town. Sophie Bennett, the teacher at Hannibal Day, was also a concern. She knew I was worried about Ian. But she knew the family well enough that she'd assume they'd locked him up somewhere. She was probably dying to tell me about it, asking at the library when I'd be back. If she started talking to Rocky, if he told her I'd vanished, that would be the worst. But nobody talks to Rocky.

Rocky could figure it out easily, all on his own. Maybe he already had. And yet somehow I wasn't worried about him. Why was that? My stomach lurched. "Because he's in love with you," it said.

When Ian was in the bathroom at a gas station, I stood in the snack aisle and dialed the downstairs library extension on my cell, knowing Sarah-Ann would answer. She did.

"I'm just checking in," I said.

"Oh!" I could picture her sitting there, surrounded by books she couldn't figure out how to re-shelve, reading a magazine from upstairs. "Are you back?"

"No, I'm not—I think it has to be a few more days. My friend is very sick, and I'm helping with her children. It's worse than I thought."

"Oh, my heavens, well I'm sure you're a blessing!"

"Can you handle everything for a while?"

"Yes. Well, we had to redo the computer, because things got in there backwards. But it's just fine now, and yes, it's wonderful!"

I wasn't going to bother imagining what that meant. "And Chapter Book Hour is 4:30 on Friday," I said.

"Oh dear, it is, isn't it?"

"Yes, it is. *The Borrowers*, by Mary Norton. The one about the little people who steal things. It should be in the top left drawer."

"I don't see anything but staplers!"

"That's the right. Look on the left."

"Oh, good! Where do I start?"

"Right where the bookmark is."

"Now Lucy, you need to talk to Rocky. He was trying to reach you. Did he reach you? There was something terribly important. Shall I connect you upstairs?"

"No, I'll call him. Tell him I'll call very soon." I hung up and bought Oreos and a box of tampons.

How to jog like a ten-year-old boy:

1. Swing your arms violently, as if shadowboxing.
2. Lift your knees very high. Remember: moving forward is not your primary goal.
3. With every step, scream the word "JOG!"

Back in the parked car, I told Ian we had to stop in Pittsburgh, but that after that he needed to pick the road. We were using my Swiss Army knife to spread peanut butter on the crackers from Ian's backpack. We watched the stream of travelers rubbing their rear ends as they walked into the Shell.

"I'm tired of deciding."

"Okay, but this is your trip. If you don't tell me where to go, I'm taking you home." I felt almost as if I were saying this for legal reasons, as if this defense would hold up in court. I never took him anywhere he didn't tell me to go, Your Honor! Except to make a brief Mafia drop in Pittsburgh!

Ian was flipping through the map book angrily, the way he'd flipped through *Blueberries for Sal* months before. "Why do you always make everything my fault?"

"I don't think anything's your fault. What do you mean, exactly?"

"You're making me do all the bad stuff, telling us where to go. You never did anything bad, just me."

"Hmmm."

"But really you're the worst one. You're the kidnapper." But he was trying not to laugh.

"I think you're the librarian-napper," I said. "And now you have to choose someplace, or I'll choose. And what I'll choose is Hannibal, Missouri."

He closed the book and flapped it open randomly. "Vermont." It was in the middle of the book, on the page with New Hampshire. "That's where the Green Mountain Boys were from, anyway. I know all this stuff about them. And it used to be its own country. Only it and Texas ever used to be their own countries. Oh, and Hawaii." I worried he'd launch into his song again, but his mood seemed to have shifted back to serious. Vermont was much, much farther than I wanted to go, but it seemed as logical a mouth to this crazy river as any. Inertia would carry us at least half the way there.

I said, "Okay. Buckle up."

"And also, it's definitely where my grandmother lives."

A few of the myriad questions you must face when transporting a ten-year-old boy and a box of illegal materials across the country: Do felony laws differ depending on which state you are apprehended in, or does it all go federal and therefore not matter? Are prolonged stress and the life of the fugitive perhaps more damaging to the child psyche than being raised by an overbearing anorexic evangelical? If you were a Cyclops, what color would you want your eye to be? If you had all your fingernails surgically removed, would they eventually grow back? Is it possible that your Mafioso father's cash is marked as illegal and the police are currently tracing your path from gas station to fast food franchise, hoping to arrest someone named Dmitri the Glove? What do you get when you cross a meatball with an elephant?

And then, at dusk, twenty miles from Pittsburgh: red lights, blue lights, that surprisingly gentle siren. We pulled over. We were on a smaller road, for the scenic route.

"Shoot, shoot, shoot, shoot, shoot," Ian whispered, only many more times, as we watched the cop talk into her radio in our rear-view. Ian was in the backseat again, thank God, having climbed back in the middle of the afternoon to stretch out. I hadn't yet sworn in front of him, not that he'd heard, and I didn't now. A long time later, she walked up to my window with that wide-legged swagger all women cops have. Normally at this point I tell the offi-cer exactly what I've done wrong—failing to stop fully at a stop sign, usually—and my honesty has won me about ten warnings and no tickets. I wasn't about to try honesty now.

"Yes?" I said.

She had short, curly hair and I could smell the mint from her gum. I wanted to trade lives with her.

"You aware your left brake light is out?"

"No," I said, in a voice like she'd just handed me a diamond necklace. "No, I did not realize that."

"Mommy, who's the scary lady?" Ian said from the backseat. I tried to shoot him a look in the rearview. "I'm frightened, Mommy."

"I'm so sorry," I said. "Thank you so much for telling us. They can fix that at a garage, right? I mean, we're from out of state as you can see, we're traveling, so we'll need to get it fixed right away. In the morning."

She chewed her gum and looked past me into the car. We looked remarkably unsuspicious, for the number of laws we had broken. "I'm gonna write you a warning," she said. "Welcome to Pennsylvania."

"We're visiting the Liberty Bell!" Ian shouted. But she'd already gone back to her car to fill out the form.

I was just breathing my relief when I realized there was now a computerized record of our being in Pennsylvania on this date. I wondered if they listed in their report the number and ages of occupants in the car, the way they listed the car's make and color. I was glad again that we hadn't taken my father's Mercedes. Who knows what would have come up on the police scanner then.

The cop handed me the warning, and we drove off. The sky had turned dark as we sat there.

"She didn't even yell at you," Ian said. "My mom gives much better warnings than that." It was the first time he'd directly mentioned his parents since we left.

"It wasn't that kind of warning," I said, although it might have felt good to be yelled at right then.

24

The Labaznikov Special

It was after seven when we got to the suburb where Leo and Marta Labaznikov lived.

"Labaznikov," Ian chanted from the backseat. "La-baz-ni-kov, La-baz-ni-kov. One Labaznikov, please."

The town was depressing, a collection of small mid-twentieth-century houses built on about five different floor plans, as if you wouldn't notice they were all basically the same if they alternated which side the chimney was on.

"Yes, I'd like the Labaznikov special with extra mustard, sir. I shot him in the head with a Labaznikov."

I found the house and pulled in behind the red and black BMWs, shiny fraternal twins that looked rather out of place in the little driveway. I knew the Labaznikovs from various parties I was stuffed into dresses for as a child, where I had run around under the tables with fifteen other children, all of whom spoke fluent Russian to each other. I knew about ten words, most of which had to do with food. My only full sentence was "*Ya ne govoryu po russki*": "I do not speak Russian."

When I reached back for the box, I realized Ian was undoing his seat belt. "You stay here," I said. "It'll be about thirty seconds."

"I have to pee!" He opened his door. "And I've always wanted to meet a real live Labaznikov!" And because I was operating with half a brain, I got my lies confused. Or rather I forgot my first lie, to my parents, that I was only watching Ian in Chicago, and was driving out east by myself to visit college friends. I remembered it with my finger halfway to the doorbell, and started to tell Ian that if he waited in the car, I'd pull over at the next bathroom.

But there was Marta Labaznikov, flinging the door open and performing the backward-leaning, open-armed welcome gesture commonly associated with movie versions of old Italian women. My father's Russian friends became more affectedly European the longer they stayed in the U.S.

"Lucy, you used to be so little!" she cried. If I were overweight, I'd have been offended, but she was simply remarking on the miracle of my no longer being seven years old. "And this is the poor motherless boy!" She swooped Ian into what must have been a suffocating hug. Marta was not a small woman. I wondered if my father had simply told her the story of Ian and she was inferring that he was the same child, or if he had known or guessed that Ian would still be with me and told her to expect two of us. In either case, I could see we weren't getting out of there anytime soon, which might have been fine but for the thick, chemical smell in the air, like cat litter but stronger. My throat was suddenly tight.

Leo appeared now behind his wife, with the same Italian-woman move. I was surprised how shriveled he'd become, how his head was covered with pale brown spots. I wanted to exclaim, like a Russian grandmother, "Look how *old* you've grown!"

Leo moved stiffly forward in the hall, pointing a swollen-knuckled finger at Ian, who had finally been released from Marta's bosom. "I have a question for you," he said. Ian looked startled and, for the first time since we'd run away, truly scared. "What is in common," Leo asked, "between furniture and a sentence?"

"I remember that one!" I said, more to calm Ian down than anything. Riddles were Leo's primary way of relating to children. He used to come up to me at my father's birthday parties and say, "Who is bigger? Mrs. Bigger or Mrs. Bigger's baby?" and I'd say, "The baby is just a little bigger!" He always seemed startled that I could answer. Now Ian looked up at me with a mixture of relief that Leo wasn't interrogating him and confusion about what I could possibly mean.

"They both have periods," I said.

Ian laughed. "Oh, I get it! Like period furniture!" He might have been the first child in history to understand that joke.

I hugged Leo gingerly.

Once our coats were off, I handed Leo the Hush Puppies box, and instead of opening it he stared at the dog on the lid. "Who wants to look at a dog that's so sad?" he said. He patted the lid with his palm and put it on the living room coffee table.

"Okay!" said Marta. "So now we eat! Leo, you give the tour, and I get the table ready." I found myself not protesting.

Leo walked us into the dining room, his left knee bending a tiny, deliberate bit with each step, like it was made of rusted metal. "This is Anya," he said. He stopped at the buffet table of photos in silver frames and held up a picture of a teenager with '80s hair and a turquoise shirt. "You remember this beauty?" I did. She was my age and I recalled my parents saying she'd gotten into drugs and run away. "Two babies now! One is five, one is two. Two boys! No husband!" Ian was squinting at a photo on the edge of the buffet. "And that is little Dora!" Leo said. Ian picked up the picture. It was a studio portrait of a ferret, its face filling up most of the frame, a mottled blue backdrop. I looked at the wall, instead, to keep from laughing.

"Is she yours?" Ian held it close to his own face.

"She died in 1998. Now this one, she still is with us. This is Clara." He pointed at another picture, this one a snapshot of Marta holding a ferret against her cheek. "And this is Levi, and this is Valentina." I saw now that almost half the photos on the buffet were of ferrets, or family portraits in which a ferret was just a fuzzy ball on Leo's lap. So that was the smell. Ferret and associated byproducts.

"Anya loved ferrets when she was thirteen, and so since then we have always had ferrets. Anya was very sad when she was thirteen, and she wrote beautiful poems. I can show you later. So we had to make her happy, and we ended up with ferrets."

"Teenagers are very dangerous," Ian said.

Leo clapped him on the back. "I like this one!" he shouted. Leo's English was significantly smoother than my father's, although they'd come to America around the same time, from the same town. Leo's older sister had been my father's babysitter and first (and unrequited) love.

After we toured the ground floor, Leo took Ian into the basement to meet the ferrets. I bowed out by offering to help Marta in the kitchen. She was making spaghetti with meatballs and a loaf of garlic bread. I expected her next to tell me I was too thin and call me *cara*.

"Your father says the boy lost his mother," she said. She was washing lettuce in the sink and shouting above the water.

"No, not quite. She made a suicide attempt, but she's okay."

Marta shook her head. "Oh, they always succeed sooner or later. How hard can it be? This is a crazy country, that people want to kill themselves. Other countries, people struggle to stay alive every day, they run between the bullets, they eat five little pieces of rice, and here the people say, Oh, stay alive in this beautiful country with lots to eat? No thank you, not for me."

I was sure there were plenty of suicides back in the country that invented Russian roulette, but now was not the time to say so.

"This is so sad," she said, "to be an orphan in America, but surely he will get adopted. People always want to adopt a white child."

I stirred the spaghetti, dumbfounded. I finally managed to explain that I was driving Ian to Vermont to stay with his grandmother. "It was a change of plans," I said. "So my parents didn't know about it. It's a good development. She's a very stable woman, very capable."

Ian came up a minute later, proudly showing me the three red marks on his thumb where Valentina had bitten him.

"Wash that out," I said. "With soap." I didn't want to think what Ian would be like rabid.

Soon we were sitting in the dining room, the smell of garlic mercifully covering the smell of ferret. We all fell silent when Leo raised his hands solemnly over the food. He closed his eyes. "As we say in the Old World," he intoned, in a voice like a priest, "Don't choke."

Ian laughed and practically dove across the table at the garlic bread. Up till then, he'd made a point of bowing his head before meals, and it seemed each prayer had gotten longer. I doubted he was really praying, the way he scrunched his face solemnly and kept flicking his eyes open to see if I was watching. But tonight he seemed to accept Leo's joke as blessing enough.

He impressed the Labaznikovs with his litany of world capitals, and he even knew all those new ones—Tashkent, Dushanbe, Zagreb. Marta clapped and gave him more salad.

After cookies, Marta said, "I'll show you your rooms." I hadn't wanted to stay, but it was a night without a hotel bill. She put Ian in a small guest room and me in Anya's old room, preserved exactly as Anya must have left it at age seventeen. Sketches of hands and feet were still thumbtacked to the walls, and romance novels and schoolbooks shared the shelves with a snow globe, an African mask, and a bottle with layers of colored sand. I wondered if she'd been back in the room since she ran away from it.

I snooped around, pawing through the clothes that still hung in the closet, the high school papers stuffed in a desk drawer: "Salinger's Use of Hyperbole in *The Catcher in the Rye*." I remembered playing Monopoly with Anya once in someone's basement, while the adults drank and had dinner upstairs. She had started to cry when I took her last five-hundred-dollar bill, and then claimed it was allergies. "They must have had a cat once in this house," she said.

It occurred to me then that no one would miss anything from this room. I went through the closet, picking out the few things that weren't baggy and black. I found a few T-shirts, three decent

sweaters, and a pair of ripped jeans. Her sock drawer had only single, unmatched socks, but I grabbed a few anyway. I got books off
the shelf for Ian—*Johnny Tremain* and a biography of Henry VIII.
There was Anne Boleyn's smiling face, lined up with the other
wives at the bottom of the cover, her head about to roll. Ian would
love it. I put these all in the shopping bag I was using as my suitcase, along with a bottle opener, a notebook, a washcloth, a flashlight, a Tupperware container, a bottle of stale perfume to cover
the smell of fries in the car, and ten cassette mix tapes that at
least would probably not contain the Australian national anthem.
I opened the bee-shaped piggy bank on her nightstand and was
surprised to find a handful of coins—what runaway leaves money
behind?—until I realized they were Canadian. I could picture her
sitting on her bed the night before she ran away, carefully sorting
out the American coins and calculating how far she could get on
the bus. I put the coins in my pocket. At least if I had to escape to
Canada, I'd be able to pay the highway tolls.

I changed into a white summer nightgown from the dresser
and put a gray sweatshirt over it. They both smelled musty, but it
was better than sleeping in my clothes again. I lay on the bed and
called Tim. Every day that went by, more mail would be piling up
in my box, until the mail lady would have to leave it on the lobby
floor. It was only a matter of time before the local press descended
on my neighbors to ask whether I was the quiet type who kept to
myself. I held my breath while his phone rang, and half expected
the police to answer.

"*¡Hola!*" Tim shouted. "*¿Quién es?*" There was loud music
behind him.

"It's Lucy," I said.

"*Who?*"

"*Lucy!*" I was trying not to yell.

"Lucy!" cried Tim. "I'm so sorry, honey. We'll turn it down."

"What?"

"I'm so sorry. It's Lenny's birthday! You can join us if you want!"

"Oh—no. No, I'm under the weather."

"Oh, honey, I'm sorry. We'll tune down so you can sleep. Anything you need?"

"No, no thanks. No. I'm fine."

"Okay, *ciao, bella!*" For a moment I wondered—I truly did—if the real Lucy Hull was still back in Hannibal, lying in her own bed reading Wodehouse or Highsmith or Austen, listening to Tim's Spanish-Italian fiesta and trying to sleep. And the real Ian Drake was cross-legged on his bedroom floor, turning a Pastor Bob worksheet into an origami aardvark.

And all the while the two of us out here, floating eastward across the country, we were phantoms, acting out what might have been, or what should have been. Or we were a nightmare in the fevered brain of the real Lucy Hull.

But no, it was the other way around. The Lucy in Hannibal was the phantom. She always had been.

> In the sad, stale room there was
> a theme paper
> and a bottle of sand
> and a charcoal sketch of a man's hand
> and there were three Russian dolls on a shelf on the wall
> and an African mask
> and a dented flask
> and a dusty window pane and Johnny Tremain
> and the sound from outside of late freezing rain.

Goodnight Anya's bed.
Goodnight Anne Boleyn's head.
Goodnight neurotic ten-year-old boy.
Goodnight piggy bank of foreign currency.
Goodnight cigarettes and goodnight shoebox.
Goodnight drawer full of unmatched socks.

Goodnight ferrets
Goodnight lights
Goodnight sirens in the night . . .

25

Runaway Nation

I tried for three hours to sleep, but the room was cold and I hadn't eaten enough and I kept thinking about the shoebox. Marta had put a night-light in the hall, and it saw me to the top of the stairs, where I stood and waited for my eyes to adjust.

It occurred to me that I could leave right then, drive away and let Ian wake up with me gone. The Labaznikovs would get him home. But then they'd have to tell the police how they met him, and I'd have to live on the lam in Canada with my $2.35 in coins. And more to the point, if I hadn't driven him home the first night, if I hadn't left him at the museum in Cleveland, if I hadn't run out on him at a gas station and called the police by this point, I wasn't going to abandon him now, either.

I walked carefully down the stairs, the ferret stench growing stronger with each step. The box was still on the coffee table. I was surprised Leo had left it here, this illicit treasure I'd so carefully stashed under my hotel bed, this fourth comrade on the yellow brick road through Ohio. My father's packing tape still secured the lid. I realized then that I hadn't even been there when my father sealed it up. Who knew what he'd slipped in at the last minute. I picked up the box and shook it gently. It was heavier than it should have been for the number of receipts he'd shown me, and something more solid than individual pieces of paper was sliding back and forth: a rubber-banded stack of bills, maybe, or a small box within the larger one. I couldn't undo the tape without ripping the whole thing. I found a pencil in the kitchen and jammed a ragged hole in one of the bottom corners, small enough that Leo could convince himself he'd just missed it before. I put my finger inside and felt around. There was something solid. I remembered the flashlight upstairs and went back up for it.

When I got to Anya's room, Ian was standing in the doorway. "I can't breathe," he said. His shoulders were up around his ears and I could hear his squeaky wheeze from where I stood. "I took my puffer, but it didn't help much. Do you think I should take it extra?"

"No, that's a bad idea."

"But I . . . CAN'T . . . BREATHE!" Now he was breathing far too quickly. If I hadn't been through this a hundred times myself as a child, I'd have thought he was dying. A light flicked on at the other end of the hall, and Leo came out rubbing his arm across his eyes. He wore a matching pajama set, white with blue stripes. He turned on the hall light, and Ian sank to the ground, crying and hugging his shoulders. Marta came out behind Leo in her bathrobe.

The Labaznikovs swept Ian downstairs, Marta making clucking noises and Leo clapping him on the back and saying, "We'll get you fixed up, good as new, all full of air!" I followed, glad I'd put the shoebox back in place.

We sat in the kitchen while Marta brewed a pot of coffee. I thought at first it was for the adults, to keep us awake, until she poured Ian a big mug of it and thinned it out with sugar and milk. My father always wanted to give me coffee for my childhood asthma attacks, but my mother refused. "You want her to end up four feet tall?" she would say.

Ian started blowing on the coffee and sipping it. "I have . . . my mom's . . . Starbucks. . . . all the time," he managed between breaths. She must have handed it off to him once she'd drunk her ten calories' worth. But no, it wasn't fair of me to think bad things about his mother now. I stomped on my own foot under the table.

The Labaznikov kitchen was painted pale yellow, with little pots of herbs above the sink. The clock on the wall said 3:10. Ian finished his coffee, and his shoulders went down a little. "It's stress," Marta whispered. "Because of his poor mother." She meant the fake, suicidal one, of course, not the real, anorexic, evangelical one. I nodded. She poured Ian another cup, poured three more cups for the adults, and put another pot on to brew.

Leo said, "Now this is not real Russian coffee. Real Russian coffee, it turns your veins black. Lucy, your father used to make coffee like molten rock."

Ian took a thick, wet breath so he could talk. "Did you . . . know Mr. Hull back . . . in Russia?"

"Ah! Jurek Hulkinov was in my class at school! He was good at math, and I will tell you why. The teacher could ask us, what is seven times eight, and Jurek would answer, forty-two. And the teacher would say, no, this is not correct. And Jurek would explain exactly why seven eights make forty-two, until the teacher agreed that he was right. He could get the teacher to apologize to him, for her errors."

"Were you part of . . . the chocolate factory?"

Marta put a wet paper towel on Ian's forehead. "Hold this here," she said. "Now stop talking."

Leo, meanwhile, looked confused. "No, the chocolate factory? No."

"But was it real?"

And now Marta and Leo were looking at each other over Ian's head, the look of perplexed and concerned movie characters silently debating how to handle a difficult situation.

But Leo surprised me: "Yes. The Leningrad Chocolate Factory. It was very real. I will tell you a secret: it was the best chocolate I ever tasted in my life. And the Hulkinov basement was full of people working, day and night, working for *free*, just so they could have the chocolate. They were like the Oompa-Loompas. It was a triumph of capitalism." He could see that Ian was about to exert himself again, probably to ask what capitalism was. "But Marta is right, this talking is no good for you. I tell you what: I will take Lucy down to see the ferrets, and you sit here quietly with Marta."

I didn't want to leave him alone with someone else, but I was too tired to argue, and too upset at the prospect of having to walk Ian into an emergency room in the morning without insurance. I found myself halfway down the basement stairs, which were carpeted in bright green and which grew somehow softer and soggier with every barefooted step. And there were the ferrets—most likely the cause of all the asthma to begin with—in their long wire cages. There was wood paneling everywhere, too, and a bar, and an ancient weight bench, and laundry, but the room was dominated by those three cages in the middle, and the three slinky animals stretching elegantly as Leo turned on more and more lights. The one I reached first was peach-colored with a white nose, and the other two were nut brown. Leo sat down on the weight bench, while I paid polite attention to Clara, Valentina, and Levi (whose cages bore brass nameplates). The more I watched them, I really did find them fascinating, the way they snaked their vertebrae around in some kind of primitive, rodent yoga.

While I still had my back to him, Leo said, "Lucy, I have heard that story before. About the chocolate factory. Your father used to tell that to Anya, too."

I laughed. "Oh, he was just trying to cheer Ian up." I poked my finger through the wires to stroke Clara, the peach one, who seemed the calmest. "It's a cute story, but I have no illusions that it's real, don't worry."

His silence was somewhat alarming. I turned around and saw the strange contrast between the weight bench and the tired old man in pajamas, too frail and arthritic to use it ever again. "Lucy, this story has always bothered me. It bothered me even that he told it to Anya. But he is still telling it, this many years later."

I shrugged and laughed and felt extremely uncomfortable. "No, I know it's not real. It's okay, seriously."

"There *was* a Leningrad Chocolate Factory, when Jurek and I were young children—six, seven, eight. But it was not your father's company. It was your grandfather's. He ran it in the basement, just like I said."

"I thought my grandfather worked for the government."

"Yes. *Yes.* You can see the problem. He worked for the Ministry of Culture, but here he was going home on the weekends to his house just barely outside of Moscow, employing half the town in his basement. And the only step he took to hide his crime was to say 'Leningrad' on the labels. But it *worked.* The idiot government searched all over Leningrad. And Roman Hulkinov shows up for work every morning, his breath smelling of chocolate, and no one looks at him twice."

The caffeine and the lack of sleep and the smell of the ferrets were swelling into one giant wave of nausea, but I was interested enough in what Leo was saying that I sat down on the moist green carpet rather than excusing myself for the bathroom. I breathed through my mouth. I was trying to piece it together. "But he got caught eventually," I said.

"Well, yes. Yes. I will tell you something about myself: I do not believe in keeping secrets about the past. I think that when we have false assumptions about the world, we make the wrong decisions. When Anya was growing up, I never told her the nasty parts about escaping, and deserting my family, and leaving my sister to marry a drunk. I made it a happy story. And so what does she do? She runs away. She thinks it sounds like fun. Because she has false information."

I wasn't sure if this was an accusation, or a warning, or a justification of whatever he was about to tell me. And I couldn't focus on the issue for more than a second, because of the nausea pulsing through my throat and face and chest. I tried burying my nose in Anya's sweatshirt, but the stale must of it went up my sinus like dust.

"So I will tell you this, because I think it is useful. You understand?" I probably managed to nod.

"Your father and I had a schoolteacher, Sofiya Alekseeva. We were eight years old, and so we were in love with her. She had a long braid, this is why we loved her. She taught us songs about Pavlik Morozov. He was the thirteen-year-old boy who turned his father in to the Soviets, and then his own grandfather killed him. Number one Soviet martyr. There were statues and plays and books. I'm sure Sofiya Alekseeva taught us the songs because she was told to. But to your father, he must have thought she really loved Pavlik Morozov."

Although I could see, starkly and horribly, where the story was going, it had the opposite effect it normally would: my head cleared, the nausea cleared, my sinus cleared.

"I get it," I said, meaning, *stop*. More for his sake than my own. He was propping himself up with his hands against his knees, and he looked wretched and pale and old. "Okay. Thank you, I get it."

"He left her a note, after school. I watched him put it on her desk, and I didn't stop him, because I thought it was a love letter. Which it really was, I suppose, in a way. I teased him about it all the way home, until he told me what it said. He had given all the details of the operation. And because he was eight years old, he illustrated the letter. He drew a floor plan of the basement with all the equipment, and he drew his father standing beside a mountain of chocolate bars. I never saw the letter, but I've had always such a picture in my mind of what he drew! It was so innocent, really, to illustrate for the teacher like this. This is to me the saddest part."

"So he ran off to Siberia then," I finished. Leo looked up at me, blankly. "My grandfather."

"No. Are you kidding? No. Your grandfather was arrested, there was a ridiculous trial, and he was sent to a work camp. He died six months later."

"Oh."

"I mean, yes, it was in Siberia. All the work camps were in Siberia."

"Right."

"Of course, they did not build statues of Jurek Hulkinov, and they did not write songs about him, and even after his father was arrested, the teacher did not say anything at all about the note. The police came to question him, et cetera, but there was of course so much evidence that he did not need to testify in the trial. Even his mother, I think, didn't know what Jurek had done. I'm fairly sure I was the only one."

There were colors swirling on the wall under the stairs, colors I was certain weren't really there, and my throat was closing from the ferrets. Even though I hadn't had a moment of asthma since I turned fifteen, my throat was closing up. I felt that I needed to rewind my life to the beginning and watch it again, to see what I had missed. For instance, the story of my father's escape. Clearly the potato in the tailpipe was a lie, just like the chocolate had been. Though I knew he really did come at age twenty, because . . . no, I didn't even know that. So I asked.

"Yes, your father was maybe twenty, maybe twenty-one. He was horrified at what he'd done. It wasn't the USSR he was running from, you see that now. I came three years later. So yes, twenty. Lucy, you look not so good."

"I'm fine."

"You know, this is not so unusual, this story," he said, as if trying to reassure me of something, but I couldn't imagine what. "This is a nation of runaways. Every person comes from somewhere else. Even the Indians, they run once upon a time across the Alaskan land bridge. The blacks, they maybe didn't run from Africa, okay, but they ran from slavery. And the rest of us, we all ran from something. From the church, the state, the parents, the Irish potato bug. And I think this is why Americans are so restless. I think about Anya, that she comes from the blood of runaways. Only that in America, there is no place left to run to. Lucy, raise up your head. You look very sick."

"I could use more coffee."

We walked upstairs to find Ian breathing much better, his shoulders down from where they'd been, and Marta telling him about *babka* and *kissel* and *pashka*.

Ian said, "We never changed the subject from desserts!" and I was relieved to hear him get a full sentence out like that. We joined them at the table and Marta poured everyone more coffee. I burned my tongue, and then managed to focus my numbed brain on that strange sensation for the next hour. I pressed my tongue against my teeth and felt nothing. I pressed it against the ridged roof of my mouth and felt nothing. I bit it and felt something. I started all over again.

We all finally went to bed at four thirty in the morning. We propped Ian up in the guest bed with six pillows behind him. "You are a prince carried on a litter," Leo said.

"Litter?"

The Labaznikovs laughed without explaining, and Ian didn't really seem to care. I was too sleepy to go back down to the shoebox, but I told myself if I got up early, before everyone else, I'd try again.

26

A Glass for Glass

When Ian woke me up, though, it was nine thirty and the house was filled with clanging and sizzling and the smell of bacon. He opened the door without knocking, fully dressed but with a towel wrapped like a turban around his hair. "Miss Hull!" he said. His face was bright again, and he seemed to be breathing well. "Just wait till you take your shower!"

"Why?"

"It's a surprise!"

When I did stumble down the hall and into the guest bathroom, I looked carefully at the bottom of the tub, checked for towels, checked the soap, and couldn't see anything unusual besides the green and orange design scheme. It was nice to use non-hotel soap. The water pressure was better here, too, and although the tub was olive colored, it seemed clean. I reached for the one bottle of shampoo on the little suction-cupped shelf, and saw what Ian meant. It was yellow and runny, like baby shampoo, with a coat of congealed soap slime covering a paper label that proclaimed FERRET-GLO! in big red letters. A beady-eyed ferret, washed pale by years of Labaznikov shower water, stared out from under the logo. I squeezed a thin puddle of yellow into my hand and sniffed it. It smelled like puppy shampoo, not totally unpleasant. I put it on my head and scrubbed around quickly, but it didn't really lather. As I rinsed and ran my fingers through my hair, everything felt sticky and clumpy.

When I got out, I wiped the mirror and stood looking at my waxy hair and then at my body. I must have lost five pounds, at least, in the four days we'd been on the road—enough to make a visible difference. It wasn't until just then that I remembered what Leo had told me about my father, and I had a few foggy moments of trying to figure out what parts I'd dreamed. I was getting used to the feeling: waking up in the morning relieved that I hadn't taken Ian from Hannibal, then remembering that yes, I had, in fact, taken Ian from Hannibal. But this story about my father for some reason seemed even darker than that other daily revelation. Here was something I wasn't *supposed* to know, and wasn't supposed to remember.

I quickly got dressed and, towel around my hair, ducked into the guest bedroom where Ian had been staying. I could hear them all downstairs, talking and eating. On a corner desk sat what I thought I'd remembered from four thirty that morning: a thick gray Dell computer, old but not ancient, its screen uniformly dusty, a phone cord running out the back and into the wall. I turned it on and managed to get online—it made that loud phone-dialing sound I'd forgotten about after a few years of instant access at the library, and I had to jump up and close the door—and ran a search on "Ian Drake" and "Hannibal" and "suspect."

My blood froze when eight links popped up, but on closer

look they all seemed to be using the word *suspect* as verb, and numbers two through eight seemed to refer to the first, an article from Loloblog.com, posted on Wednesday night. Loloblog was a very artsy, very liberal online magazine I used to read occasionally in college and had all but forgotten about. The writers were all around twenty-three years old, living in the same square mile of Brooklyn, and hopelessly opinionated. They were smug about being smug, and they had, apparently, no fear of being sued. They also tended to be horrendously ill-informed, but not this time:

THE BIGOT AND THE RUNAWAY

by Arthur Levitt

Smoking gun of the week:

In Loloblog's obsessive stalking of Reverend <u>Bob Lawson</u>, founder and director of <u>Glad Heart Ministries</u>, one of the most egregious of the many organizations that claim to turn gay adults and children straight, we found the following item, posted Wednesday: "Please pray for Ian D., a young sheep in our St. Louis fold that the Lord has allowed to let wander. We pray for his return, and for his loving parents who have been my loyal supporters."

Okay, let's ignore the awkward syntax. Let's ignore the obvious sheep jokes. Let's start collecting circumstantial evidence.

1. Our tireless interns found the <u>St. Louis Post-Dispatch</u> reporting Tuesday that Ian Drake, a 10-year-old

resident of Hannibal, MO, has gone missing, and that no criminal play is suspected. (Read: runaway.) No Amber Alert issued, no parents arrested. (Again, read: runaway.)

Conclusion: Well, let's not jump to any, quite yet. Let's just note the interesting coincidence, and the fact that what has always singled Glad Heart Ministries out for our especial vitriol is the fact that they start brainwashing young lads at the age of ten.

2. The Post-Dispatch article and all others we could find mentioned the Drake family's involvement in <u>Olive Branch Evangelical Bible Chapel</u>, which is less of a chapel than a converted airplane hangar with movie screens and a whole lot o' fire and brimstone. (Read Blake Andersen's amazing article on megachurches and megachurch architecture <u>here</u>.) Loloblog intern Andrea D. called Olive Branch, posing as a young lesbian hoping to join the congregation. She was told by an unnamed representative that "All are welcome. Basically our belief is, love the sinner but hate the sin. And we have several counseling and recovery groups." Ummm, okay . . .

Conclusion: The Drake family's beliefs would appear to be consistent with those of someone who would send their son to get un-gayed.

3. Ian is a fairly uncommon name among ten-year-olds. Bear with me here. The Social Security Administration

<u>website</u> lists the name Ian as the 74th most popular
for boys born ten years ago—and it consistently ranks
in the mid-seventies throughout the 1990s (the pre-
sumed range of birth years for a "young sheep"). In
other words, it's a relatively uncommon name. Add
to that the odds of the last initial being "D"; add to
that the date of Lawson's posting; add to that the geo-
graphical proximity.

Conclusion: If we're not talking about the same kid, it's
one hell of a co-inky-dink.

Admittedly, it's a hike from Hannibal to St. Louis—
<u>MapQuest</u> puts it at exactly two hours—but what's a lit-
tle two-hour drive to de-gayify your child?

Dr. Ken Washington, director of New York's private Kohl-
man Children's Mental Health Center, wrote to Loloblog
in an email this morning that "in recent studies, up to
42% of all homeless teenagers identified themselves as
gay, lesbian or transgender. Of America's 1.6 million runaways, that's a staggering number."

While most of these cases involve kids kicked out of their
parents' homes, the Drake case is clearly not that. But
Dr. Washington writes that "a desire to escape a hos-
tile family environment and the mental abuse of sexual
'reprogramming' would certainly be consistent with the
patterns of homelessness we've seen with young runaways, although typically we are looking at adolescents."

The article went on to break down the history and philosophy of the Pastor Bob phenomenon, such programs in general, and the number of unreturned calls put in to Glad Heart Ministries over the previous twenty-four hours by hapless interns. It was eight pages long, and not much of the rest had to do with Ian.

I sat back in the desk chair and attempted to react. I wasn't sure what to think, except that (1) this wouldn't necessarily point any fingers in my direction; but (2) it would possibly raise some interest out there in the case, which wasn't exactly good; and (3) if the Drakes had any sense and a good lawyer, they could easily sue the pants off Loloblog and Arthur Levitt in particular for all kinds of libel.

I went back to Anya's room, tried to run a comb through my hair, and gave up.

Downstairs, Ian was sitting like a king at the Labaznikovs' table. Marta stood at the stove, an actual apron around her waist, and Leo sprawled in a chair, drinking a bottle of beer and smoking a cigar, the smoke from which he was mercifully blowing away from Ian, turning his head every few seconds to puff it through the door to the dining room. Ian didn't seem to mind. He looked positively gleeful. There was a platter of thick Canadian bacon on the table, a dish of eggs scrambled with onions and peppers, two whole salamis, a pot of coffee, a plate of bread slices, a brick of muenster cheese, jams, mustards, peanut butter, and three more unopened bottles of beer. Ian beamed up at me and put a forkload of eggs in his mouth. His hair stuck up in four separate Ferret-Glo cowlicks.

"I *love* Russian breakfast!" Ian said.

"This is not Russian breakfast!" Leo shouted. "This is how Russians eat in America!"

We ate better than we had since we left Hannibal. Leo forced two beers on me, after which I knew I couldn't drive yet. And Ian didn't want to leave. He went down to see the ferrets again, asked Marta if she had any pictures of Russia (why, yes, she did) and asked Leo to explain what, exactly, communism was. This took about an hour of monologue, but at least did not include my father's joke about the cat and the mustard. I'd helped Marta with the dishes, Leo had smoked another cigar, and Marta had started putting out plates for lunch, but apart from Ian's foray into the basement, we hadn't even left the kitchen. I suddenly wondered if the shoebox was still there. I hadn't noticed it on my way down.

Marta put a glass of milk in front of Ian, and he beamed up at her. This might well have been his idea of heaven. "There!" Leo said. "A glass for Glass!"

"What?" Ian said.

"A glass for *Glass*," I repeated, willing him to hear the capital G.

"I don't get it."

I said, "Your last name. Is Glass." But by this point, Marta and Leo were glancing at each other, amused.

I knew, though, that I didn't need to worry. This was the thing about people who did favors for each other, who passed illicit shoeboxes in the night: they didn't ask questions if you didn't. And if anyone in a uniform ever came looking for you, they wouldn't say, "My God, is she okay? I have an envelope with her last address!" They'd say, "We no speak good English. No, we never hear of such a young lady. We—how you say?—never met."

It was two o'clock when we got up from the table. I reminded Ian that his grandmother was waiting for him and thanked the

Labaznikovs for their hospitality. Back in the living room, I saw that the shoebox was gone.

Of course it was, I realized. It was nothing more than the cigars Leo was smoking at breakfast. Cuban cigars that my father must have picked up in Argentina, a thank-you gift to Leo for some favor, past or future. Then again, there was probably some money stuffed in there for padding, too, maybe a few illegitimate receipts. I didn't have the energy to care anymore. Who was I to blame him for his cigars, his money laundering—I, who was laundering a child?

When we had our coats on and bags in our hands and were almost out the door, Marta said, "We have to take a picture!" She scurried upstairs for a camera, and for a moment I considered sprinting out the door with Ian before our presence could be immortalized. If Leo hadn't been there, I might have. I tried to catch Ian's eye, but he was systematically squeezing the leaves of all the plants in the Labaznikovs' living room to see if they were real. Leo said to me, "Lucy, we will see if you remember. What is three Russians?"

"A revolution."

"Very good! And here we are three Russians in this house!"

Marta appeared again with the camera and arranged us in a row, me and Ian and Leo, and backed up to snap the picture. Just as she said, "One, two, three!" Ian put his hands in front of his face and peeked through the slits of his fingers. The camera went off, and Marta said, "Oh, one more so we can see you!"

"I'm very self-conscious," Ian said. Of the thirty or so pictures of the Winter Book Bash that were currently on the display board at the Hannibal Public Library, approximately twenty featured Ian Drake sticking his face in front of someone else's and displaying a happy mouthful of orthodontia. "I'm afraid the camera will steal my soul."

"He's just shy," I cut in before they could ask what they were teaching, anyway, in the schools these days. I thought what a strange photo this would seem in the newspapers, if we were ever caught. *Hull, Drake (behind hands), and unidentified Russian man at private home near Pittsburgh. Note suspicious cowlicks in hair of both kidnapper and victim.*

Marta let it go at that, and we got out the door with a series of smothering Russo-Italian hugs and a brown paper bag full of sandwiches. "What is the difference between a piano and a fish?" Leo shouted from the porch when we were halfway to the car.

"You can't tune a fish!" Ian called back. He beamed at me. This was clearly the finest individual moment of his life.

"*Poka!*" the Labaznikovs called. "*Udachi!*"

As we backed out, I caught a look at myself in the rearview. My hair was even worse than I thought, greasy clumps jutting out from my head at odd angles. "We look pretty terrible," I said.

"We're the Ferret-Glo twins!" And he proceeded to make up a song about it.

27

The BFG

It felt awful being back on the road. With every mile, our car was starting to feel more like a submarine, something we weren't even allowed to emerge from. Outside our little capsule was a different element, a substance from which our lungs were not suited to extract oxygen. Inside, we were cramped and coated with grime and cracker crumbs. Our bodies had taken on the contours of the car seats.

I realized I had to bite the bullet and call Rocky when I knew he'd answer. He never worked Friday afternoons, even when we were short-staffed, even on those rare occasions when the children's librarian vanished to commit a felony. Ian and I stopped for milkshakes at a McDonald's with an outdoor playground, and I sat on a picnic bench to call while Ian swung from the monkey bars. He wasn't able to pull himself across them, just swing from one bar until his arms gave out and he landed in the wood chips. Then he'd climb back up and do it again.

"Rocky!" I said when he answered.

"Yes?"

"It's Lucy." He never needed me to identify myself. Had he written me out of his world this quickly, or was he just mad that I hadn't called yet?

"Oh. You sound hoarse. Are you okay?"

"I'm fine, just a little exhausted. Still in Chicago." I told him again about my sick friend, even said her name was Janna Glass, and made it sound like a planned trip. An extended illness. I said I'd donated bone marrow yesterday, but left out anything about her son or driving east. I felt like I should be making a list of what I said to whom. "It hurt like all hell," I said.

"Right."

"Is everything okay downstairs?"

He was quiet, which was my opportunity to act surprised and concerned, but I didn't have much air in me. I managed, "What's wrong?"

"Look," he said, "I have to ask you something. Okay, Ian Drake? The boy who hangs out downstairs all the time?"

"Sure."

"He's—no one exactly knows where he is."

"What do you mean?"

"He's missing."

"Do you mean the *library* doesn't know, or his *parents* don't know?"

"Neither. He's, like, officially missing. Police and everything."

"Shit. Did he run away?"

"Well, there's some kind of note, but they're not saying what it was."

"So what did you need to ask me?"

"What do you mean?"

"You started by saying you had to ask me something."

"Oh. I guess I meant tell you. Are you okay?"

"No. Not really. That's pretty awful. How long has he been gone?"

"A few days. I think he vanished while you were still in town, even. Did you see him on Sunday?"

I tried to think, honestly. Monday was when I found him . . . He must have been there Sunday afternoon to hide, but Sarah-Ann was working at closing, not me. "No. He came in Friday, I think. He only returned books, which is really unusual for him. But the records would be in the computer." They actually would, this time, since the books he returned were ones for his school report on the Cherokee. "Didn't you look?"

"Yeah. I just thought you might have talked to him or something."

"No. He was just in and out. If he were running away, you'd think he would have checked out some books. Have they—have the police, like, come into the library? Have you talked to them?"

"It was weird. They talked to Loraine for a couple minutes, and then they specifically asked to talk to Sarah-Ann. They said the mom wanted them to talk to her."

"How bizarre. Did they?"

"For about two seconds. If I could've rolled downstairs to eaves-drop, I would have. My guess is they realized pretty fast how batty she is and just gave up. She was asking me later if Ian was the Asian kid with the crutches. Seriously, I would have paid cash money to see that police interview."

I wanted to laugh, but I reminded myself I was supposed to be in shock. "Do they think he ran away?"

"I don't know what they think. *I* think he ran away."

"Why?"

"I don't know. It's just a feeling. Didn't you say they were so terrible to him? The parents? And there was that weird letter you found."

I was silent for a while, which I figured was the best way not to talk myself into a corner.

"Lucy?"

"I'm okay."

"I know you two are close."

I said, "I have to go," and hung up while I was still ahead.

Ian was navigating us in a straight line now, right along the interstate, where before he'd been taking loopy detours. He had the atlas open on his lap.

About forty miles later, when I thought my right foot would fall off, Ian started a game. "So, you know how a white horse is worth fifty points?"

"In what?"

"When you're driving. It's fifty points. That's the most you can get. And a pink Cadillac is also fifty."

"Okay," I said, remembering this vaguely from my childhood.

"A car with one headlight is ten points. But these are all only if you see them *first*. You have to call it out."

"Right."

"Well, the way I play, there are a couple others. Any word you see that rhymes with either of our names, first or last, that's worth thirty. And it's forty-five points if you see our exact same car. But it has to be the *exact same*, not just the same color."

He was talking so fast it was hard to understand him. "What's wrong with you?" I said. "Why are you doing that?" He had his hands crossed over his chest, grabbing opposite shoulders.

"It's just a little hard to breathe still," he said. "I don't think it was just the ferrets. I'm actually low on my puffer."

"Is it albuterol? Like an emergency inhaler?" I realized I hadn't really looked at his inhaler, or asked his entire medical history, or even monitored his breathing since we left Pittsburgh. And now I'd let him exercise on the monkey bars. I wasn't even an adequate babysitter.

"I just take it when I need it, but I've had to use it a lot lately."

I stared ahead at the road in panic a few moments before assessing my options. At least it wasn't a regular medication that his asthma would spiral without. I could get him something over the counter, or in the worst case I could take him to an ER and say we had no insurance, maybe call my father for the bill. I could eventually use it as an excuse to take him home.

"How bad does it get?"

"It gets as bad as last night. My doctor said I should take this purple kind that you take every day, but my dad said I'd just get addicted to it, so I'm not allowed to."

"Jesus Christ."

"What?"

"I said, 'That's nice.'"

"It's just that really you shouldn't say religious words unless you really mean them, because that's one of the Ten Commandments."

"Right. Sorry about that."

I spent the next ten miles making myself a mental Ten Commandment scorecard for the past month, which looked something like this:

COMMANDMENT	YES	NO
Murder		X
Failure to Honor Sabbath	X	
Theft	X	
Bearing False Witness	X	
Adultery (dependent on exact definition)	X	
Failure to Honor Mothers and Fathers	X	
Coveting of Neighbor's Property (dependent on definitions of "covet" and "property")	X	
Creation of Graven Images		X
Worship of Pagan Gods		X
Taking of Lord's Name in Vain	X	

I had a hard time remembering them all, but the hours spent helping my rather slow childhood friend Brooke with her CCD homework had apparently added *something* to my cultural literacy, if not to my actual moral code. For good measure, I added the Seven Cardinal Sins:

FAUSTIAN ERROR	AS MEASURED IN . . .	YES	NO
Sloth	calories not burned	X	
Lust	untalented musicians slept with	X	
Avarice	apparent sense of entitlement	X	
Gluttony	Oreos	X	

FAUSTIAN ERROR	AS MEASURED IN . . .	YES	NO
Pride	self-righteousness	X	
Wrath	vehemence of judgmental monologues against Pastor Bob	X	
Envy	desire to trade lives with everyone I saw, including the man who washed our windows for two dollars under an overpass	X	

Consider it quantitative proof. I have horns for a reason. And yet what criminal, in the midst of the crime, really and deeply believes she's evil? In our minds we're all Jean Valjean, Martin Luther King, Henry David Thoreau. I was Gandhi, marching to the sea for salt. Look at the blisters on my poor, bare feet.

Somewhere on Route 80: "Let's talk about books."

"That's a great idea. Okay, books. What's the next thing you want to read?"

"Well, I think I want to read *The Hobbit*. This one guy, Michael, in this class I go to, he said it was very good. Have you ever read it?"

"You haven't read *The Hobbit*?" I practically screamed it at him, missing my chance to talk about his "class." Of *course* he hadn't read it, I realized. He wasn't allowed to read books with wizards. Not real wizards, at least. Oz the Great and Terrible was probably only acceptable for being a humbug. I said, "Once we're back in Hannibal, I'll check it out for you." But I really couldn't envision a scenario anymore when both of us would be back in Hannibal and I'd still have my job and Ian would gallop down the steps every day to see me. "So you said your friend's name was Michael? Is he your age?"

"Yeah. But that's not really what I meant by talking about books. I mean fun stuff, like if you go to heaven and it turns out that one of the things you can do there is you can be anyone in any book, whenever you want to, but you can only choose one person, who would you pick?"

"Wow. I have no idea. What about you?"

"I think definitely the BFG. Because then you could be in *two* Roald Dahl books. Because the BFG is in one chapter of *Danny, the Champion of the World*, right? Except I wasn't allowed to read it, but I remember after you read us *The BFG* you showed us that part. Do you remember that? You held it up to show us." I liked the image of a big, friendly giant Ian stomping through the streets of Missouri, crushing Pastor Bob underfoot.

I thought for a while. "In that case, I think I'd be Theseus. Do you remember him?"

"Was he the guy with the Minotaur, and he had the ball of string?"

"Right. And my reason is, he shows up in probably hundreds of different books. He's in a Shakespeare play, and all the Greek and Roman writers used him. There are probably some battle scenes that would be too violent, but I'd spend most of my time in Shakespeare, anyway."

"And you could be in *D'Aulaires' Greek Myths*!"

"Definitely." It didn't take a psychoanalyst: I wanted to be the guy who could get himself back out of the labyrinth, the guy who could roll the string back up to where he started.

"Okay, the other thing is, if you're a *writer*, and you go to heaven, you get different rules. Then you can be in any story you ever wrote, and you can jump between all the different people. So Roald Dahl could be the BFG one day, and then he could be Charlie, and then he could be the centipede in the peach."

"So tell me more about your friend Michael."

"He's really not my friend. He definitely picks his nose."

"Do you have other friends at your class?"

"We're really very busy the whole time. They don't really let us have a lot of just conversations. And the good part is, sometimes they give us doughnuts. You know what's good? If you ever went to prison, you could just keep your same job. Don't they have libraries in prisons? Hey, about ten seconds to New York!" We could see the large signs ahead, advising us of local traffic laws and tourist information. Ian took off his hat and started singing "Erie Canal."

I wondered if each individual state line we crossed was an additional felony charge, or if crossing the first was as criminal as you could get. I could feel the quality of the tar become smoother under the wheels as the New York Highway Commission took over. It made it feel somewhat more official and monumental, although I always wished there would be a big arch to pass under. "Buckle Up" signs just don't have the same appeal as passing through city gates or checkpoints. I tried to imagine Persian emissaries following the Via Appia into Rome, greeted by nothing more than a "Check Your Harness" sign. It would never do. Something had been lost. Not that I wanted a checkpoint right then.

Crossing the border into Russia in a college choir bus, postcommunism, I'd felt ridiculously privileged, and tried hard to think about my uncle, who died trying to get out, and my father, who ran and swam and broke his leg. And there I was, getting my passport cursorily checked by the burly border guard who had mounted the bus. He wouldn't have known by my truncated surname, my straight teeth, my sneakers, that I considered myself Russian. That the stolen dry cleaning, the head on the pike, the horrible joke about the cat and the mustard, made me feel more Russian than American. I had tried very hard, at the time, to think something profound about expatriation.

Now, older, running away—if not from my country, then from everything I'd ever known—I felt something perhaps a little more real. To tell the truth, it was still an effort, in this age of cheap flights and e-mail and long-distance phone calls, to imagine what it meant for my father and his brother to pack up and leave, to understand that everyone they'd ever known in twenty years of life they'd never meet again, that they'd either die in the sweaters they were wearing or live in them for the next three months, that they, who had spoken such beautiful Russian, would become awkward, accented foreigners. That their children would belong to some other place.

I wondered if (when they started looking for me, plastering my face in the post office) I could really leave my country—send Ian home and flee to Canada with Anya's coins and never come back. It would be nice, in a way. To look at America from the outside, to feel like the underdog instead of the overlord. Or I could move to Australia, land of criminals and exiles. I already knew the song.

As we pulled into the next gas station, my cell started ringing. "Don't," I said, because Ian was reaching toward the dashboard, where the phone was balanced. I picked it up myself as I parked next to the pump.

"It's me," Glenn said. I handed Ian a five-dollar bill and nodded toward the Speedee Mart. He skipped up to the doors.

"So I had this crazy day," I began. I got out of the car and started half-consciously pumping gas.

"When are you going home?" His voice was too loud and too thick, and if I'd been the one to call I'd have thought I woke him up. I managed to remember that I was supposed to be in Cleveland, still.

"Soon, I think. I mean, I can give you a lift back, I'm just not sure quite when."

"I found a bride."

"I'm sorry?"

"I already found a ride."

"Great. I mean, that's fine."

He let out a groan or a yawn, I couldn't tell which. "I take it you're not my date next weekend for the thing." He had another concert, a second performance of the Mr. Clean Remix, which apparently was getting critical acclaim in whatever limited-circulation music news zines reviewed minor modern orchestra pieces premiering in St. Louis. "I mean, you said my piece sounded like a cartoon song, so . . ."

"I'll make it if I can," I said. "I'm probably going back to Chicago for a while to help my friend. That's the issue."

"I'm sure," he said. "Speaking of which, that guy called."

I immediately thought police. "Guy?"

"Your retarded friend. Rambo, whatever. He asked if I knew about a kid from the library."

It didn't make sense, and I needed to know more—for instance, when exactly did this call take place?—but all I wanted to do was get off the phone, which was suddenly slipping out of my hand with sweat. Somehow, the only question that came out was "How did he get your number?"

"Fuck do I know? Because he's in love with you and he stalks you. Look, do I need to call the cops on you, Lucy?"

"What in the hell for?"

"You tell me."

"For not going to your stupid concert? For helping my sick friend? I know about the library kid. I talked to Rocky, and I'm incredibly upset."

"It just seems strange. I mean, that guy said you already gave the bone marrow." So he'd called Glenn *after* our conversation just a few hours ago. A very bad sign.

"He was wrong." The gas pump clicked that it was done. Ian would be coming back out any second.

"You're not a very good liar."

"I'm an excellent liar. I told you I liked your orchestrated commercial jingle."

I said it on instinct, if only to get rid of him. It wouldn't be a bad thing for him to be gone and silent and so angry that if Rocky called him back, all he could say was that he hadn't heard from me in days and hoped I burned in hell.

What he said to *me* was "Don't ever call me again."

I pulled back up to the doors of the store and waited for Ian. Despite the vague and inexplicable urge to cry, it was all a relief. Because now that there was no more Glenn, and now that Rocky was probably realizing what an awful person I was, there was nothing really to go home to—except Ian, who wasn't even there but *here*, coming out of the store with his coat on backward, arms and sleeves tucked up so it looked like his wrists were sprouting from his shoulders. It seemed strange now even to think of Hannibal as home. Chicago was home, the Labaznikov house was a sort of home, and certainly my car was home. Hannibal was a distant memory.

We went a few more exits, Ian reading aloud to me from the magazine he'd bought with his five dollars—some sort of off-brand teen star-stalker with a photo of a shirtless movie star on the cover, one whose name I didn't know, although I recognized his scruffy goatee and alarmingly pale eyes. ("What's a fiancé?" Ian asked. "What's a rehab?") Every car had started to look like a police car, every noise sounded like a siren. I wondered if Rocky had taken his suspicions to the Hannibal PD, or if he was working freelance, sorting out the clues on his own. He would have been the one to find the lights on, the one to know how close I was with Ian.

Ian had collected thirty points in our game for rhyming Lucy with "goosey," and thirty more for insisting that "librarian" rhymed with "Ian," when he fell asleep—his head tilted back and his glasses falling down his face. I leaned toward him every few minutes to hear if he was wheezing, but all I heard was the gurgle of someone sleeping with his mouth open.

Not long after, I noticed a car behind us on the highway that was a copy of mine: powder blue, rusted, Japanese. I thought of waking Ian up to claim my forty-five points, but I was enjoying the quiet and he needed his rest. I couldn't tell if it was a man or a woman driving—the low sun reflecting off the windshield completely washed out the face—so I couldn't help but imagine it was a woman who looked like me. My twin—only her greatest guilt wasn't riding shotgun, her mind wasn't playing a constant loop of grieving parents and vindictive ex-boyfriends, she wasn't starring in the next act of her family saga of shame and flight and idiotic idealism.

After the sun was down I looked for her again, but couldn't tell if the bright little headlights behind us were hers or not. I didn't wake Ian until we were pulling into a motel.

28

The Emerald State

The next morning, Ian's asthma was better. Before we got in the car, I listened with my ear pressed to his back. He couldn't stop laughing, but what breathing I could make out sounded clear.

We started toward the wrong car. There, again, with a better parking spot than mine, was a copy of my car, Japanese, powder blue. A man with dark hair and sunglasses reclining in the driver's seat. When we got on the highway, he did, too. I gave myself a silent lecture about paranoia, and we headed east for a few hours until we finally passed a sign that said "Welcome to the Green Mountain State!" "So," I said, "what town does your grandmother live in?" It was mean of me, and I don't know why I did it, except that I was in a rotten mood, and I'd been up all night thinking about my father, alternately enraged at his betrayal and devastated for the guilt he must have carried his whole life, and confused about why Leo Labaznikov had taken it upon himself to fill me in.

It had been a long time since we'd mentioned Ian's grandmother outside the Janna Glass fiction, and it took him a second to remember what I was talking about.

"Oh," he said. "I didn't understand at first, because I call her my nana. My *grandmother* would be my *mother's* mother, and my nana is my father's mother."

"Okay. Which town does your nana live in?"

Suddenly he was screaming at me, his face red. "IF I TELL YOU, YOU'RE GOING TO TAKE ME THERE WITHOUT LETTING ME SEE THE TOURIST ATTRACTIONS!" It was a fake temper tantrum, the kind I'd seen in the library. Not half as scary or real as the one the day we left. He flung his face down onto his own lap, then looked up and whimpered, "I want to see about the Green Mountain Boys."

"All right," I said. His screaming had at least brought me back to the present moment, to the problems at hand, the ones that weren't forty-seven years in the past and out of my control. "Then where do the Green Mountain Boys live?"

"*Lived.* They were in the 1700s. I don't really know."

"Why do you like them so much?"

"We had to do this report on something about the Revolutionary War. And I wanted to do Betsy Ross, but that was taken." He was drinking a spinach and apple smoothie, and pretending to like it. We'd managed to find a health food store out there in the middle of nowhere, a sort of gingko-and-mung-bean oasis. And it worked: I felt extremely healthy, for the first time in days.

We drove through little towns composed of two or three stores and a handful of houses that had shed most of their paint and started to sag. There were homemade signs hanging on bedsheets from windows: "Take Back Vermont." I'd heard an NPR story about it that winter, this ongoing grassroots movement against the recent civil union law. They'd played a phone interview with a Burlington resident who'd sounded young and energetic and pierced. He said, "This state is the most happily polarized place in the country. Half the people are way liberal, and the other half are so conservative, it's like, 'You can be gay if I can have my guns.' It's this sort of balance of extremes." The angry clots of paint on these weathered sheets looked anything but happy, though. And I remembered that the man on the radio had said his own car bore a bumper sticker reading "Take Vermont from Behind."

Right then, Ian asked what the signs meant. I started to make something up, something about the fight against pollution, but I decided to be honest. I'd been looking for opportunities to bring up the subject, and it would be dumb to turn one down. I said, "Vermont is really a good place to live for people who are gay. Like men who are in love with other men. And they even sort of let them get married, in a way, but there are a few angry people who don't like that. So they made these signs."

Ian said, "Those are probably the Christian houses." I glanced over. He looked proud of the Christian houses, and he also looked like that was going to be the end of the conversation.

I said, "Well, they might be Christians, but most of the Christians don't have those signs out. Most of them think people should be happy the way they are. These are the hateful people. Like the Nazis. The Nazis didn't like gay people, and they sent them to the concentration camps with the Jews."

On my mental instant replay, I realized that obliquely comparing his family to the Nazis was maybe not my finest moment.

He was quiet a second, and then he said, "Did you know that Hitler wanted to be an artist, but since he couldn't get into art school, he turned into a Nazi?"

"Yes, I remember that."

"Just imagine if he got into art school, the whole world would be different."

I said, "It just shows that people should be allowed to be who they are. If they can't, then they turn into nasty, sad people."

He started to laugh. "What if you went to the art gallery, and the guy was like, 'Here you see a beautiful Monet, and here on your left is an early Hitler.' Wouldn't that be weird?"

I couldn't think of any subtle way to turn it back around again.

He said, "You would go to the gift shop and buy Hitler postcards, and you'd go, 'Oh, look at this beautiful Hitler. I'm going to hang it in my room!' And people would wear Hitler T-shirts."

"Yes," I said. "That would have been better."

Staring at the soft mountains in the distance, thinking about Leo's "nation of runaways," I was considering how running away was a childhood rite I'd missed out on—the angry flight to the tree house, the backpack full of candy bars—when I suddenly remembered that I *had* once run away, or something close to it. I hadn't thought of it for years, but there I was at ten years old, crouched under my desk. All that morning I'd been down one floor playing with Tamara Finch, and when I came home there was such a silence in the hall, as if the entire building were in a trance, that I wanted to be a part of it. I let myself in as quietly as I could and curled under my desk, where I could look up and watch the snow falling outside in giant flakes. I held a book but didn't read it. I imagined my grandfather vanishing into the Siberian wilderness. I wasn't angry at my parents, wasn't even sad—I just didn't want to break the spell. Even when they started asking each other if I'd

come home, even when they called Mr. Finch, I sat there para-
lyzed, refusing to exist. It was only when my mother picked up the
phone to call the police that I came out of my room, yawning, and
told them I'd been asleep under my desk. They couldn't be mad at
me for that, and they weren't.

Perhaps if I'd been caught then, if they'd sat me at the table
with their hands in their laps and grounded me or cried or hit
me with a stick, I might not have ended up in this mess. I'd have
learned my lesson the easy way: you can't disappear. Not in America, not at this late date. You could disappear into a snowy Russian
field, I'd thought at one time. (And maybe this was why I'd agreed
to drive Ian north, every twenty miles dropping us another degree,
every new day bringing more ancient, packed heaps of roadside
snow.) But no, even that was a lie. There was no more Siberia.
There was no more dropping off the face of the earth.

We stopped around dusk in Bennington because Ian remembered
something from his report about a Battle of Bennington. Downtown was closed up already, and there was no one around to ask.
A foldout flyer we picked up at a gas station said there was a Revolutionary War museum in town, but when I said we could wait
until the next morning, he didn't seem too excited. "I don't really
love museums, because I'm scared of setting off the alarm." I wondered if he cared at all about the Green Mountain Boys, or if it
was just the only thing he knew about Vermont. We took the flyer,
bought some snacks, and Ian bought a pair of green-framed, green-
lensed "I L♥VERMONT" sunglasses with what was left of his own
money.

We drove just a little more, up north, and stopped at a hotel on the block-long Main Street of a town we never learned the name of. The floors were slanted and hollow sounding, and Ian convinced himself the place was haunted. We were the only people staying there, but while we had dinner in the bar downstairs, the place started to fill up. They were all looking at us, but it was probably just because we weren't local, or because Ian insisted on wearing the sunglasses over his regular glasses throughout the entire meal so his milk would look green.

I found I was hungry, for the first time since we arrived at the Labaznikovs'. Hungry and tired and cold, despite all the junk I'd eaten since we set out, despite cranking the hotel thermostat up to eighty every night, despite the adrenaline and caffeine that had replaced my blood. I wanted to eat warm bread and wrap myself in blankets and go to sleep. I wanted to eat an entire blueberry pie. I suppose I felt homesick, but it was unclear what home I was sick for. One that didn't exist.

On Monday, the bewildered librarian and the very strange child had a 3 Musketeers bar, a Coke, some Pringles, a greasy pepperoni pizza, and two cheeseburgers. But they kept driving.

On Tuesday, they had six powdered doughnuts, two pale fast food salads, some spinach ravioli with marinara, and a pilfered bottle of expensive Syrah. But they kept driving.

On Wednesday, they had two plates of eggs, six glasses of orange juice, two large cherry-flavored Slushees, one BLT with frilly toothpicks, one quesadilla, several pocketed restaurant mints, and one cigarette. But they kept driving.

On Thursday, they had two doughnuts, a cup of orange juice with two creamer packets added "for texture," twelve Oreos, two turkey sandwiches, Marta Labaznikov's spaghetti and meatballs and garlic bread, and an inordinate amount of coffee. But they kept driving.

On Friday, they had some Canadian bacon, eggs scrambled with vegetables, cheese, bread, jam, peanut butter, salami, milk, mustard and beer (which is how Russians, apparently, eat breakfast in America), two milkshakes, sandwiches, four Tylenols, and some M&M's. That night, they felt like crap.

The next day was Saturday. They drank two organic green smoothies and felt marginally healthier.

And that was all. They did not construct an impenetrable chrysalis.

They failed to metamorphose. They failed to fly away.

We had agreed earlier to save money by sharing a room that night, as long as I promised never to tell Ian to turn off his reading light and go to sleep. I was willing to accept that if I were put on trial, the rooming arrangement really wasn't going to make or break me. And it had turned out to be a lot easier, checking into one room. We seemed more like mother and son to the very talkative woman at the desk, who asked Ian what grade he was in and what was the name of his school. ("Saint Mary's School of the Church of God," he answered. "Wasn't that good?" he said later. "So she would think I'm Catholic.")

At eight thirty, after we'd eaten our dinners and two whole baskets of bread, I walked Ian up to the room and then decided I wanted nothing more than to go back downstairs and get drunk. Not so drunk that I would start telling everyone in the place what I was doing there, but drunk enough that for maybe a minute or two at a time, I could forget about what was happening back home, why Rocky had called Glenn, what Loraine had told the police, whether the Drakes were five miles behind us with a state trooper. I told Ian I was going to make phone calls.

I sat at the end of the bar, and I took the small spiral notebook and pen out of my purse and put them in front of me on the counter, as if I were busy making a list—an old trick to keep friendly strangers away. I turned my stool so I could see the rest of the room. The men were all extremely skinny, and the women wore fleeces halfway to their knees. The bartender was the same woman who'd checked us in, with her big blue cardigan, a yellow bird stitched over the left breast. I ordered a vodka tonic, and then another. In the corner of the room, facing away from me, was a man who didn't seem to fit the room. His black hair was slicked back, and he wore a dark blazer. I tried to angle myself to see his face, but all I could see was his plate of chicken fingers, sitting untouched on the table, and his very expensive new phone resting next to that. I turned as slowly as I could to the window that looked out over the lamp-lit gravel parking lot. There was my car, but not where I'd parked it. And not with my license plate. It was a Pennsylvania plate, with that keystone thing in the middle.

I wanted to run away, to drive fast to another state or another country or another planet, but waking up Ian and then being seen with him as we fled the hotel was maybe the worst possible decision. I couldn't think what was better, so I opted for smoking. I started to light a cigarette, my hands shaking, but the bartender scurried over. "Sorry, honey," she said. "We're on the historic register now. Won't let us smoke."

The man next to me spoke up, his voice already sloppy. "Make you hope the librarians take over, practilly."

He was staring in a strange way. Was it an "I'm an undercover officer with a concealed weapon" kind of way? An "I saw your picture at the post office" kind of way?

"Yain't the librarian I heard about," he asked. He meant me. I took the unlit cigarette from my mouth, afraid I'd swallow it.

"*Libertarian*, Jake." The bartender gave me a smile and walked down to the other end. She'd heard this particular rant before.

Jake had a thick beard and was the only fat man in the room. He wore an actual lumberjack shirt, as if he were an extra in a movie about Vermont and his job was to stand endlessly in the background tapping a tree for syrup.

"Just passing through," I said. It was probably best not to attract suspicion by speaking in full sentences.

He snorted. "We got a *libertarian* just moved to town. Couple years back, though, they had some plan come up here, take over. Chose New Hampshire instead. Good choice. Here, they woulda got shot. Want to all move up there in New Hampshire at once, then they're gonna secede. Nation of New Fucking Hampshire."

"Libertarians," I agreed, nodding. I looked at the same window again, this time checking the reflection. The black-haired man was still at his table, too far away to hear our conversation. I could tell Jake that that man right there, the one in the preppy blazer, was the libertarian, and send him over thirsty for flatlander blood while I made a run for it. But Jake was too drunk to do much good.

"Everyone wants to come Vermont, make it something it ain't.

Got all these hippies in the sixties, built solar shit, tried to farm llamas. You seen those communes?"

We actually had passed a star-shaped, wooden structure, with clotheslines sticking out in all directions and some old Volvos parked in front. "Sure," I said. "Saw one on the way here."

"Got gays come get civil-unionized now, got college kids come in to ski. Everyone comes up, thinks they discovered the damn place, like they're Christopher Fucking Columbus. Plant a flag in Montpelier, claim it for California. Turn us into Disneyland."

The bartender was back. "Jake," she said, "leave the young lady be."

Jake snorted again and drank the rest of his beer. It left foam on his mustache. I turned back to my notebook before he could start talking again, and began making a list, the only list I could think of. It read:

> *Rocky*
> *Loraine*
> *Glenn*
> *Sophie Bennett*
> *Labaznikovs*
> *Mom, Dad*
> *Drakes*
> *Man*

I wasn't even sure what it was a list of. People who might betray me? People I feared? I looked at it awhile, then added Ian's name to the bottom. A good half hour later, the black-haired man paid his bill, leaving his chicken fingers completely intact on his plate. He put the phone in his pocket and walked through the door that

led to the rest of the hotel, not out to the parking lot. He was staying the night. Before the door swung shut behind him, he looked
straight at me and nodded crisply. I'd had four vodka tonics by
that point, more than I could afford, but I was thankful for the
dulled nerves. I managed to stick to the barstool drinking water
for another hour and a half, long enough that I figured even if the
man had been waiting on the other side of the door with a crow-
bar or a television camera or a police badge, he would have given
up and gone to bed.

I walked upstairs still drunk, checking for the man around every
corner, worried my feet would break through the rotten boards of
the staircase. Ian was asleep, wheezing again, and I managed to
turn his light out without waking him. I counted how many days
we'd been gone (six, almost) and realized, suddenly, that it was
my father's birthday. Or rather it had been, all that day, and I had
missed it. But it was an hour earlier in Chicago, and my father was
a famous insomniac, and—more to the point—in my sloppy, liq-
uefied state, I was glad for the excuse to call him. One of the things
on my increasingly desperate and random to-do list was to give
him an explanation for why Ian had come with me all the way to
the Labaznikovs' house, which he surely knew about by now. And
even more than that, for some unexamined reason I wanted to feel
him out about Leo Labaznikov's story, to see if I still recognized
him as the man I'd left in bed with his ice pack, or if the interven-
ing time and incriminating information would make him sound
somehow different. I wondered if I'd be able to hear a layer of guilt,
of patricide, behind his accent.

But he was tremendously cheerful, wide awake, and his usual
self.

"Lucy! What is the story!"

I was sitting on the hard, moldy bed, talking barely above a whisper, because I was too scared to go out in the hall. I told him I'd ended up driving Ian to Vermont to stay with his father's mother. Woodstock, Vermont, I said, because I was fairly sure such a town existed, and I said the grandmother was in her fifties, a mosaic artist, perfectly capable of looking after Ian. "But he got to meet the Labaznikovs!" I said. "So that was fun! Little asthma attack, but he ended up just fine."

"Yes, yes, a birdie told me this."

"So Leo filled you in. Oh, wait, happy birthday! That's why I'm calling!" I realized I must have sounded fairly drunk, and I tried to slow down my speech and enunciate, as if that trick had ever fooled anybody in the whole sorry history of drunkenness.

"Yes! No present necessary!"

I dove right in. I was in that particular state of functional drunkenness when you see the decisions you've just made flying past you like telephone poles on the highway. "So Uncle Leo told me the real story of the chocolate factory. Finally."

"Okay, yes." He didn't sound surprised. More like nonchalant.

"The *real* story. Does Mom know?"

"Listen, I tell you something. You think you don't need your father's help, and look, you do. You need the money, and you should take the car."

"Dad, I'm in Vermont. I can't take your car."

"You should not be so surprised by this. The stupidity of children. This is the moral of the story, yes? Children think they know, and what do they know? Never as much as the parents."

I couldn't rearrange his words to make sense. He seemed angry, but whether he was angry at me for not magically knowing the true story sooner, or just angry at himself, or (was it possible?)

angry at Ian for betraying his own parents, for thinking he knew better than them, it was impossible to tell.

"Crap," he said, and I could hear a glass breaking. It finally occurred to me that *he* was drunk, that it was almost midnight on his sixty-seventh birthday, and I was the soberer end of the conversation.

"Dad, we can talk about this later." Over on his bed, Ian rolled over and made a little squeaking noise.

"No, I will tell you now about the stupidity of adults. Okay, so we already know about stupid eight-year-olds, yes? This same boy Uncle Leo tells you, he grows up to be twenty and realizes what he has done. You realize something once, when you are nine, and then you realize it again when you are ten, and you realize when you are eleven, twelve, but every year you see that what you thought you understood a year ago, no, wait, it is ten times worse. And your heart fills up with lead." He was almost shouting, and I found it miserably sad that he was speaking in everything but the first person, and I wanted nothing more than for him to stop, but stopping him would be the only thing crueler than having started him in the first place.

"And by the time you are turning twenty, you have two choices: you can suicide yourself, or you can take out revenge on the world. So I write a little book, eight pages long, about the brainwashing of Russia's children, and I stick it into every doorway in Moscow in the middle of the night. Not every doorway, but okay, five hundred. And then I take potatoes and cram them up the tailpipes of the Party leaders outside the government buildings. Not to kill them, because in USSR no one is so stupid to turn on their car without an inspection. But I put my little book in the handle of the car door and I shove the potato, so it's a clear message, okay?

I have a huge sack of potatoes in my hands, and no one questions me. No one notices this young man with his sack of potatoes. To me this is a surprise because I thought I would get shot. Lucy, listen: I thought I would get shot, and I did not care. Not because I was suiciding myself, but because I knew I was right."

I lay down on the bed and tried to see only one window on the far wall instead of two, and absorbed that last sentence. If there was a common thread between the great warriors and runaways of my Hulkinov ancestors, and my father the pathological expatriate, and me, it was just that: hotheaded self-righteousness. And not the bad kind, either. We actually *were* right. We just cared more about *being* right than *doing* what was right. And we cared more about being right than about our own lives.

"That's why you ran away," I said.

"No." I could hear more things in the background crashing, falling, breaking, getting shoved out of his way. "This is why Ilya ran away. This was your uncle Ilya, your real uncle, not some fake uncle, okay? Someone tells the police, I don't know, something like 'The Hulkinov boy did it.' Or maybe they just say his name, because we look like peas in the pod. So he is sleeping with some girl in the woods, and the police come to our door at five in the morning asking for Ilya, and my mother proves that I am not Ilya, and by the grace of God they do not arrest her. Many times they did that, arrest the mother. This young stupid police says they are coming back the next night, and the older police slaps him on the face, *pow!*"

I said, "So Ilya took off for Romania."

"He was shot in the chest at the border, six times. Our cousin Anton found this out, and he told my mother."

I said, "Dad, it's not your fault."

"You are my psychologist now? I tell you something psychological: this is America. There is nothing here to run away from. This is why I come all this way."

I probably should have pretended he wasn't talking about me, but I didn't have the energy. "I'm not running away."

"And here is a furthermore. You see what happens when we do not trust our parents. Children do not know what is their best interest."

"Are you calling me a child?" I asked it mainly to ascertain whether he was talking about Ian.

"Sure. You are a child and I am a very old man on my birthday. I go to bed now. I hit the hay."

I hung up when he did, and hoped my mother was still awake over there to make sure he got to bed safely. But I knew she wasn't, or I'd have heard her voice in the background, telling him to calm down and hand her his glass.

The only thing I dreamed that night was Leo Labaznikov drowning in a river, shouting something upstream. I had to come right down to the water to hear him, when I should have been running for help. "Lucy, what is half a Russian?" he shouted. "What is *half* a Russian?"

I woke up, hyperventilating and sweating under the three heavy blankets I'd piled on the bed, and looked around the room in the red glow of 4:24 from the digital clock. Half a Russian was half a nihilist, a fourth of a game of chess, one sixth of a revolution. It felt accurate. Half a Russian was someone who carried inconsequential shoeboxes through the night, who played games with no strategy. Whose only revolution was to run.

29

Scam

How to brush your teeth like a ten-year-old boy:

1. Attempt to apply Crest to the brush in a perfect, swirly-ended cylinder, like in the commercials. When it doesn't work, scrape the paste into the sink and reapply. Repeat three times, until perfect.
2. Ask the nearest adult if she has a camera with which she can photograph your masterpiece.
3. Sing your toothpaste the "So Long, Farewell" song from *The Sound of Music*.
4. Brush vigorously enough to work up an impressive pale-blue lather.
5. Ask the nearest adult if you look like a rabid dog.
6. Stand three feet back from the sink and announce that you are going to spit like a camel.

7. When mouth is clean, intentionally drop toothpaste
   tube on the floor, and say, "I'm so crestfallen! Get it?"
8. Floss.

That day, Sunday, we drove up to Burlington. I'd been there
once before, when I was visiting colleges with my mother, and I
remembered all the bookstores on Church Street. I told Ian about
them and promised we could buy some books on local history and
eat lunch in an Italian restaurant. I was hung over, but the throb-
bing in my head felt appropriate and necessary. This was how I
should have felt all along, from the minute we left the library. If I
threw up, all the better.

We parked, and I let Ian fill the meter. "I never, ever, ever got
to do that in my entire *life!*" he said, as if this were the major problem with his upbringing. We walked to Church Street, where no
cars were allowed and where even in the dead of late New England winter, people filled the cobblestone arcade between stores
and lit the space with their colorful coats and tasseled hats, and
where a bundled-up vendor was selling coffee and hot chocolate
from a cart. We bought one of each and began ducking in and out
of shops. Ian picked out a sketch pad and colored pencils at an art
store. "Just don't draw *me*," I said. I had a vision of the prosecuting attorney holding up as Exhibit H a picture of a woman with
my face, and a head of pale, stringy hair not yet entirely recovered
from the Ferret-Glo.

He said, "I'm going to draw some pictures for my grandmother,
to give her as a gift when I see her. Because I forgot to bring her a
present."

He said his breathing was fine, and it sounded okay, but his shoulders were up around his ears, and his face was pale. But that could have been from stress, who knew.

After Ian used the bathroom in the basement of the courthouse (an irony that seemed lost on him), we headed back north to the independent bookstores down by the big Unitarian church. We bought a book on Vermont history that must have been a required seventh grade public school textbook at some point in the 1970s. Each chapter was followed with a page of questions like "What is the job of the Lieutenant Governor?" and "Name the three major patterns of settlement." We also found a guidebook called *Highways and Byways of the Green Mountain State*, and I bought him the two Lois Lowry books he'd been too afraid, back in Hannibal, even to sneak home in his pants. He'd once told me his mother had read something about Lois Lowry believing in Satan. Lois Lowry, the sweet white-haired Newbery winner from Maine. ("Doesn't your mother believe in Satan?" "Yeah, but she doesn't *like* him.")

He started *Number the Stars* before we were even out of the store. "The only problem is, I already know how it ends," he said. "Because once when I looked at it back at the library, I found out."

"I do that too," I said. "It's a bad habit."

"But I never *mean* to." He was walking, talking, and reading all at the same time. "It's that I always have to look back and see how many pages there are, so I know when I'll be exactly halfway through, but then when I see the last page it's like my eyes suck up all the words."

I said, "At least you know there's a happy ending."

I was glad for Ian's sake that half the people we passed would have been stared at in Hannibal, Missouri. Mohawks, piercings, a man in a sarong, girlfriends in matching green hats holding hands. UVM was in session, and there were lots of dreadlocked nineteen-year-old boys making their slow ways up the street to the coffee shops under the snail shells of full backpacks, nodding along with their headphones.

After a while, he said, "People here have dirty hair."

"It's just a different hairstyle."

"No, that guy actually had a *twig* sticking out of his hair."

"I see your point."

When we found an Irish pub, Ian decided that was better than Italian. We sat in a booth made of what seemed to be ancient church pews. I told Ian I wasn't hungry. He said, "My mom only ever eats tomatoes." I ordered a coffee, knowing it would come with bottomless refills and I could get some calories from the cream and sugar. When Ian's food came, he bowed his head over his cheddar soup for a suspiciously long period of time. I went ahead and kept drinking my coffee, because you never knew how long he'd stay like that.

When he looked up, I said, "I gotta tell you, we're almost out of money. I have some saved for getting back. After we see your grandmother. But we only have about a hundred dollars left besides that."

"What about your credit cards?" He was blowing so hard on his soup that it was flying off the spoon in little droplets and landing all over the table.

"I'd rather not use those," I said. "Because then someone could find where we are."

"Don't worry too much," he said. "I have an idea for later." He took the Vermont books out of their plastic bag and laid them out on the table. "But for now, we definitely have to find out where the Green Mountain Boys lived."

I opened up the history book and he took the tourist guide. Skimming through the first few chapters, it appeared that Jake the drunken lumberjack had been correct. The state was a constant battleground, from the Iroquois chasing out the other tribes to the French claiming the land for New France, to the Dutch, to the English, to the French, to the English, to Massachusetts and New York and New Hampshire. Vermont was its own country for fourteen years, long enough to print its own money, long enough that its brave citizens had every reason to think they'd made it, to think that hundreds of years into the future, schoolchildren would look back on the Green Mountain Boys as founding fathers and visionaries. They were independent enough to be their own strong military presence in the Revolutionary War, to fight someone else's battle for freedom.

And then they buckled, joined up, state number fourteen. Not early enough to get one of those bright-minted first white stars, not late enough to be a frontier. And then, Jake was right, people kept on coming. Farmers tried the land and mostly failed. Hippies in the sixties, communes in the seventies, and though the book stopped there, with its "hope for a bright new future for the state of Vermont," I could see on Church Street what had happened next: the skiers, artists, backpackers, political idealists, runaways, all coming to contend with the Jakes of the world. And here we were too, trying to claim it in the name of—what? Sanctuary, maybe.

Ian finished his soup, but asked the waitress for more of the crusty white bread that had come with it. He put two slices on my coffee saucer and started spreading the other two with butter and shoving pieces in his mouth like he was preparing for hibernation.

When he came up for air, he said, "Miss Hull, I have to ask you something."

"You can ask me anything," I said, and my hangover was gone in a flash of adrenaline.

"Okay." He asked it through a mouthful of bread. "Had you expected Jesus in a tart?"

"Okay, I can only *answer* if I can understand what you're saying."

He swallowed deliberately, several times, as if to clear out any crumb of food. "I said, have you accepted Jesus into your heart?"

"No." The hangover was back. I didn't want him to get his hopes up, but I also didn't want to make him angry. "But listen, I already know all about it. It's probably not worth your time to try."

He shrugged. "It's okay. It's just I have this assignment for my class, and we're supposed to witness to three different people." It really didn't seem to bother him. I was relieved to see that it wasn't, as I'd briefly worried, the real reason for his bringing me all this way, some perverse and elaborate scheme approved by his parents.

"Well, did that count?"

"Probably. And also before we ate I prayed for your soul."

"Fabulous."

"Actually, I was supposed to pray *with* you, but I didn't think you'd want to."

"That would be correct." After a second, I gestured at the graffitied church pew seats and the stained glass behind the bar. I said, "Maybe you get extra credit for bringing me to this lovely cathedral." He rolled his eyes. "Okay, I have a question for *you*. Do you like your class that you go to? On Saturdays?"

"There's this one workbook that has cartoons."

"Right. But does the class make you feel better about yourself, or worse?"

He took his glasses off and wiped them on his napkin. "It's

probably not the kind of class you're thinking of," he said. "We don't really learn stuff. I'd rather do, like, an art class."

"I think I know which class it is. Isn't it Pastor Bob?"

He looked surprised, then happy, then absolutely mortified. "It's kind of supposed to be for boys who haven't really grown yet. Like, maybe they're not as tall as everybody else."

"You're pretty tall for your age."

"Yeah, but I'm not, like, good at sports. So it's supposed to help with that. And getting along with people."

"Has it helped with those things?"

He took his empty inhaler from his pocket and puffed up whatever molecules of medicine were clinging to the bottom of the canister. He held his breath for ten seconds, putting down one finger for each second that passed until he was holding up two little fists. Then he let all the air out of his cheeks in a small, slow, noisy stream. "Actually, I really kind of hate it."

Finally, after six days, the chink I'd been waiting for. I said, "You know, Pastor Bob is pretty notorious."

"Doesn't that mean criminal? He's a criminal?"

"No." Although who was to say. "It just means famous in a bad way. There are lots and lots of people—like journalists, and lawyers, and other ministers—who think that what he tells people is very, very wrong."

He pointed his soup spoon at me and said, in a voice like a news anchor, "That is a rather interesting observation, ma'am."

I charged on before he could launch into other voices or turn this into a talk about lawyers. I thought of phrasing this very vaguely, very tactfully, something about people loving each other. But I was tired of our tentative conversations, and I was hung over, and I apparently came from a long line of suicidal freedom fighters, and who was I to break with tradition? I said, "Basically, he tells people that if they're gay, they're going to go to hell. And he tells people that it's a choice, to be gay or not. But almost all the scientists in the world disagree about the last part, and the first part is based on two little Bible verses that are in the middle of all kinds of other things that everyone ignores. Like right near there, it says you can't ever eat pork or shellfish, and women should cover their heads, and you can't plant two crops in the same field. But Pastor Bob ignores all that, and he spends his whole life telling people they can't be gay."

Ian was shaking his head. He looked mildly irritated, but other than that, I couldn't tell what he was thinking. "We don't really talk about that stuff, like—*gay* stuff." He was whispering. "We mostly talk about families, and how to be a dad someday, and like what to do at a dance, but my school doesn't even have dances for two more grades. It's just that it gets really annoying and boring, and then my mom always makes me tell her everything we did, and she yells at me if I can't remember. And then on the way home she always cries."

I just said, "Oh." Of course, if Pastor Bob was hoping to get to these kids before the "secular media" did, he wasn't going to bring up the gay issue himself, not in so many words. And so if I pushed it, I would be the one making Ian uncomfortable. I'd lose him. Also, I didn't want to be the one to break it to him: Hey, your parents think you're gay. They're probably right. The next eight to ten years are going to be hell.

So I said, "The problem is that he tells people they can just change the way they are, the way they were born. And it's *not true*." I realized as those last words came out that I was saying them on the presumption that Ian would end up back there, that he'd be in the Glad Heart rehabilitation program until he either turned out to be straight, or ran away, or shot himself, or overdosed, or married some miserable, lonely woman. It killed me to think it, but at least I'd said something. And at least we had a little more time, even if it was only the five minutes before I was arrested. If I hadn't been so dehydrated, I might have been crying. I said it again: "It's not true."

Ian's face was dark red, and he kept glancing around the room. I'd been talking too loudly, and I had probably embarrassed him so badly that he hadn't absorbed a word I'd said. He had scrunched his napkin up into his empty soup bowl, and now he was poking it with his fork. I thought of apologizing, but instead I paid the bill. As we stood up, he said, "Is shrimp a shellfish?"

"Yes."

"I saw him eating a shrimp at the Christmas party. Pastor Bob."

"Well, there you go."

Back on the cold street, Ian suddenly seemed positively bouncy, and he was breathing more slowly and deeply. He handed me his green sunglasses and said, "Okay. Stay very far back, like you don't know me. And only come get me if I'm in trouble." He was jamming his pockets full of the mints and toothpicks he'd filched on his way out.

I leaned against the side of the restaurant. The coffee had woken me up but dried me out even more, so I felt wired and empty. He walked up to a college student, actually the same kid we'd seen before, with the twig in his dreadlocks. They talked for a few seconds, Ian's voice sincere and urgent and compellingly distressed, although I couldn't make out what he was saying—and then the student set his backpack on the ground and knelt down to unzip a little pocket on the side. He handed Ian something, punched him gently on the shoulder, and walked away. Ian pocketed what looked like paper money, and approached two teenage girls walking together with shopping bags. How he knew which people to hit up—how to avoid mothers, for instance, who would try to march him home—I had no idea, but I guessed it had less to do with street smarts than instinctive childhood manipulation tactics. He tried a young professor type, a girl on a skateboard, and two waiters on break. After about twenty minutes I even closed my eyes, confident I'd recognize his voice if anything went wrong.

When I opened them he was still there, talking to a stoned-looking woman with a guitar. But across the street, leaning on the window of a children's clothing store, was that man. I couldn't check for his car, of course, but the dark blazer with jeans, the slicked-back hair, the wraparound sunglasses, were all the same. He was turning his phone over and over in his hand like a worry bead. He didn't make any move toward me, and he didn't move toward Ian, although he was close enough to snatch him up before I could get there. So I stayed still and used the wall for balance and hoped the pale, oblique sunlight could bake some of the alcohol from my body. I wrapped my fingers around the car keys in my pocket, in case I needed a weapon. But Mr. Shades looked pretty calm over there. I sang the Mr. Clean song in my head, with new lyrics.

Now that I was sure I wasn't paranoid, I tried to work out who this could possibly be. If he were police, he'd certainly have reclaimed Ian by now. But he could be a private detective, hired by Rocky or Glenn. Or Rocky *and* Glenn. He could be an agent for Pastor Bob, watching over Ian and reporting back, not wanting to create a scene and unflattering media attention. He could be an intern for Loloblog, only he wasn't quite young or hip enough. That slick hair was receding, after all. He could be my uncle Ilya, watching from beyond the grave to ensure that I paid for the sins of my father.

The man checked his watch, then entered the store and pretended to examine the racks of jumpers and rompers in the window. I looked back to the road and saw Ian galloping toward me.

"Guess how much!" he said.

"Let's hope enough for dinner." My real guess was around twenty-five. Twig boy hadn't looked terribly rich.

"One hundred sixty-something!" He scooped it out of his pocket and handed it all over, a big wad of bills that looked like mostly singles. "It helped that the guy with dirty hair gave me a hundred-dollar bill and some other stuff. I told them I had to go see my grandmother in Boston on the train, and if they asked why, I said my mother tried to kill herself. I think I can get more!"

It occurred to me finally, through the haze of my hangover, that the main street of Vermont's largest city was probably the worst possible place to panhandle. There were bound to be police everywhere. I said, "Let's quit while we're ahead." In fact, the two waiters he'd approached were now looking at us and talking. They thought we were a scam. We *were* a scam, I had to remind myself. We dodged around the corner and walked fast back to the car, where the meter had almost run out anyway. If our stalker wanted to follow us, he'd have to find us again on the road. His car was there, just a few yards from our own, but he was nowhere to be seen.

———

I didn't see the black-haired man for the rest of that day—not on the road, where we put thirty miles between ourselves and Burlington, not at the cheap hotel with wet carpets, where I checked the parking lot frequently from our window, and not in the cheap restaurant, where we filled up on free breadsticks and split a plate of spaghetti.

That night, I used the computer in the hotel lobby to check e-mail, although I swore I wouldn't search Ian's name again. I had remarkably little mail, but there, at the top of the list, was one from Rocky, sent yesterday. It said, in its entirety, "I thought you'd find these interesting. Take care." After that were links to three articles. The first was the same Loloblog one I'd found myself. I noticed this time, though, that 273 people had commented on the article since it had been posted. I didn't bother looking at what I knew would be angry and uninformed tirades from both ends of the political spectrum, dissolving, predictably, into personal attacks on the authors of the other posts. The second article was the one from the *St. Louis Post-Dispatch* that Loloblog had referenced: *Hannibal police are asking for help in locating a 10-year-old boy missing since Sunday afternoon*, et cetera. It gave Ian's address, which I might have found helpful six days ago, and told me he would be wearing a red T-shirt, which I was relieved to note that he was not.

The third link was also the *Post-Dispatch* but it was a new article, posted Saturday morning: "Amid Cries of Child Abuse, Pastor Defends 'Gay Rehab' Ministry." I had trouble focusing on the words of the article itself, not because it said anything particularly horrifying, but because I was at that stage of fatigue and stress where words refused to link together into coherent relationships. I read each sentence five times, giving up on most of them. But what I did manage to put together was that the Loloblog article had incited a St. Louis LGBT group both to picket the "three-story former office building" that housed the headquarters of Glad Heart Ministries, and to launch a phone campaign wherein volunteers would call the Department of Child and Family Services hotline every ten minutes, reporting Pastor Bob for suspected verbal and sexual abuse of minors. (The president of the LGBT group stated that "Of course we don't mean sexual abuse in a physical way, at least not that we know of. But we do believe that inflicting severe sexual identity disorders on underage children can produce the same lasting damage as hands-on abuse, and we believe that when this case goes to court, it will set a new and essential precedent to protect children and teenagers.") Of course the case would never go to court. Even the author of the article implied as much, when it would have made a much better story to suggest that this was something with half a chance of happening.

The reporter had managed to confirm Loloblog's assertions that the missing Ian Drake and Pastor Bob's "Ian D." were one and the same. There was a brief statement from the Drakes about just wanting their son to be safe. "We continue to support the good work of Glad Heart Ministries," they said.

Only after I read the last paragraph for the sixth time did I absorb that Pastor Bob had responded by "expanding his current East Coast tour" and apparently milking any media coverage he could get, however minor. The original point of the tour, it seemed, had been to fire up and organize the dwindling number of East Coasters who actively opposed same-sex marriage, in those states where civil unions were finally evolving toward it. He was awfully brave, I reflected, marching into Boston with his hate flag flying. Of course, he might really be going there for the gay bars. "Lawson spoke with us by phone," the article ended, "from Brattleboro, Vermont, where he will be attending worship services Sunday morning and speaking that evening." Tonight.

I swore at the computer, loudly enough to attract giggles from the teenage girls behind me in the lobby, checking into the hotel in their basketball uniforms. Burlington is pretty far from Brattleboro by Vermont standards, but not far enough, and for half a second, I wondered what Ian's motivation in directing me to Vermont had really been. But no, why would he run away from someone just in order to run back to him?

I looked at Rocky's message again, at that insultingly stiff "Take care." He had never even signed his e-mails before, and that fact made this formal little sendoff almost eerie. As in, "Be careful." As in, "Watch out."

Back in the room, Ian had carefully unpacked all his things, and I wondered if he'd been doing this every night. The night before, the first night we'd shared a room, I'd been down in the bar when he got settled in. I watched now as he put his inhaler in the drawer of the bedside table, then pulled from his backpack a stack of cable guides and restaurant flyers he'd apparently been collecting along the way, and arranged them in an arc on the dresser along with the Lowrys, the Vermont books, and a Hannibal Public Library copy of *The Egypt Game*. "I'm sorry I didn't check this out," he said when I saw it, "but I wouldn't have been allowed to anyway. I tried to read it when I was in the library, but it got too scary. The library is definitely haunted at night."

"Who's haunting it?"

"Probably the ghosts of dead librarians. Not like you, but like old ladies who never got married."

Lying in bed that night, I thought what a wonderful children's book that would make: a library haunted by friendly old librarians. They would fly around the stacks, leaving clues in dusty books, helping three stalwart young children find the treasure beneath the floor. And what better hiding place for anything mysterious than a library? Thousands of closed books, hundreds of shelves.

And perhaps it was what I would do myself, after they shot me, or after I died of grief. I'd float and sneak and haunt, dropping clues like snowflakes. When children came to hide, I'd put them under a spell so they could crawl inside the picture books. If the cops or reporters or pastors came searching, I'd jump out of my little puppet theater, ghostly fingers twitching, and scare them all away.

30

Where's Ian?

E verybody is looking for Ian. Can you help find him?

Is he under the bed? Lift the flap!

No! That's a cat!

Is he on the BobMobile?

No! That's an evangelical windbag!

Is he drinking coffee with Shapko the Ukrainian on a couch in the high-rise apartment?

No! That's the patricidal Russian patriarch!

Is he in the library men's room, whispering to the FBI on his cell phone?

No! That's Rocky the Friendly Librarian!

Is he circling the hotel in a rusted blue car with Pennsylvania plates?

No! That's a strange man with slick hair and ominous sunglasses!

Is he zigzagging across northern Vermont with a would-be revolutionary, sporadically bursting into impressions of Julie Andrews?

Hooray! You found Ian!

31

North

My phone wasn't working here in the mountains or I would have called Rocky the next morning, to tell him I'd gotten the e-mail, to ask if there was any more news of Ian. Instead, we drove farther north on Route 89. Ian was giving the directions.

"Your grandmother better not live in Canada," I said. "That's where we're headed." We were whispering in the aisles of a little country store where we'd stopped to get food for breakfast.

"Why can't we see Canada?"

"We don't have passports. Not going to happen." Although mine was right there in the zip pocket of my purse. "And you can't get in with your pool pass."

"I just meant I want to *see* Canada. Like, with my eyes. Can't we do that?"

"I think the border gets pretty crowded with traffic. I don't know how close we can even get." The last thing I wanted was to drive straight into a police checkpoint.

Instead of Pop Tarts, Ian chose to buy a cheaper, one-serving box of cornflakes so he could afford Handi Wipes to clean off his sneakers. He knelt down there in the middle of the store, in front of the little wall of post office boxes, and scrubbed the white leather until the shoes, apart from the laces, looked brand new. "That's *much* prettier," he said, standing up and folding the Handi Wipe. The bearded man behind the counter, the postmaster, granola- and gasoline- and *Penthouse*-seller who was probably also the mayor, raised an eyebrow at me. "Something *wrong* with that kid," said the look on his face.

We kept heading north, listening to one of Anya Labaznikov's mid-'90s mix tapes: Nirvana and Pearl Jam and The Cure. I spent five futile minutes trying to explain to Ian the concept of grunge. I could hear him wheezing beside me. We were down to about three hundred dollars, including escape money, and this part of the state wouldn't be very fertile begging territory. Trucks were parked in front of farmhouses that should have been abandoned fifty years ago, places with walls so rotted and curved, they looked like Dalí paintings. I knew that unless we found a pile of cash lying around, we'd only last about one more day.

"I completely miss the library," Ian said.

"I'm sorry."

"Mr. Walters said he'd show me his Purple Heart, but I never got to see it."

I couldn't imagine what he was talking about. "Rocky Walters, at the library? His what?"

"His Purple Heart for getting injured in the war."

"Ian," I said, and took my foot off the accelerator so I could turn and see his face for a second, "what are you *talking* about? What war? Mr. Walters from the library?"

"Yeah, he was in like the first war in Iraq or something. I thought you were friends with him."

I looked ahead at the empty road, at the dead leaf scuttling across on its points like a cartoon lobster. "So," I said slowly, "by injury, do you mean his wheelchair?" This must have been what Ian had meant, weeks earlier, by "red cross." But I couldn't get any of it to make sense.

"Yeah. Before that he was completely normal. My mom knew him in school, and he used to mow my grandpa's lawn when he was little, so he must have been normal."

"What the *fuck* are you talking about?" I said. And there, I did it. I swore at a ten-year-old child. Classy. Fabulous. Ian stopped talking and opened his Henry VIII book, burying his face in it and breathing fast. He thought he was in trouble. Or maybe he thought the hand of God was about to reach down and smite me, and he wanted to look like we'd never met.

I had never asked Rocky about his condition, but that was only out of tact. I thought I was being laid-back and understanding about just taking it for granted, not considering it worth conversation. I tried to remember anything he'd ever told me about his childhood, about high school or Boy Scouts or his brother. He'd talked once about relay races at camp, when we were preparing for Family Fun Day, but I'd pictured twenty little boys in identical wheelchairs, baseball cards stuck in the wheels for the flapping noise. It was almost as if he'd deliberately avoided any stories of sports or learning to swim or bunk beds or broken legs or driving a car that wasn't a van. Or the entire United States military. I wondered if he did it to punish me for never asking, or if it was too painful to talk about a time when he could move through town with his head above people's waistlines, a time when he didn't live with his mother.

As we drove along I asked Ian stupidly, every five minutes, if he was sure, and he'd tell me he was, that he'd seen Rocky's picture in his mother's high school yearbook, and he was on the baseball team. I felt sick. Maybe from hunger, but more likely from the realization that Rocky and I weren't nearly as close as I had thought. My nightmares had thus far been tempered by the distinct possibility that although Rocky might play detective and solve the whole case of the stolen boy, he would still want to protect me. This whole time I'd thought Rocky was in *love* with me, and he was barely my friend. I couldn't even see straight. He'd gone to high school with Janet Drake. What if he knew her well? What if he'd been her boyfriend? Why hadn't he ever mentioned this?

There was another matter, beyond the shock of it all, beyond my new fears about Rocky's loyalty: if I didn't really know anything about Rocky, if I didn't really know anything about my own father—if my perceptions, in short, were this inaccurate—what if everything I thought about Ian and his family was wrong? All I'd really seen with my own eyes was the time Janet Drake dragged him upstairs while he shrieked that he'd already repented. But who knew what he'd done wrong that day? He could have strangled the cat. And since Ian said the fork marks on his head were self-inflicted, what exactly did I think I was rescuing him from? He was a ten-year-old boy who didn't think his parents were always fair to him. Big trauma.

But Pastor Bob was very real, and I saw for myself the way Ian had fallen apart that winter. I hadn't been making that up. I didn't think I'd been making it up.

One of the only thoughts I could keep in my head was how glad I was to be heading away from Brattleboro, away from where Pastor Bob would be waking up, congratulating himself on last night's speech, heading off in the BobMobile to the next New England town that needed rescuing from tolerance. Wherever he was going, it couldn't be this far north, unless he intended to preach to the cows. That was yet another thing: if I'd misjudged everything so far, what if I really *had* been wrong about Ian's reasons for coming to Vermont? What if Bob, in his repressed and slightly psychotic state, had started manipulating young boys into coming to meet him on the road, however they could get there? What if he threatened them until they ran away and forced naïve young librarians to give them rides? But that made no sense. Of course, logic didn't seem to be a prerequisite anymore for events in my world.

Ian hadn't spoken much since I'd sworn at him. Partly to make it up to him, and partly to get even farther away from Pastor Bob, I said, "I'll make a deal with you. We *will* go look at Canada. We'll see if we can see all the geese and bacon and hockey. And the socialized medicine." He looked at me blankly, as well he should have. I really was being obnoxious. I was dehydrated and hungry and operating solely on adrenaline, but that was no excuse to talk over his head. I took the only deep breath I'd taken in several days. I said, "But first we need to get you some medicine. What pharmacy do you normally go to?"

"Walgreens. The one in Hannibal."

"Perfect." I had checked online the night before, in a rare moment of foresight, and found that the state of Vermont had a grand total of three Walgreens. One very far south in Rutland, one in Brattleboro, where we might run into Pastor Bob himself, and one in the middle of pretty much nowhere, about forty miles east.

I knew I was making the decision right then that we wouldn't stay in Vermont more than one or two more days, even if we had the money to. I doubted the Walgreens computer would be rigged up to the Hannibal Police Department, but even so, a charge on the Drakes' insurance plan would eventually tip someone off. But if we were leaving Vermont anyway, this would just throw them off the trail.

Within an hour we were standing at the pharmacist's counter, and I was giving them Ian's real name. They had us sit and wait, and while Ian flipped through a copy of Bon Appétit rating each picture ("Yummy!" "Icky!" "Yummy!") I silently panicked that it was taking so long only because they were holding us here until the police came. How long could it take fill an inhaler prescription, anyway? It wasn't like they had to wait for the machine to count the pills.

But they called us up after twenty minutes, and the co-pay was only thirty dollars, plus seventy-nine cents for the chocolate bar that would probably be my lunch. The woman asked if I had any questions for the pharmacist. No, I did not. Lots of questions for the ethicist, but none for the pharmacist.

As we walked out the door, Ian squirted the inhaler into the air three times, then put it to his mouth and puffed up his cheeks like a blowfish. Now that the prescription was filled, and so easily, too, I knew we should have done this days ago, and I was furious with myself for waiting. I reflected that my revolutionary temperament might be better served by an equal helping of Russian courage, or at least foolhardiness, than by my maternally genetic Jewish-American carefulness. Imagine Woody Allen leading the Charge of the Light Brigade. That was me.

My key did not fit in the door of my car. I tried again, and Ian yanked on the passenger side door handle. I tried it again, and, idiotically, again. Then Ian said, "Why is there fifty coffee cups in the backseat?" We ran like hell to my actual car, three spaces down, Ian dove into the backseat, and I sped back onto the main road and north out of town. Ian probably thought we were racing away out of embarrassment, worried the car's owner had seen us from inside the pharmacy. I was worried he'd seen us too, but for much darker reasons. I was somewhat relieved at his ineptitude, that he'd get out of the car and shop for toiletries when he was supposed to be on our trail—unless he'd followed us in there to apprehend us, or take our picture, or grab Ian away. But no, I willfully pictured Mr. Shades filling his little green basket with cotton balls and hair gel, unaware that we'd left.

It was good, I reasoned, to have a time line for getting out of Vermont now. On the other hand, on some level it was probably bad that there was no longer any compelling medical urgency to getting Ian home, no unassailable excuse if I needed to get rid of him in a hurry. At some point, I might try asking, casually, if he was ready to head back to Hannibal. But it needed to be the right moment. If I had to ask the question more than once, he'd get stubborn and never say yes. Also, we had to be *done*. Done with what, I wasn't sure. Done with fixing him, maybe. Saving him.

I broke off half the chocolate bar and handed it to him. I bit off a tiny corner, just like Charlie Bucket, and let it dissolve on my tongue. It was awfully good, that confection that had cursed my family. ("In Soviet Russia, chocolate eats *you!*")

Ian ate his half in two bites. "I feel way better now," he said. "But Miss Hull?"

"Yes?"

"One thing that's bothering my breathing is that I don't know why, but you kind of smell like smoke."

32

Humbug

At about eleven o'clock, just as the town names were all turning French, Ian reached forward from the backseat and put a fifty-dollar bill on my shoulder. "I think you dropped this," he said.

"Where was it?"

"Sticking out of this pocket back here." He meant the one on the back of my seat.

I took the bill and stared at Ulysses S. Grant as if he'd tell me exactly where he'd come from. "It must have been part of the money from Church Street," I said.

"No. The one guy gave me a whole hundred dollar bill, but everybody else just gave me regular stuff."

I wondered for a moment if Ian had stolen it from the country store cash register, or if he'd had it all along in his backpack, but it was the crispest, cleanest bill I'd ever seen, the corners still sharp. If a ten-year-old had held it even for five minutes, it wouldn't have looked like that. Likewise, it didn't seem right that it would have sat undiscovered in my car for the past two years, a pristine relic of the fast-food-eating fan of Australian soccer. It could only have been Glenn's. I'd been locking my car in even the smallest Vermont parking lots. I set the bill on the dashboard like a lucky charm.

The road that led to Canada was just a small country highway with farms right along it, but it was fairly busy, and the traffic was slow. I could tell Ian was getting antsy back there, but he didn't want to admit that he was bored, that a visual of the Canadian border might not be worth another twenty minutes in the car. He pointed straight east, away from the main road, to a tall white church in the distance. "A big green church!" he shouted. He was wearing the green glasses again. "Let's go over there!"

"Sure," I said, and found a road that cut over that way. It might well have been the last turnoff before the border, and I was relieved that we wouldn't be going any closer, pulling off the road suspiciously or doing an illegal U-turn in front of the heavily armed and presumably well-informed border security.

"And besides," he said, "it's Sunday. We might get to hear the end of church."

"It's Monday. We've been gone a whole week."

He gasped. "You let me miss church!" Not the way most children would have said it, in joyful astonishment, but in horror. As if I'd fed him poison.

"Okay, so we're going today."

I took a few false turns before we found it. Up close, it wasn't nearly as tall or as white as I'd thought. It was dirty, almost gray, and still decorated for Christmas, three months past, with crumbly brown wreaths and garlands tied with bows that remained a violent red against the faded needles. There was a little graveyard off to the side, the kind with wafer-thin stones that nobody bothers tending anymore. "Parish of St. Bernice," the sign in front said. "All are welcome!" How brilliant of me, to drive this particular child halfway across the country just to introduce him to the Catholic Church. I tried to think of a way to back out of it. But he was so happy, bouncing up and down on the seat as we pulled into the empty gravel parking lot between the church and the graveyard. I turned the car off and put on my coat, but Ian was already out there, still with the green glasses on, cutting across the heap of leftover snow to get to the side door. He rang the bell and said something into the intercom, and by the time I reached the door it was buzzing and Ian was tugging it open with both arms. We stepped inside and Ian stomped his shoes on the mat.

A pale, skinny man in jeans and a red sweater and a clerical collar came down the hall looking mildly surprised. He squinted at us as he walked, to see whom he'd just let in, and then for the last three yards held his hand out for Ian to shake. "Father Diggs," he said, as he finally reached Ian and pumped his arm, then grabbed my hand from my side and shook it too. "Or Father Oscar, whatever you prefer. Or just Oscar!" A man named Diggs this close to a graveyard was almost too Dickensian to be true, but here he was, tall and pockmarked and gangly. "Sorry for my informality here. We don't get many visitors during the week. We're a small parish." He straightened the sweater on his knobby shoulders. "But I assume you're here to see the finger."

Ian looked at me and then back at the priest. I reached over and plucked the green glasses off his nose. "Yes," Ian said. "We would definitely like to see the finger." I nodded, bewildered, but glad Ian was taking charge. I was busy panicking over the possibility that the priest would offer Ian confession, and he would go into the little booth and tell Father Diggs exactly who we were.

Father Diggs smiled at me, over Ian's head. "I figured. I'm always happy to show people. Did you read about it in the guidebook? Someone put it in a guidebook a ways back. Why don't you come into the sanctuary, and you can have a look around while I get the keys." We followed him around the corner. He flicked a row of four light switches, and the narthex lit up around us.

"Are you from these parts?"

"Yes," Ian said. "Well, we're from Concord, which is the capital of New Hampshire. It's just that we're not a Catholic family. We're a Protestant family. But we wanted to see the finger, out of curiosity."

Father Diggs went to a long table and moved aside a stack of bulletins and flyers. He handed us two pink sheets. *The Legend of St. Bernice*, they said at the top. They were hard to read, with the speckly gray letters that come from Xeroxing a Xerox.

"Personally," he said, more to me than to Ian, "I don't know much about this whole relic thing. I came here in ninety-two, and it was old news by then. I came all the way from Omaha, Nebraska, if you can believe it. Still not sure how I ended up in the great state of Vermont. But Concord, right? Concord's a great town." He opened the big double doors to the sanctuary: dark wooden pews, a broad isosceles of stained glass at the front, Stations of the Cross along the sides. Father Diggs started down the middle aisle and we followed. "It was a gift in the early nineteen hundreds. Some wealthy parishioner did his grand tour of Europe and got the finger somewhere in France." I managed not to laugh at his choice of words. "I mean, the fact that they even sold it to him means they can't have valued it very much. Or perhaps they were starving. It's a bit of a white elephant now, but the older women in the church, they've grown up with it. It's important to them." We had reached the front of the room. "If you'll excuse me a minute," he said, "I ought to tidy up back there first. You can poke around."

He opened a door behind the pulpit and ducked under the low frame. I looked down at Ian, at his face turned up into the streams of colored light from the stained glass. His cheeks were yellow, blue, orange, with lines of shadow in between. I left him there and started down the side aisle.

I didn't know where the stations of the cross were supposed to start, so I just looked at each painting as I came to it. Christ Meets His Mother. Christ Falls for the First Time. They were poorly painted, and in several Christ bore an unfortunate resemblance to John Lennon. Ian was watching me now. I worried he was waiting for me to have some kind of religious revelation.

My purse beeped loudly, twice, echoing through the whole sanctuary. Ian jumped back and took his hand off the altar, apparently thinking he'd set off an alarm. I had a message, and one bar of connectivity. When I moved a foot forward, the bar was gone. I moved back, and it was still gone. I held the phone out in front of me like some modern-day divining rod until the bar appeared again. I finally stood half crouched under the arched wall of a little stone alcove near the back of the sanctuary. Ian was busy pulling down the kneelers in the pews. I entered my voice-mail code and listened.

"Lucy, hello? It's Monday morning, and you're not back. I suppose this is your answering machine. You have no idea what I went through to find this number. Rocky had to dig it out for me, from under I don't know how many files and papers, and it's been a tremendous inconvenience. For everyone."

I held Loraine a little farther from my ear, or rather I moved my entire head away while holding the phone perfectly still so as not to lose the connection.

"And I need a firm date on your return, Lucy, because it's just chaos downstairs. The balloon man showed up yesterday, and no one had any idea he was coming. Now, Rocky said he told you about the whole Drake family situation, and apparently Janet Drake told the investigators they should interview Sarah-Ann, Lord knows why. I told the man that *you* were the head children's librarian, not Sarah-Ann, but now you're not even here, which is terribly embarrassing for us. Sarah-Ann is absolutely refusing to do Chapter Book Hour again this Friday, because the children were just *beastly* to her last week. So I'll have to do it myself, if you aren't back. Of course I love working with our little cherubs, but I'm *very* busy, as you know."

That was the end of the message. No farewell, no ultimatum, unless I was meant to take Loraine reading to the children as the threat. I'd been so busy keeping all my stories straight that I'd forgotten the details of that original, simplest one: I'd return on Monday. I considered calling her back, but what would I say? Not wanting to waste that one bar, that one chance for communication with the rest of the world, I decided to call Tim.

"Lucy," he said, "where *are* you?"

I told him the same story I'd told Rocky and Glenn: bone marrow, Chicago. I said I'd be home by the weekend.

"Your phone was ringing off the hook yesterday. I finally went in and unplugged it. It was driving us crazy."

"Oh, I'm so sorry."

"And there was this guy looking for you yesterday. He came here."

"A guy in a wheelchair?"

"No, and not your boyfriend. He was this old guy, very Charlton Heston. He knew your middle name and everything. Look, are you okay?"

"Did he say who he was? Did he have black hair?"

"No, white. Like Charlton Heston. The old version. He gave me a name and number, but I threw it away. I figured he was some kind of stalker."

I said, "It's probably just a friend of my dad's," although I knew it wasn't. "He has strange friends."

"But you're cool?"

"Yeah. He just came once?"

"Right. Are you in trouble?"

Thinking rationally, I knew it was just the same detective who'd come to the library, checking out every possible lead. He probably got my address from Loraine. If Rocky had really figured it all out and told the police, there would have been local news coverage, a public search, something more than just one guy knocking one time. But what this did mean was that I'd showed up on their radar screen, and I didn't like that at all.

"I'm not in trouble. It was just kind of unexpected. The trip, I mean."

"Cool. If you're back soon, you should know we're all gonna be gone for the weekend. We canceled Friday rehearsal so we could all go down for that thing in St. Louis. We felt it was more important. The whole company's going."

"Thing?"

"You saw the flyers downstairs, right? About the kid who ran away? The rally?"

"Oh, right."

The phone cut out right then, and I couldn't get the bar back, not that I wanted to. The walls of the little alcove seemed to be pulsing, cold and wet. Here I was at the lip of the country, unreachable, unknown, and yet the world was closing in around me. There were detectives at the library, detectives at my apartment, and the one person I counted on to be there through my living room wall, the man who was the heart and soul and loud, irrepressible voice of the building, was heading to a rally for the boy I'd stolen, presumably encouraging him to run harder and faster. I looked around to find Ian and half expected to see my father sitting there in the pew, next to Rocky and Glenn and Charlton Heston and Mr. Shades and Loraine. *This is your life,* they'd say. *You have the right to remain silent.*

"Miss Hull!" Ian was whispering loudly from down the aisle, waving his Xeroxed sheet. "It says it's the only officially recognized relic in all of New England! And we just came here by accident!"

"That's tremendously lucky."

"What's a relic?"

Father Diggs stuck his head back through the door and coughed pleasantly, a fake cough. Ian looked up at the ceiling, crossed himself (backward, I thought) and walked solemnly through the little door.

"What's she the saint *of?*" Ian asked as I joined them.

"Well, not every saint is exactly in charge of something. But you could consider her the patron saint of this parish, and of the village in France where she lived." We had walked down a hallway crowded with cardboard boxes, and now we entered a small room filled with a rack of choir robes and a heap, in one corner, of what looked like the detritus from a Christmas pageant: angel wings, shepherd staffs, jumbled piles of dirty white cloth. Father Diggs walked backward toward the far brick wall and something resembling an aquarium. There was a little purple curtain covering the front. He rubbed his hands together. "Well, here it is."

He pulled back the little curtain and flipped a light switch, and a fluorescent light buzzed on in the aquarium. Ian pressed his nose to the glass, and I had to look around his staticky hair to see what was in there. There was a faded blue cushion in the center of the box, and on top was what looked like a small, white, shriveled breakfast sausage.

"It still has a *nail*!" Ian squeaked. Father Diggs leaned over the box, studying it with him. I felt the blood flush from my head and I leaned my cheek against the cool bricks of the wall.

"No," said Father Diggs, "I don't think that's a nail. I think it's pointing the other way."

"Why?"

My eyes were closed and I could hear my pulse.

Father Diggs was quiet a moment. "I think that's what I remember. I think they had it pointing southeast, toward the Holy Land."

"But it could be pointing northwest, and that would point to the Holy Land, too. It would just be a longer way to go."

Father Diggs chuckled. "Good point, good point."

"Because I really think that's a fingernail. Miss Hull, *look*. Don't you think that's a nail?" I opened my eyes, mainly to see if Father Diggs had noticed that Ian hadn't called me Mom. They were both staring through the glass, which was partly fogged up by Ian's breath. I thought, the finger could be pointing to Canada or Mexico or Russia or Jerusalem, but it didn't matter. There was no place safe to go, and there was no place safe to stop. Only what does a pointing finger mean, but *go, go, go*?

"Don't you think?" he said again.

"I have no idea."

Father Diggs looked back at my face. "Uh-oh," he said, taking my arm. "Young man, I think we need to get your friend outside."

Ian flipped off the light switch, crossed himself again, and picked up my purse from where I'd dropped it.

"I'm sorry," I said to Father Diggs, as he propelled me out the door and down the center aisle of the sanctuary.

"Not at all, not at all. Matter of fact, that's why we keep it hidden away. Most people like knowing it's there, but they don't want to see it on a weekly basis, you know?"

We stepped out the front door, and the cold air made me feel better.

"You could lie down on the snow," Ian said. He had stuck his head and one arm through the strap of my purse and was bumping it with his hip as he walked.

"I'm much better now." I hoped the color was coming back to my face.

"I don't know if you ought to drive." Father Diggs held me by the elbow as I walked.

"I could drive!" Ian said.

I found myself leaning against the rail fence that bordered the little graveyard. "No, you could not."

I closed my eyes, and when I opened them the priest was standing right in front of me, smiling. "Why don't you just wait and get some fresh air for a bit?" he said. "You breathing okay? Look, I'll show you something fun. You see all that stuff down there?" He pointed down the hill I hadn't realized we were on, back toward the main road. About a mile to the north was a hazy complex of large buildings, close to the road and distinctly unfarmhouselike, with cars and logging trucks stopped around it in both directions.

"That's the checkpoint for the Canadian border. America ends right there."

Ian stared at it through the green glasses that he must have just fished back out of my purse. "That's so weird. I always thought there was a wall or something."

"You think *that's* funny," Father Diggs said, "you ought to see what happens to *this* road. You go up a mile or so farther north, and it just stops dead in the middle of a field. Then there's some dense trees, then there's the actual border, where they mow through every so often to keep it clear, and then on the other side the road starts up again. Only on that side, it's called Rue de la Something. All the roads do that here. They just stop. Back in Nebraska the roads went on forever and ever. I'll never get used to it."

"I'm going to be fine now," I said. "I just got squeamish. But thank you so much for your time." I knew I'd feel even better if he went back inside, if he left us alone with the cold air and pale sun and dead grass.

"You take care of this fine young lady now," Father Diggs said, smiling at Ian. "You're both welcome back anytime. We don't parade the finger around during Mass!"

"We're Protestant!" Ian called after him. "But thanks!"

33

O Canada

After a few minutes I felt stable enough to move toward the car, but when we got there all I could do was sit down on the hood. It was warming up a little, and it wasn't too cold to just sit there, soaking up the sun and staring toward the border.

We were quiet, which was fine with me. I halfheartedly willed my feet to move north, but they didn't, as I knew they wouldn't. They stayed planted on the front bumper of the car. I had several simultaneous, ridiculous visions: Ian and me trekking north and into the hills, *Sound of Music* style, a choir of nuns bidding us to find our dream; me running across the border, leaving Ian to stumble down to the police at the checkpoint; the Mounties forming their swords into some kind of arc that we could pass through. But I did also, much more seriously, consider what would happen if we got back into the car and headed to that checkpoint. Ian would have to hide in the trunk. I'd have to be prepared for them to search the car and find him. I'd have some story about needing to flee an abusive husband, about my son not having a passport, how we were going to go stay with my uncle Ilya, just for a few weeks, just till the restraining order could be processed.

What was so special about Canada in my mind, I wasn't sure. It wasn't as if they had no extradition treaty. It wasn't as if they were any freer, any happier. A little less inclined to religious extremism, maybe. A little more welcoming to the Ians of the world, a little less welcoming to the Pastor Bobs. But not much. Growing up hearing all those stories of expatriation, of running across the borders with nothing but your clothes, my younger self must have set some strange, romantic standards of adulthood: in one's twenties, one is to leave everything behind and start over. This preferably involves gunfire and land mines. One's mother stays behind and weeps. Only, as Leo Labaznikov had pointed out, "In America, there is no place left to run to." I was born too late.

A single car passed us on the smaller road: powder blue, rusted, Japanese. Black hair, black sunglasses. He was going twenty miles an hour at most, not even looking at us. He disappeared over the hill.

Ian said, "For a second, I almost thought that guy stole our car. And then I realized we were sitting on it!"

A minute later, the man came back over the hill and passed us again and vanished onto the main road, going south. If he had wanted to grab Ian or shoot me, it would have been the perfect chance. Whatever he had planned, I actually wished for him to get it over with. Ian said, "I guess he found the end of the road."

I lay back on the hood, which was still warm, or at least warmer than the air, and watched the traffic. After Bush's reelection, a lot of people had talked about moving to Canada, although I didn't know anyone who actually had. It was something Tim and his actor friends would shout when they got drunk. I imagined that all these people in trailer trucks and Subarus were launching out on their new lives—their pockets full of Canadian coins, their radios blasting songs of freedom. They were like settlers, heading off to colonize Canada as the new America, the land of infinite possibility. They would camp on the prairies and coastlines. They'd live on cod and seagulls. I would join them. I would leave Ian, not with the border police, but maybe at the parsonage door. Then I would join my fellow pilgrims.

But I would be the one with the secret, the one I'd learned from my father: you always take your country with you. You think you can leave Russia? You find yourself stealing someone's dry cleaning, buying the black market cigars that support Cuban communism. You think you can leave America? Go ahead and try.

What is three Americans? A revolution. What is two Americans? A divided nation. What is one American? A runaway with no destination.

I would keep my secret, though, and watch what I already knew would happen. We settlers would proclaim ourselves a city on a hill. We'd slowly push the native Canadians onto reservations in the Yukon. The friendlier ones would teach us how to drill for oil. They'd trade us Montreal for a handful of beads.

Within a few generations, the sight of a real Canadian would be rare. Our children would dress like them for Halloween. We'd name our country clubs after their fallen chiefs.

Our brave little nation would grow. Global warming would make our weather tropical. America, scorched and obsolete, would fall into disrepair. Other countries would come to envy New Canada. But could we help it if our children had beautiful teeth? Could we keep from shining our glorious light for all nations to see? *Someone* has to dominate the world.

Soon, our president would claim divine right and bomb things. We would develop a deep self-loathing.

Things would fall to shit. Also, we'd run out of trees.

Some of us, the dreamers, would pack ourselves in dinghies and set sail for Greenland. Greenland, land of opportunity. The first two hundred years would be fantastic.

I had somehow, in the last couple of days, fallen under the illusion that I was in charge. I felt I had a decision to make—fight or flight, stay or go—when really Ian had been calling the shots all along. And the natural end of our journey was not the dead end of this winding Vermont road, but whatever Ian decided it was.

"Listen," I finally said, "what is the name of the town where your grandmother lives?" I waited for the meltdown.

"Mankson," he said, and slid down onto the car's front bumper and grinned up at me like he'd won a game, although I couldn't imagine what he'd do when we got there.

"Okay, let's go."

"We're *there*!" he said, and started clacking his teeth together like a monkey. "I just can't *wait* to see my grandmother!"

"We're there?"

"There was a sign! Didn't you see it? It said 'Mankson, Vermont, Home of the Mankson Township Mighty Moose!' I memorized it."

"So what's her address?"

"Well, I forgot to tell you something. She's dead. I only wanted to visit her grave. And guess where her grave is!"

"Is it right here in this graveyard?"

"Yes! Probably!"

The way he hopped down off the bumper, the way he made a huge show of walking back to the rail fence and surveying the graveyard as if trying to remember something, he couldn't have fooled the world's dumbest substitute teacher.

I felt stable enough to walk, although I really did need some food. I followed him to the fence and opened the swinging gate so we could walk in, onto the brown frozen grass and the furrows of half-melted snow. It was a small graveyard, with only thirty or forty graves. Ian was squinting at the writing on each marker, although none of the stones seemed recent, and the once sharp-edged chisel marks had eroded to the soft, shallow traces a finger would leave in sand.

"So Ian, what's the name of your poor dead grandmother?"

"Eleanor Drake," he said, but then opened his mouth again as if he wanted to change it. "But she had this other maiden name. This is definitely where she was buried, though, because I was here when I was little."

I wanted to stop him, to tell him he didn't need this lie, but he seemed to have a plan worked out, and he wasn't acting desperate or trapped. I told myself I should let him work this out, but I knew my real motive for staying quiet was selfish curiosity. It was like finishing a horrible new children's book just to see how the author would rescue the imprisoned babysitter and her dog from the pirates. Ian stalked between the graves, reading the legible ones out loud.

"Thomas Fenster! 1830–1888! That is definitely *not* my grandmother!" He stopped in front of another and counted on his fingers. "This girl only lived to be six! She probably died in a fire!" Had he really needed his fingers to find a difference of six? I'd always assumed he did very well in school, based on his reading, but math must have been another story. Math, logic, problems with solutions: they didn't really fit into Ian's world.

I watched him as I followed behind, waiting for the first sign of a breakdown so I could tell him to give it up, that I would have driven him anywhere in the world anyway.

After about five minutes, he stopped in front of an old thin rectangle of stone and squinted. I stood behind to look over his shoulder. The writing was almost completely illegible, especially at the top where the name should have been.

"I think this is it," he said.

"How do you know? You can't read the name."

"Oh, because I think I saw a picture of this gravestone once. And also I was here, even though I was pretty young. And these are the right dates." He pointed to the only clear part, where it said 1792–1809.

"You know, Ian, that was a really long time ago. This person died almost two hundred years ago."

"Well, yes," he said. "Also I forgot to say that this was like my great-great-great-great-great-something-grandmother."

"Mm-hmm," I said, and felt more than anything that I wanted to go to sleep. He squatted down in front of the stone. I would have sat beside him—would have lain down on the ground—if it weren't for the slush and snow and mud.

"What does the rest of it say?" he asked.

"I can't really read it." There were two words under the dates, and both seemed to start with Ds or Os. On the next line were four words. The first and third were very short, and the second looked like "town."

"I have an idea," he said. "Miss Hull, if you stand there above it, you could cast a shadow, and it would be easier to read." He was right. The sun was shining directly on the stone, making any indentations practically invisible. I stood with my body blocking the sun, and he crouched down, shading his eyes with his hand. "I think the first word is 'died.' That would make sense, right? Because she's dead. The second one is like 'deafening' or something. It's a lot longer. I'm sure the last letter is a G."

Suddenly I had it, before I'd even looked down myself. "Defending," I said. "I think this was a soldier."

"Cool!"

"Your grandmother was a seventeen-year-old soldier?"

He didn't answer. "Stay there! I still can't read the last part, but I have an idea!" He ran a few feet away to the big leafless tree between the last row of graves and the church, and began to climb up. "I think I can see better from here!"

And those were the last words he said before he plummeted to his death, went the movie voice-over in my head, but he was fine and up on the low bottom branches in seconds.

He shook his head. "No good. Why don't you try? I can block the sun."

"I won't climb the tree," I said, "but I'll look." We switched places. I was sure now of those first two words, and together with the word "town" in the next line it probably read "Died Defending the Town of." I stared at it a long time, and as my vision went fuzzy it all came together to form a blurry but readable word. "It could be Howe," I said, "but I think it's Havre. I think he died defending the town of Havre."

"*She*. My grandmother was a *girl*."

Ian memorized the gravestone, or at least what we thought it said, and asked if we could go find a library so we could look up the dates and the town. And so we got back in the car and headed

west and then south, without saying good-bye again to Father
Diggs, without heading over the border to a new life.

We could still do it. I could put him in the trunk and gun it.
I could drop him at the church and do the same. But I knew I
wouldn't. I'd lost any momentum I'd had, not that I'd ever had
much to begin with. I was almost ashamed of myself, of my inability to unstick from America, when I had so little here to stick to.
I had my parents, true, but they would come see me anywhere. I
had Ian, but not for long. I didn't have friends. Even the ones I'd
thought I had, I didn't. What is half a Russian? Half an American.
What is half an American? Only half a runaway.

34

The Battle of Havre

We found a white brick library two towns over, in Lynton, with a golden retriever sleeping in the doorway. I told the librarian about the gravestone (avoiding pronouns, in case Ian decided to pitch a fit), and asked if she knew of any local battles in the early 1800s. She was a blank-faced woman with dull hair, and she looked sleepily at my shoulder as she talked. "All I know is there was off-and-on fighting all throughout, with the Canadians, over where the border would be. Some of the disputes would have been pretty small, just one family against another, really. Not much written up, but you could try."

"Have you ever heard of a town called Havre?" I asked. "Or possibly Howe? Here in Vermont, presumably?"

She sighed and looked at Ian's shoulder. "Well, all these names would have changed a lot. Sometimes when they kicked the French out they'd give it an English name. So it could be anything now, or it could have just vanished. A lot of settlers would come up

different times and try to farm the land, and then they'd see how
harsh it was with the winters, and then they'd leave. They'd sometimes just abandon a whole town."

"We read about that," Ian said.

"I don't mean to discourage you, but if you can't find it on a
map, my guess is it just isn't there anymore." And she left us to our
piles of books.

We searched all afternoon with virtually no luck, except that
the books and the Internet seemed to back up the librarian's state-
ments about constant border fighting. We looked not just for
Havre and Howe but anything else of that length starting with
an *H*, and nothing fit. We tried Haven, which I was fairly sure was
the translation of Havre, and we tried Harbor, because I thought
that might be it too, and I was too lazy to get up and find a French
dictionary. There was, indeed, a town called New Haven, presumably smaller and less erudite than the one surrounding Yale. It was
a good forty miles south. "That's my best guess," I said, showing it
to Ian. "And it makes sense that when they won they'd give it an
English name. And call it 'new,' to celebrate." It didn't sound right,
but I was more interested in giving him an answer he'd be happy
with than being correct. But he just shook his head, still staring at
his book, and held up one finger as if he were about to say something, which he never did.

"I have a theory," he said at about 4:00, taking his glasses off
and wiping them on his shirt. "I think that Mankson and Havre
were the same town. That makes the most sense. Because when
they won, they would definitely have changed the name, like to
celebrate their new freedom. Like you were saying. But your town
wasn't even anywhere near the border, so it doesn't make sense to
have a battle there. And also, I think that if she died fighting, they

wouldn't have carried her away very far. They probably just buried her right near where she died. She would have been bloody and possibly amputated."

I closed my book. I was so out of ideas that I'd actually looked in the index for "Drake, Eleanor." "Maybe," I said.

"Anyway, she was a war hero, and that's what matters. She helped save her town."

I was glad he was happy, and he seemed genuinely proud of this fake ancestor. Sitting there pushing his hair back, he grinned the way Tim did when he'd pursued some ridiculous scenario all the way to its absurd end, forgetting it was never real.

We returned the books to their dusty reference shelf and checked out a few chapter books for fun.

(How to check out a book without a library card:

 1. You, to young teenage trainee behind the desk: "I'm afraid we forgot our cards. My last name is Anderson."
 2. Trainee, concentrating on pushing right buttons: "Joan Anderson or Jennifer?"
 3. You, with swish to your hair: "Jennifer."
 4. "Can you just confirm your address for me?"
 5. "Oh, we just moved! Let me give you the new one!"
 6. Jennifer Anderson can sort it all out later.)

In the car, Ian leaned his head back smiling and stared out his window. I drove aimlessly southeast and thought about the inscription. Now that Ian had constructed his story, I had to make mine. There was more than one way to read it. Die defending. Defend thy beliefs even unto death. Defend your country from the Pastor Bobs of the world. But what compelled me to keep doing this, reading it like a personal message to me, as if some teenager died in 1809 just to give us a cryptic direction?

Maybe the problem was that I'd had no signs so far. Or no intelligible ones. My family crest, with its conflicting symbols, was too ambiguous: Head on a pike! Or maybe just stay home and read a book! The finger in the church was pointing west and east and north and south; home, away, Canada, hell. And here, finally, regardless of the unclear direct object, was a firm directive: Die defending. Do not go home. Do not give in. Do not abandon this child on the steps of the Lynton Public Library. Fight, not flight.

We checked into a disintegrating motel twenty miles south, the cheapest place we could find. We were almost completely broke, and I wasn't sure we had money for gas to get back home, or even bus tickets. I paid while Ian nosed around the little table of things for sale: candy, maps, French-English dictionaries, soda, gum. He stuck his finger into the change slot of the pay phone. I turned and watched him while the manager fiddled with the computer, and it struck me how normal this seemed, how practiced: Ian with his nose to the glass by the Snickers bars, my elbow on the wooden counter, his left shoelace fraying on one side so he couldn't tie it properly if he tried. Yes, this is what we do. We do this every night. I check in and look casual. He stares at the candy. His shoe falls off.

We collapsed on the beds with books we'd checked out, and I felt a strange combination of deflation and energy. I thought of Tim and all his friends heading down to the rally this weekend, and what they'd think of me if they knew. If they only saw my actions and not the equivocal, self-loathing thoughts that accompanied them, they'd take me for a kind of hero. And I thought of my father's flight—the original one, the self-righteous, potato-stuffing, tract-writing one, before Ilya died, before things turned from revolutionary to desperate. It was in my blood, in the thick Russian veins of the Hulkinovs, this need to fight. I'd have it tattooed on my back, in prison: Die Defending.

I looked over at Ian, lying flat on the bed with his arms straight up, holding *The 21 Balloons* above his head, already a third of the way through. His arms were streaked with dirt, and his bare feet looked like they hadn't been washed in weeks. I said, "Ian, do you mind my asking when you last took a shower?"

He scrunched up his face. "I don't like hotel showers, because they might be slippery, and it's very dangerous to fall in a tub. But I took one at those ferret people's house, remember?"

"We'll make a deal. You take a shower now, and if you're not out in half an hour I'll call an ambulance."

"When I finish the chapter."

I couldn't argue with that. When he finally went into the bathroom, I called my father collect from the room phone.

"You are out of money? Listen, I have Ophelia, my black secretary, put a thousand dollars to your bank account, okay?"

"I don't want money." I wasn't sure that was true, but I could always change my mind later and he'd still jump at the chance.

"Ha! You already ask for money by calling collect! Who is paying this call?"

I asked how he was and apologized for upsetting him the other night.

"You don't call people when the people are drunk."

"But I think what you did was very brave, and I wanted to make sure I said that. You could have used your past to get in good with the Party, and you didn't. And I didn't get to say that the other night."

My father began speaking quietly, at least for him, a sure sign that my mother was in the next room. "Lucy, you think this is hero stuff, this running around like crazy with the potatoes and this ridiculous book? The problem with you is you read and you read, but you don't listen to anything someone says with the *mouth*. And you don't understand what I'm saying: it was stupid, this fighting. What did it accomplish? Ilya gets killed and I waste some potatoes. Do I end communism? Do I make Khrushchev give a state apology to my poor mother? And my mother loses *both* sons. Because after this I can't go back, and she can't come out." My grandmother had died when I was two, before she ever met me. I hadn't thought much about that part of the story, about the woman who lost her husband, and then her son, and then her other son. But then I'd been fairly preoccupied. And perhaps I'd successfully blocked whatever part of the brain it is that deals with parents and their missing children.

I couldn't think of any reply that wouldn't sound ignorant or make things worse. So I said, "There is one thing you can do. If anyone calls there looking for me, can you forget that I ever came through Chicago? I just need some time away right now, in peace, and I don't want anyone tracking me down. From work, or anything."

"I already did this!" He sounded proud of himself. "Some boyfriend, he called here and asked for you. He sounded no good."

"Rocky Walters?"

"Yes, some ridiculous name like this."

"Thank you."

Ian came out of the bathroom, his wet hair sculpted into a Mohawk. He had put on his red T-shirt, the one from the police report, but I couldn't ask him to change without explaining why. And I was still too busy seething at my father, at his puncturing my little balloon. But he had to be wrong. Or maybe he'd just forgotten what it felt like. There's a reason revolutionaries are young. Three *young* Russians are a revolution. Three *old* Russians are just a bunch of people sitting around the kitchen, arguing how much cabbage to put in the soup.

Ian lay back on the bed and began reading again, but after a few minutes he rested the book on his abdomen and stared at the ceiling, where water leaks had stained the paint.

"Miss Hull, can I have some coins?"

"It's too late for candy."

"No, it's not for candy, it's something else. I can't tell you. It's a secret."

"How much?"

"A couple dollars, I think."

I remembered the pay phone in the lobby, and my heart sank through the bed and onto the floor underneath. I tossed him my coin purse anyway, lay back and closed my eyes, heard him count change in a stack and leave the room.

So it was over.

He wasn't calling the police, or he wouldn't have asked for money. Unless he didn't know that it was free. More likely it was his teacher, his parents, some kind aunt or uncle. The library, for all I knew. Pastor Bob. All I could really do was breathe, and so that's what I did for the next five minutes. It was over. If he came back and said that we were through, that someone was on the way to pick him up, then that was it. I couldn't cross the line to *actual* kidnapping.

When he came back with paper in his hand, I thought it was a small phone book. Even when he unfolded the whole thing on the bed, I couldn't comprehend the lines, the tiny lakes, the words. It was a subpoena, a picture of jail, a mass of pink and green hell. Really, it was a map of Quebec.

"No," I said. I sat up. "We are *not* going to Canada. We've been over that."

He rolled his eyes. "Do you think I'm stupid? They'd arrest us at the border. I think I figured something out, though."

"What?"

"No, just read your book. I'll tell you in a second."

I lay down and held the book above my head, the other hand fingering the spongy polyester of the comforter. Soaking it in: it wasn't over. The book was *Anna Karenina*, from the Lynton library. I suppose I had wanted a book whose horrible ending I could see coming from page one, a book where I wouldn't hold out hope for a happy resolution that never came.

"I got it," he said. He started giggling, red-faced. He picked up a pillow and held it on top of his head with both arms. Glasses falling off, laughing.

I went over to look, and he pointed his pinky at a small dot by a big green patch, a few miles north of the Vermont border. *Havre*, it said.

It took me a second. "So you think this all happened up—you think your grandmother was Canadian."

"*No.*" He was laughing the way no one would unless they'd just won something impossible—a kingship, a lottery. Or maybe the way they would laugh if their house burned down. "Don't you get it? They *lost.*"

When he disappeared to brush his teeth, I felt like crying. It was hunger and fatigue and stress, and more than anything, it was the writing on the wall. I'd been looking for a sign, looking for the dead grandmother soldier to tell us something, and here it was. Not *Run for it*, not *Trust that he'll be okay*, not *Keep fighting*, but *You're going to lose.* And it was true, and my father seemed to agree, and it was the only thing I could see clearly right then. The wall-paper of the room was a blur, the numbers of the digital clock were a single red stripe, the mirror was a glaring yellow spot, but this was absolute: you can't keep going, you can't go back, and you can't stay here. What did you think, with your bag full of potatoes? How did you think this was going to end?

Ian came out of the bathroom, his toothbrush still in his hand, and said, "What's really so funny is that *no one* was right. Isn't that weird? I thought it was the same town as Mankson, and you said it was New Haven, and that librarian said it probably stopped being a town at all. And the answer was something totally different! It's like, I thought you might be right because you're really smart, and I thought that librarian might be right because she lives here and stuff. But *no one* was!"

"Except for you," I said.

He thought about it a second, then raised his toothbrush tri-umphantly in the air and bowed.

When he lay down again on the bed, he didn't even pick up

The 21 Balloons, which surprised me a little. Judging by the spot where he'd stuck the hotel channel guide as a bookmark, he must have been right at the most dramatic part, where the gull makes a hole in the hydrogen balloon and the professor crash-lands on the mysterious island. Instead, he lay there looking around the room as if he expected more mysteries to solve themselves, more revelatory maps to unfold.

I found myself at an utter loss—for words, for action, for decisions. I'd just come crashing down from the height of my revolutionary fervor, and here was Ian sitting across from me, apparently elated by his discovery. I decided to throw it all back on him, once again. Letting Ian call the shots had started as a way to assuage my guilt, both moral and legal. Now it was simply a way out of paralysis.

I said, "Since you're the guy with all the answers, you need to decide what's happening next. We're pretty much out of money. I can get some more if we really, really need it, but right now we're almost out. We barely have enough to get back. And we're not going to beg in the streets anymore." I wasn't trying to lead the witness, but I did want to give him an excuse, if he was ready to go home. The whole day, except for my brief inspiration from the gravestone, had felt like the end of something. The end of our money, the end of the country. And hadn't Ian been telling me we were done, by letting us find his grandmother? He could have kept us circling Vermont for several more days, if he'd tried. Or he could have said, "Oh, did I say Vermont? I meant Virginia!"

He looked at the ceiling, as if he were deciding what he wanted for breakfast in the morning. "The thing is that the auditions for the spring play are next week, and I definitely want a part."

"Okay."

"Only the eighth graders get the leads, but I still want to do it, even if it's just the chorus. So I think we should probably go back now."

He kept looking at the ceiling. I assumed it was because he didn't want to look at me.

"Miss Hull, I'm sorry if I'm changing the subject a little, but why do bagpipes only ever play that one song? You know the one song they always do, like at the parade?" And he began a fairly decent impression. He still wasn't looking at me.

I said, "I have no idea. Most composers don't really write for the bagpipe."

"I'm going to put them in my symphony. They can have a whole section of the orchestra. Or the bagpipe players could be hiding all through the audience with their bagpipes under their seats, and then suddenly they all pull them out and start playing, and everyone's totally startled. Only they couldn't wear those kilts, because that would sort of give it away."

"It would certainly look a little suspect."

I went into the bathroom and put a cold washcloth on my face.

I was surprised—and surprised to be surprised—but I couldn't figure out what it was that I'd expected. Was I really going to raise him myself and enroll him in school somewhere? Homeschool him? Sign us up for the circus? Somewhere in the back of my mind there had always been a fantastical and illogical ending to the story, as crazy as Ian's story about his grandmother, and if only I had bothered to examine it first, we wouldn't be here. I'd forgotten that all the runaway stories end like this. Everyone goes home. Dorothy clicks her way back to Kansas, Ulysses sails home to his wife, Holden Caulfield breaks into his own apartment. Huck didn't go home, at least—but what happened to Jim? Probably something terrible. I couldn't even remember.

What happy ending could I have been nursing, this whole
time? It lurked there like a dream, half remembered. There was a
picture from somewhere of a place I would take him, maybe a place
from a book: a white-walled, sunny house where people took care
of children, where they would explain everything and let him stay
there forever or until he was strong enough to face his parents. Or
we would all launch out together in our happy little boat and forge
a new country on new land rising from the ocean foam: an ideal
America finally or again.

35

Outstanding Fine

I was up once again at four in the morning, my pillows unbearably hard, my heart beating fast as a hamster's. For better or worse, Ian was going home. That was settled. But where was *I* going? The room was pitch-black with the thick hotel curtain drawn, so I got up and opened it and let the parking lot lights illuminate the room. There, in the lot, side by side, were my car and its twin. I had stopped being surprised. I was really just impressed. I wondered if he'd follow us all the way back to Hannibal. And then what? Turn me in for a reward? And what if I didn't go back to Hannibal at all? Would he follow me or follow Ian? Who was he really after?

Even if I did go home, and even if Mr. Shades went back to whatever dark rented basement he'd crawled out of, I knew eventually Ian would slip up. Or even more likely, Pastor Bob would drag the story out of him. And there I'd be in Hannibal, behind my little desk, ready to arrest.

Then there was this: I didn't really *want* to go home. I wouldn't see Ian anymore, I knew. His parents would keep him away from the library, even if they didn't suspect me. I couldn't quite picture what would happen if we ran into each other, if I saw him at the Fourth of July parade. It would be different and diminished and sad. In addition to which, Rocky wasn't my friend anymore, or maybe never was. And minus Rocky and Ian, I didn't even like my job.

I lay down again and waited for morning. Ian would have to go home alone. If I drove him back myself, we'd get pulled over twenty miles outside Hannibal for the brake light I still hadn't fixed. The cops would recognize Ian, and not even my father could invent a story good enough to get us out of that one.

I counted the hundred and twenty dollars left in my purse, and then I turned on the TV with no sound. I watched the weather channel, watched the bands of color sweeping eastward across the nation again and again and again. When Ian woke up at seven, I turned it off. I said, "Have you ever been on a Greyhound bus?"

No, he had not, but he had seen them, and he was visibly excited by the prospect, even when I told him he'd have to do it alone, and overnight. He might have to get off in St. Louis and call home or the police from there. I told him I'd come back separately. My major concern, though, was his safety over the two days. I thought of giving him my cell phone and having him throw it out the window as soon as he crossed the Mississippi, but there were too many ways that could go wrong. I had to trust that Ian would find the most helpful adult on the bus, the grandmother on her way to St. Louis, and latch on to her. I remembered the way he'd swindled half of Church Street. He'd be fine.

As soon as I found the address of the Burlington Greyhound

station in the phone book, we started packing up. I didn't want to call Greyhound from the front desk—it would be like tying everything up in a nice little bow for the prosecuting attorney. And of course the hotel had no Internet. Lots of mold, but no Internet. We'd have to get to the station, see the schedule and wait it out.

On the drive back to Burlington, we tried to solidify the details of the plan. Ian was jumpy, and he kept rubbing his ears with his shoulders. He had dark circles under his eyes, and I wondered how much he'd really slept. He'd seemed pretty out of it from four to seven, but of course those might have been his only hours of sleep.

I said, "Are you sure you want to do this?"

I didn't know what I'd do if he said no. He said, "I probably missed a lot of quizzes." I took it as a yes. I didn't have to, but I did.

So I changed the subject. "People might be looking for *me*," I said. "Either right now or later. Even if you don't say anything at all."

Even as I said it, I saw Mr. Shades pass another car behind us and come up right on our tail. He was getting bolder in his espionage, if that's what it was. Either he was planning his big move, or he figured I was onto him and had decided to drop any pretense of subtlety.

Ian was pulling a hole in the knee of his khakis wider and wider. "I *swear* I wouldn't say anything. But they could have found a clue. Like, maybe I dropped something in the library, like a sock or something, and they did a DNA test."

Oh my God.

My hands went numb on the wheel. "Ian, did you clean up your origami?" I didn't mean to shout.

"What origami?"

"The origami in the plant! Remember, the plane crash and the people? When you were hiding?"

He sucked his lips straight into his mouth.

"Did you clean it up when we left?"

He shook his head no.

The truck in front of us slowed to turn, and I almost crashed into it. Mr. Shades almost crashed into me. When Ian and I both had our breath back and the seat belts had slackened again, I said, "Maybe they'll think it was from a craft class. There wasn't anything with your name, was there?"

"Because those other ladies who work down there wouldn't even know. They're both kind of stupid."

"Right." They wouldn't fingerprint origami, would they? And Rocky couldn't go downstairs. It was horrible to be glad for that, but thank the Lord, Rocky could not wheel himself down the stairs.

We both relaxed a little, and Ian started counting all the cows we passed.

I said, "So even after you're back, you might not see me in Hannibal a lot."

"That one other librarian always loses her place when she reads, every single time."

We hadn't figured out yet what Ian would say, and when he reclined the passenger seat all the way and closed his eyes, I was glad for the time to think. We'd probably have time in Burlington, too—who knew if Greyhound would have tickets for anytime soon? We might have to live there a few more days, camping out in the middle of Church Street, stealing bread crusts off the café tables.

I hadn't thought of anything brilliant by the time we got there.

I started to wake Ian up as I parked, but he opened his eyes on his own and began organizing his backpack and the plastic bag he'd been carrying when the backpack became too small. I saw, as he rearranged everything, that he still had all the Vermont books and the Lynton library books. I made him give them back to me.

"Because it would be like a trail?" he said. He was getting good at this.

"You can finish *The 21 Balloons* at the library," I said. "I know we have two copies. And you have to promise me you'll check out *The Hobbit*, too. But you could read *Johnny Tremain* on the bus."

As we climbed out of the car, he said, "You know the whole thing about the shrimp? That means, like, lobster and everything too? Didn't the Pilgrims eat lobsters, from the Atlantic Ocean? I thought the Pilgrims were very Christian."

Mr. Shades was suddenly nowhere to be seen, but I doubted that would last very long.

"That's what it says."

"Are you sure?"

"You can look it up when you get back. It's in Leviticus, I think."

He opened the back door of the car and searched under the seats to make sure he hadn't missed anything. His voice emerged from the car floor: "But it's just, like—that can't be *right*."

It was a small triumph, but I was enormously happy. Those stupid shrimp and lobsters might, in the long run, be the crucial wedge between Ian and Pastor Bob. We crossed the parking lot to the small, quiet building.

I reconsidered his amazement the night before at no one but him solving the mystery of Havre. It was the universal revelation of adolescence, that the adults around you do not have all the answers—and like all children growing slowly and painfully into their mature selves, he'd realize it again and again over the next few years. But in Ian it was more than a simple disillusionment. It might well be what would save his life. It had saved the lives of thousands of people before him, the ones who, unlike my friend Darren, had looked at those outdated moral codes, at the judgments of their parents and aunts and priests, and said the same thing: *Wait, no. That can't be right.*

I was no moral relativist. I couldn't have been, or I'd have believed that Pastor Bob was entitled to his opinion, that the Drakes should raise Ian however they saw fit. It had always bothered me that fundamentalists would assume, when you argued with them about gay rights or abortion or assisted suicide, that you were arguing that there was no absolute right. When really I do believe in an absolute right; I just don't believe in *their* absolute right. I don't believe that the universal truths are encoded in a set of ancient Aramaic laws about crop rotation and menstrual blood and hats.

We approached the counter inside the Greyhound station, and Ian himself spoke to the attendant, a smiling old man who seemed thrilled to talk with a child. There was a bus leaving at 10:45, in only an hour and a half, and if he transferred just twice he could stop right in Hannibal, and yes, there were seats still available. Ian didn't seem surprised at all—and no wonder, Hannibal being the center of his world—but I was astounded. And vaguely insulted, as if the universe had just slapped me in the face. Not only did the universe want him out of my hands and back home, it wanted it *immediately.*

"How old do I need to be to travel by myself?" Ian asked. I was impressed—I wouldn't have thought of it.

"If the trip's more than five hours, you gotta be fifteen."

"Oh, thank goodness," Ian said loudly. "Because I just turned fifteen last Tuesday. And I got a learning permit for driving a car!"

The man raised an eyebrow at me. I nodded. Yep, really fifteen.

"You might think I'm kind of short," Ian went on. I willed him to stop talking. "But that's because I drank too much coffee. It stunts your growth."

The man tapped his fingers on the counter, a lot less amused now. "I'm gonna need some ID to that effect."

Ian and I looked at each other. I didn't even have enough money to come with him if I wanted to. Besides which I'd be abandoning my car. And I'd have to get off the bus early, in Illinois somewhere, with no car and no money, and nowhere near Chicago. "This is really an emergency situation," I said. "His mother—I'm not his mother—his mother is very sick." The man shook his head.

"Hey!" a voice behind us said. "No worries! I have got here in time!" A thick Russian accent.

It was Mr. Shades. The shades still on, even indoors.

I stared at him, at the forehead above the sunglasses, at the cheekbones and stubble and thin lips below—but he was no one I knew, no cousin or family friend, no shady business associate from my father's Russian Chicago. He said to the ticket agent, "I go with the boy. We go to Missouri, yes, okay?" My instinct was to grab Ian and dive through the "Staff Only" door and blockade ourselves, but Mr. Shades's left hand was in the pocket of his blazer, and I figured he might have a gun.

"Okay, then," the man behind the counter said, glancing at me to make sure it was all right, which I must have indicated it was. "One child ticket, one adult." He rang it up, and Mr. Shades pulled an alligator skin wallet out of the left pocket. He paid with three crisp hundred-dollar bills. Ian looked even more terrified than I was, and only slightly impressed by all the money. I planted my hands on his shoulders.

Once the ticket man handed the tickets and receipt over to our Russian interloper, we all three walked to the far side of the station, awkwardly, slowly, each of us glancing constantly at the other two to make sure we were cohering as a group. A loud trio of older women in matching green T-shirts separated us now from the ticket counter.

"Listen," said the man, "I no hurt him. They tell me, Mr. Hull will kill me if I touch him. I no want to touch him to begin with, okay? I just sit in the back of the bus. I be like Rosa Parks, okay? Yes? Back of the bus. I am not wanting to mess with Mr. Hull, you believe me."

Ian said, "You know Mr. Hull? The guy with the horns?"

I said, "You gave us fifty dollars. At the Walgreens." I realized I'd been holding Ian's shoulders this whole time, digging my nails in.

He took off the sunglasses, finally. He had small green eyes. "Look, I was not intend to scare you! You are very pretty lady, okay, and I was not wishing to make scared!" He handed me a business card: *Alexei Andreev*, it said. And underneath, in place of an occupation: *Reliable, discreet*. He said, "I work many times before for Mr. Leo Labaznikov, and I never make mistake."

I had been so stupid, assuming the cigars in that shoebox had been for a past or future favor. They were for a *present* favor. There had probably been a stack of money in there, too. And that morning at the Labaznikovs' house, the way they'd kept us there so late, they must have just been waiting for Mr. Shades to show up. Though how my father had figured anything out, I didn't know. How had I fallen for his lies for twenty-six years when he didn't fall for mine for ten minutes?

Alexei Andreev reached into his other blazer pocket and handed Ian a shiny black cell phone, one of the skinny new ones. "This is extra, okay? The boy can test this, you see it works, he can hold this in his hand the whole way."

I said, "What are you going to do with your car?"

He laughed. "It's a disposable."

I had relaxed significantly by this point. Whoever this man was, whatever his training or criminal background, he was clearly, irreversibly, on my side. And as loath as I'd always been even to accept my father's money, tainted as it was with the illicit dealings of his Russo-Chicagoan black market, I was in no position to turn down help. A little assistance from one criminal to another.

"You both go outside," he said, "in the good weather. You test the phone, okay, and say bye-bye, and smoke a cigarette. I be here when the bus is going."

Slowly, incredulously, we walked outside into the cold to go over our plan. Now that it was really going to happen, now that the tickets were bought, it seemed far too sudden. But there was no reason to wait, and no excuse, either. The sooner Ian got back home, the sooner the police would stop looking for him and amassing evidence. They'd move on to more pressing cases.

"Are you okay with this?" I asked.

"That guy was so cool! Why is he afraid of your dad? Do you think this really works?"

I took the phone and dialed my own cell with it. It worked. I programmed my number in, under the name Laura Ingalls, and we sat down on a gum-covered bench, out of earshot of the four other people waiting for the bus with suitcases.

"We need a story," I said. "And it needs to be a good one."

I remembered a project I had to do for high school Spanish,

where we pretended we'd been accused of murder, and each set of partners had to come up with an airtight alibi, in Spanish. Then the rest of the class interrogated both of you alone, while your partner waited in the hall: "Which restaurant?" "What was the soda?" "What was the weather?" Rajiv Gupta and I thought we came up with the perfect story: we drove to the beach and watched the waves. Nothing happened, we didn't talk, it was pleasant weather, we drove back to town in a red Ferrari, and that was it. We went over our clothes, how I wore my hair, and even whether the car's gas tank was full. I answered my questions first, brilliantly, then went to wait in the hall and do my calculus. I remember just having turned on my calculator when the room broke into laughter and Señora Valdez called me back in. She explained, in heavily enunciated Spanish, that while I had answered the first question, "What body of water?," with the geographically logical answer of "el lago Michigan," Rajiv had answered "el océano Atlántico." The whole time we planned, he'd been picturing his family's trips to Maine. I'd been picturing the graffitied section of concrete waterfront across from my family's building.

At least with Ian our stories didn't have to match, because, God willing, they'd never ask for mine. "What do you want to tell them?"

"I thought I could say that I ran away to the Metropolitan Museum of Art, like in *From the Mixed-up Files of Mrs. Basil E. Frankweiler*. Because that sounds like something a kid would do, especially a kid that reads a lot."

"No one's going to believe that. They must have updated their security since that book was written. And it was fiction to begin with. I don't think it was *ever* possible." But on very little sleep, sitting in the cold shadow of a Vermont bus station with a detective waiting for me back at my apartment and a Russian henchman waiting inside for Ian, I couldn't think of anything better.

"I could say I did all the things exactly like the kids in the book. Not the exhibit where they slept, because that might be gone now, but like I could say I hid in the bathroom stalls when the security guard came by. And I could say I took a bath in the fountain!"

"How would you have gotten there?"

"On a Greyhound bus! Because I'll be an expert by the time I'm home. I could say I saved up my allowance. And I could say the guy believed I was fifteen. I can tell them the whole route I took, just backwards! I'll memorize all the towns!"

I slapped my cheeks so I could wake up and think, but it didn't work. Time was running out, and we had to pick something. "They probably won't believe you no matter *what* you say. But if you stick to the same story about the Met, and keep repeating it over and over, and never change it or say anything about the library or Chicago or Vermont, at least they won't know the *truth*. You just have to have a sense of humor about it. If they prove you wrong, if they say the Met burned down last week, you can laugh, but you just have to repeat the same story. Again and again and again. Even if they threaten you. And eventually they'll give up. You just can't tell them a single thing that's true."

"Because of you. Because you'd get fired."

"Yes." I wondered if I should tell him that I would probably never go back to the library. If he found out later that I'd left town forever, he might think he was free to tell the truth, or feel betrayed and do it in anger. "Even if I don't come back," I said, "you still have to stick to your story. I wouldn't just get fired, I'd go to jail. For a very, very long time." I wondered suddenly if this was even true. How bad would the real story actually be? I tried to drive him to his grandmother's house. She turned out to be a dead soldier. I sent him home. They'd send me to jail, sure, but for how long? It wasn't Russia. They wouldn't drag me away in the dead of night. They wouldn't poison my vodka.

Without knowing I was going to, I started to laugh, a crazy laugh like Ian's the night before, and at first he looked worried, but then he started too. Even with the wind whipping past the station, even with Ian hugging his backpack to his chest for warmth, we were laughing, and not a laughter of release or a laughter that was really sadness in disguise. It was the laugh of the absurd. Your grandmother is a seventeen-year-old boy? That creepy Russian man just paid for your bus ticket? Ferret-Glo?

We eventually lost our momentum and sat in silence for a few minutes, and then I quizzed him on his story. ("What did you see at the Met?" "Well, the most interesting part was definitely the ancient part." "Ian, we know you're lying. There are motion detectors all over that place." "I'm afraid they must have been broken when I was there.") The plan was for him to get off the bus in Hannibal and keep hidden as well as he could on the walk downtown, where he'd finally turn himself in at the library. This was Ian's cleverness again: because why would he turn himself in at the very place he'd run away to? And where would Ian Drake turn himself in *but* the Hannibal Public Library? I imagined him diving through the book return slot, Rocky scanning him back in, the computer blinking all caps: OVERDUE!

I told him only to call me with an emergency, and to give Mr. Andreev his phone back before they reached Hannibal. Or, better yet, throw it away somewhere, after deleting my number from the speed dial.

Before it seemed possible, the bus was there, wheezing and dirty and urgent. I gave Ian all the cash I had left so he could buy food at the truck stops on the road without the help of a sinister Russian. Alexei Andreev came out of the building and stood a few respectful yards away, hands folded, eyes forward, like a Secret Service agent. "I call you when he is deposited," he said.

Ian counted and pocketed the money, and now he stuck his hand out for me to shake, which I did. I wondered if I should hug him. Probably not—he was ten. I punched his shoulder for luck, and we grinned at each other, more like people who were going to meet up in a week or two to laugh about this than people who would never see each other again. It would have been a wonderful moment to think of something perfect to say, something to last him the next ten years.

I couldn't come up with a single word.

How to say good-bye like Ian Drake:

1. Do the Charleston, or a gross approximation.
2. "Sayonara!"
3. Bow like a geisha.
4. Ask your creepy Russian chaperone if he has any ChapStick.
5. Spin in circles, arms extended, all the way to the bus.
6. Walk backward up the steps, looking at the sky.

Ian and Mr. Shades disappeared into the bus together, and I watched for Ian's face in the windows, the glow of light off his glasses that would somehow let me know he was going to be all right, but his face didn't appear. He must have found a seat on the other side.

The bus pulled off, and I turned and walked fast back to my car. Even as the bus disappeared down the street, half my mind was consumed with the thought that there were probably security cameras around somewhere. With luck, no one would ever think to watch those tapes with Ian in mind.

I sat in the cold driver's seat a minute before I stuck the key in the ignition. I expected myself to cry, but I was still grinning. And I felt a freedom like I was about to burst through the roof of the car. I'd never quite felt it before. Not when I got to college, where I was too scared to do anything with freedom but drink beer; not when college ended, and I was busy landing a job and denouncing my parents' money and finding an apartment I could afford. I wondered if, despite his guilt, this was how my father felt plunging into the river, getting off the plane: anchorless, homeless, inexplicably jubilant.

36

In Which Lucy Clicks Her Heels
Together Three Times

I drove back to Church Street, sat in a sandwich shop, and
ordered a cup of coffee that I had no idea how to pay for. I
thought how to spend the rest of my day. Maybe go back to those
bookstores and browse. Sit in on an art class at the university. Find
some kind, adventurous sophomores who would let me sleep on
their couch.

I knew that as soon as I found a plan, the sense of endless possibility would be over. But then for me, for my librarian's sensibility,
fifteen minutes of boundless freedom was probably enough. I had
a vague notion of lighting out for the territory or doing something
final. The idea came down on me like a warm halo as I stared
out at the street: I would open a children's bookstore, a wonderful place with couches and a dog and fortune cookies, right there
on Church Street. But I had exactly zero money—zero to the millionth power, as Ian might have said—so the store would have to
be in a cardboard box in the park. I could sell the Lynton library

books and the Vermont books. Then I'd be done. Going-out-of-
business sale.

As if it would help, I took everything out of my purse and put
it in front of me on the table, like a crazy lady. Lip balm, wallet,
Swiss Army knife, gum, pen, passport, useless date book. I had just
enough clarity of mind to leave the tampons in the purse pocket.
I checked my coin purse. Everything was still Canadian. I opened
my wallet. Driver's license. Gas and hotel receipts that I really
should destroy. Credit cards that of course I could use if I had
to, but that would still link me, in a court of law, to Vermont on
this particular day of history: an airline Visa, my bank card, and
my parents' sparkly platinum card, forced on me by my father the
year before and never once removed from its pocket in my wallet.
Which, come to think of it, would not necessarily link *me* to Vermont on this particular day. It would have been nice to think of
earlier. I tried to wish that I'd thought of it earlier, that Ian was still
here with me, that we had endless money. But I couldn't wish it,
not now with relief pouring over me like a hot shower. I ordered a
club sandwich and chips, so I wouldn't be paying a two-dollar tab
with a platinum card. I was ravenous, I realized once the sandwich
came, and I ate so fast I jabbed my lip with the toothpick that held
the thing together.

I paid and watched the waitress walk away with the black plastic receipt book, my father's little strip of silver sticking out the
top. This, I realized, was not a story of independence and rough-
ing it that held up next to the plunge into the river, the potato in
the tailpipe, Ilya's run for the Romanian border. It was more along
the lines of Anya Labaznikov's pathetic, drug-fueled flight to London. I was spoiled. I was born too late, in too comfortable a place.
Here I was with my coffee and my platinum card, my parents a

speed-dial away. I picked up my phone and called them. What the hell.

When I told my father I wanted to stay with them for a week or two, he said, "So finally you see that this Hannibal town is a nothing! Your smarts will be appreciated in Chicago. You use the credit card, yes? Buy yourself a plane ticket."

But I didn't want a ticket with my name on it, and as much as I hated the car right then, I wouldn't mind the time to stare out the window in silence. It would only be a two-day drive. I'd stop along the way to return the books to the Lynton Public Library, like a responsible member of society.

I said, "That Alexei guy was really something."

"Aha! Yes, he is *very good*! I never meet him, but he calls me every day to tell me how is it going. He thinks you are very beautiful, and if you are ever in Pittsburgh, he would like a date!"

"Dad, he scared me to *death*. You could have warned me."

"You weren't supposed to see! He was KGB once, but he's not a bad guy. He is a good egg. Moldovan, very smart. But the KGB guys can't get work. Putin can only keep a few around, or it looks bad. And nobody else will touch them. So here in U.S.A., here there is world-class KGB on the cheap!"

"How did you figure it out?" I asked, still not knowing what, entirely, he *had* figured out.

"Okay, well, you are twenty-six. So this Janna Glass at the Latin School, she would be twenty-six also. And here is a ten-year-old boy. This is not impossible. There are many pregnant teenagers on the Oprah show. But your mother says, okay, so how come she never tells us about this pregnant high school sophomore? And then I think, yes, this is right, because when anything happened at the Latin School, your mother knew all the story. Your mother is the town crier of the town of Chicago. She is like the barbershop, where all the gossip comes. And if your mother does not know about this pregnant Janna Glass teenager, then it never happened. So she goes and finds out. She calls the alumni office, and your Janna Glass friend lives in Prague."

"So then you called the Labaznikovs."

"Yes, I tell Leo to have a heads-up, and then he calls and says you have the boy with you still, and so I say, okay, what can you do for us?"

I looked around the sandwich shop. Two boys were playing cards with their father, and a woman was reading a book with a German title. Everyone looked happy and calm. I tried to be happy and calm, too. I said, "Has anyone else called there for me?"

"No, no. Here is an idea: if you are in trouble of any variety, we can print up a receipt that says you were in Argentina with us. You remember my friend Stepan, the travel agent? He can do this. He can do receipts, ticket stubs, even baggage claims, et cetera. He can't get in the United Airlines computer anymore, but this is just the terror protection bullshit that does not work anyway. But I tell him to do this printing, yes?"

"That might not be a bad idea." In that it might be as far as the Hannibal police would think to look, and if they looked deeper than that, I was screwed anyway.

"Listen, I tell your mother you just had a bad breakup with a boy, okay? This is okay? She does not know quite what is afoot."

"Well you don't really know either, do you?"

"I know nothing! I am an ignoramus!"

———

I walked out onto Church Street in the brilliant afternoon light. It was one of those winter days that look warm and sparkling from inside, until you step out into air so thin and brittle and cold you know that the earth has been abandoned by all its blankets of atmosphere, that the sun only looks so bright because it's flashing good-bye.

I walked up and down the street until my feet ached and my cheeks burned from the wind. Now that I knew I was going home, and probably for good, it felt like all this time in college and in Hannibal had been the real running away. Here I was, just like Ian, just like Dorothy and everyone else, heading back home at last. And I was heading right back into the protective arms of the Russian Mafia, which was probably what I'd been running from to begin with. You think you can't go home again? It's the only place you can *ever* go.

There was something else I'd missed, along with the fact that twenty-six minus ten equals sixteen: I'd known all along that when Pastor Bob said you can change who you fundamentally are, he was horribly, dangerously *wrong*. Yet hadn't I tried to change Ian by changing his circumstances? I had failed to understand that one reason you can't change who you are is that you can't change where you're from. I could have taken Ian to Pluto, but his mother would still be his mother, and his father would still be his father, and Pastor Bob's voice would still ring in his ears for the rest of his life.

When I got back in my car, I noticed Ian had left the Australian anthem tape on his seat, as if it would replace him or make me laugh. I didn't put it in. I wanted instead the Russian anthem, with its heroic sadness, or the American one—that song whose pompous tune and confident beat had always made me forget, at parades and ball games, that it ended with a question mark.

37

Away from Earth Awhile

Two days later I was home in Chicago, high above the ground. I didn't leave the apartment for a week, and I loved knowing that in that time, my feet never touched planet Earth. My mother kept saying things like, "Whatever his name was, you forget him. No one like that is worth it," and bringing me sandwiches. My father would wink at me over her head. I stared out at the lake a lot. I slept late.

After ten days, I still hadn't heard from anyone in Hannibal. No calls, no e-mail, no subpoenas. Halfway through Indiana, on my drive home, I'd gotten a call from Alexei Andreev. "The boy has got off the bus in Hannibal, Missouri," he said. "Is this town named in honor for the great conqueror Hannibal?" I told him I supposed so, and thanked him, and said I'd commend him to my father. I was relieved that he didn't ask for my hand in marriage. Ian never did call me from Alexei's extra phone, which was presumably a good sign. It also meant I'd probably never hear his voice again.

There was a frustratingly brief article in the papers online: "A missing ten-year-old Hannibal resident has been reunited with his family. Ian Drake was last seen on Sunday, March 19th, and returned by himself to Hannibal on Wednesday, March 29th. The police investigation of his disappearance is ongoing." I expected an outraged response from Loloblog and the activist groups that had rallied for him, but there was very little response to his return, aside from a few comments added to the message boards of previous articles. The fight against Pastor Bob continued, though, and although the recent news articles only mentioned Ian in passing ("spurred to action earlier this month by the disappearance of a ten-year-old boy enrolled in Glad Heart's youth program," etc.), it was clear that Ian's flight had focused the activists' efforts almost exclusively on Pastor Bob. That was something. They were still trying to bring him to court, and it was still going to be impossible. I was a little disappointed that they didn't seem terribly interested in the child himself, especially now that he'd come home, now that the drama was over. Not that I wanted them to descend on Hannibal and hold up signs outside his house. It was bad enough that his savvier classmates had probably found these articles, had probably told the whole school that Ian ran away because he was secretly gay. I didn't want more attention for him. Maybe I just wanted someone else to be as worried still as I was.

Pastor Bob's Web site, meanwhile, was predictably oblique and self-congratulatory. "A lot of media attention has come our way since the disappearance and blessed return of a young man in our flock. We always welcome the chance to spread God's word to a wider audience, especially those with contrasting points of view, who have yet to see the light of Jesus. God is challenging us, to be sure, right now, but we know that the return of our precious sheep is a sign from Above, and that just as the Prodigal Son returned to his father with understanding and humility and grace, our young friend has returned to his Heavenly father and to our ministries with a Glad Heart." I rolled my eyes and flipped my middle finger at the computer screen, as if someone were watching me and caring what I thought. No one was watching, and no one cared.

I had the stomach, finally, to look through every single page online, every false lead, every link to a man named Ian Drake who was a plumber on Cape Cod, every Class Notes link: Ian Drake, Colgate class of 1985. Ian Drake, Berkeley class of 2000. I found Ian Drake married to Elizabeth Westbridge in 1888. Ian Drake had a criminal record in Amarillo, Texas. All day, while my father went to meetings in empty Greek restaurants and my mother volunteered herself around town, I lay on the couch reading magazines, unable to tolerate anything as long as a book, and when I got tired of that I'd make a peanut butter sandwich and plant myself in front of my father's computer.

I had been waiting, really, for someone to come and get me. I took each day that passed as a sign that Ian hadn't ratted me out, that he was still telling them all about the Met. I made myself wait ten whole days, and then I made myself call.

"Loraine wants to know if she should go ahead and replace you." It was the first thing Rocky said when he heard my voice.

"Well, probably." I didn't have time to think, but I didn't need to. I couldn't conceive of going back there. I said, "I need to be up here with my parents now. My father had an accident, and I'm here with him. Lots of medicines."

"*Lots and Lots of Medicines*. By Robert McCloskey." It wasn't even funny, and he knew it. "So Ian Drake came back."

"He did?" I was really asking. "I mean, I saw it online, but I wasn't— So he really did?"

"He just showed up, a couple weeks ago." He didn't say that he showed up at the library, and I wondered if Ian had changed his mind, had walked home and rung his own doorbell. More likely, he was spotted on his walk from the Greyhound station.

"Where was he? Is he okay?"

"No one's saying, except that he ran away. It's not exactly the kind of thing the *Hannibal Herald* would cover in detail. In that it's not about a bake sale or an Eagle Scout."

"Right. Why didn't you call me?"

"And then apparently the parents took him out of the Day School, and no one's seen him since he's been back. He hasn't shown up here at all. I talked to that teacher from his school, the one who comes in all the time."

"Sophie?"

"Maybe. She said the family called the school the day after he came back and said they'd be homeschooling him. She was a little freaked out. I think she's worried they're locking him in a closet." He paused, but I was afraid to react in any way. "She told me that one time last year, he came into school with a big rug burn on his forehead because they made him kneel on the carpet all night with his head down to repent for something. I'm thinking you were right about him." I wondered if it really was Sophie, since she'd always told me he'd be fine. But of course, that was back when he'd had the school and the library.

I was quiet. I couldn't accept, suddenly, that I didn't know where Ian was or what he was doing. I imagined him kneeling in a closet or packing for a yearlong retreat with Pastor Bob. What killed me was that two months ago, if these things happened, it was horrifying and wrong, whereas if they happened now, they were not only horrifying and wrong but also my fault, because I'd let him go home.

I could have turned myself in right then. I could have told Rocky and the police and the Drakes that none of it was Ian's fault, that I'd taken him against his will. But I couldn't, or at least I didn't. And I honestly don't think it would have made much difference. I don't even think Ian would have gone along with the new story. Of all the things that happened, this is the one I refuse to feel guilt over. It might also be the one thing that sends me to hell.

"I gotta be honest," Rocky said. "Until he came back, I thought he might have been with you."

"*What?*"

"Lucy, you disappeared the very next day. And you were crazy about him."

I said, "I'm not a kidnapper, Rocky."

"I know that." He didn't sound sure.

"Maybe he was with that pastor. That guy does sound extremely creepy. Look, tomorrow I'll send Loraine instructions for the summer. You know you'll need to help her get into her e-mail, though. And tell her to go ahead and start hiring. I'll pick up all my junk sometime."

"Call when you're here." He said it as if he doubted I ever would be.

38

... And It Was Still Hot

Two months passed before I had the nerve to go back. My
father had been sending Tim rent checks so they wouldn't
throw my things in the street or raid my wardrobe for costumes.
It was June, 7:00 at night, and after a long, cold winter and spring
it was finally warm out. I drove slowly into town, looking at each
person I passed, at all the kids outside the ice-cream shop, not rec-
ognizing anyone.

I actually knew Ian's address now, courtesy of the *Post-Dispatch*'s
crack reporting. I drove down the street slowly, but not too slowly.
I didn't know what he'd do if he looked out and recognized my
car. He might laugh, or he might run screaming to his mother, or
he might dash out into the street and fling himself on my hood.
The house was lovely and white, peonies and irises blooming out
front. There was a large window downstairs, but the curtains were
drawn. A white SUV in the driveway. I turned at the end of the
block and passed it again. There were no protesters on the lawn,

no prayer groups camped on the porch, no taunting classmates throwing pebbles. Ian's face was not pressed to his bedroom window in agony. There were no screams, no hallelujahs, no loud strains of Christian rock. The recycling was by the curb. I kept driving. What else could I do?

I parked behind the library, which had been closed for over an hour. My key still worked. The sun was low in the sky, sending thick yellow beams through the windows. Things were different: new books out front, the five-cent cart moved. I slipped my shoes off when I went downstairs, because it felt better to be silent. The beanbags were rearranged. In this light, a thin layer of dust glowed over everything. I took the brown bear from the puppet box and ran it along the edges of all the shelves, and then I grabbed a rolling stool and stood on that to get the tops of the fiction shelves, where it looked like no one had dusted in a long time. I half expected Ian to whisper my name from down below, from deep in the science section. "I've been living here for months," he'd say. "What took you so long?"

I saw that *Heidi* was coming apart at the binding. I got the roll of adhesive book cloth from the desk drawer and sat down in the middle of the shaggy blue rug. It felt good to sit there working. It was almost dark down here, with the lights off and the sun hitting the high street-level windows only obliquely. Overhead, I could see a hundred cobwebs that must have been invisible in the day, reaching between the wooden ceiling beams and windows. They shone across the shelves, stretching for impossible distances, as if the spider had leaped off the window ledge in some great suicide and trailed her silk behind her, a failed parachute. I thought of Charlotte's web, and the silkworm in James's peach. I could see why Ian had wanted to sleep in the library. It must have been like heaven.

That night, absorbing the silence and the stillness, was the first time it hit me that I seemed to have thrown away more of my life than I'd intended. I understood that I could never have my own children, because if I did, I would realize, finally and fully, what it would mean to lose them. The more I loved them, the more it would hurt, and I knew I couldn't live my life feeling the Drakes' pain. Not because I didn't want it, but because I couldn't survive it.

I will be the thirty-five-year-old who pushes her boyfriend away. I will be hounded at parties by well-meaning friends with vital information about the biological clock. I will write a book: *What to Expect When You're Not Expecting.*

Maybe it's for the best, really, to end the Great Hulkinov Lineage once and for all. My father is the only Hulkinov left, at least the only one in America, and I am his only child. There will be no more legacy of flight and betrayal and fabulization. Or at least not in this particular family. So Hulkinov gets shaved down to Hull, then down to nothing at all. Thousands of years of Russian winters, Russian food, Russian survival, and then one day, finally, a child was born in America. The end.

I made myself stand up and ransack the desk for any artifacts of my life there. Half the drawers were empty, and the other half were full of someone else's folders and sweaters. I finally found my own things in a cardboard box down below. To-do lists, pens, Thermos, Ian's origami e-mail from that Christmas (still refolded, as I'd left it), Tylenol. I filled the rest of the box with the few things I wanted from the closet, and then before I left I got a pen and found our most ancient copy of *The Hobbit.* It was a hardcover, the plastic protector turning yellow and splintering and taped together. It was the copy Ian would have chosen, out of all of them. It was the most likely to be haunted. On the old, forgotten name card in the front, underneath "Matthew Lloyd, 4/2/91," I wrote "Ian Drake," followed by the date we'd left town. I wasn't sure why I was doing it, and it felt almost like one of those notes serial criminals leave for the cops, the kind that seems like a taunt but is really a prayer to get caught. It wasn't that, though, I was sure. Nor was it a message to Ian—it couldn't be, if he was never coming back to the library.

I imagined him finding it when he was thirty, maybe, coming back to town for his father's funeral, revisiting his childhood haunts. By then, I hoped, he'd have read the book, and maybe this would remind him that I'd meant something, however vague and inept, by directing him to a novel about a small man who sets out on a journey and conquers all the monsters. But really the metaphor didn't fit, and now that I thought about it, *I* was the one who had more in common with that unwitting burglar who has adventure so forcefully thrust upon him. I looked across at the title page and saw the subtitle, which I'd surely known at one point: *There and Back Again*, it said. Of course. You always go back again. And I hadn't even killed the dragon on the way.

I drove to my apartment next. It had been almost two months since Tim had said Charlton Heston was there to question me, but even so, I didn't want to risk going in my usual door. I went instead through the theater entrance, through the empty red-carpeted lobby, past the framed programs and the basket of cough drops.

I got my things, but just a few boxes' worth. My father promised he'd buy me new furniture, new clothes. I didn't want to know where he got the money, but I'd take it. I didn't even want my old things. They were dusty and so still, and they hadn't been touched in months. It was like a haunted house: someone used to live here, but she's long gone. Careful not to disturb her ghost.

I brought the boxes through the lobby and out to my car one at a time. There was no show that night, but I heard the buzz of rehearsal in the theater. On my last trip out, I stopped in the doorway and watched the actors on the stage, knowing they couldn't see me. They weren't acting—they were all crouched down looking at something, and when my eyes adjusted I could see they had about five CPR dummies spread out there. A big bald man with a Blackhawks jacket and a clipboard was shouting instructions: "Pinch them noses, or the air will go right back out again! You gotta pinch them noses!" I wondered whether they were all learning this for some legal reason, for the potbellied baby boom playgoers of the greater Hannibal region, or if it would be used in a play. Or maybe it *was* a play. Or just Tim's idea of a party. Tim, kneeling downstage, puffed air into his dummy's mouth, and as the dummy inflated it rose from the floor. He plunged his hands into the rubber chest again and again, his hair falling out of its ponytail in blond streaks.

Across the stage, the red-haired actress was laughing as she felt her dummy's neck for its nonexistent pulse. She picked it up by the shoulders and shook it. "For God's sake!" she screamed. "Don't leave me, Clyde! Don't leave me now! Who will look after the *baby?*"

"Okay," the coach said, "you don't wanna *shake* your victim. You're checking the airway now. Okay, lay that on down."

But she had an audience. She wasn't stopping. "You!" she cried, pointing at empty seats, "Don't just stand there, call the ambulance! You! This man is my *lover!* I didn't mean to shoot you, baby! You know I need you!"

The other actors had abandoned their dummies and circled around her to weep and laugh and flail, except for Tim. I watched him pumping away alone in the yellow light, as if he could blow life back into the plastic form, could restart its blood. For the smallest moment, I believed he could.

39

Tim Ex Machina

In my car, the conditioned air blasting my cheeks, I felt suddenly jolted awake, as if for the first time in months. It felt like the summer in college when I'd broken my leg and then finally stopped the Vicodin and realized how out of it I'd been for the past week, without even knowing it.

What I'd forgotten this time, what I'd been too fogged-up to see, wasn't what I'd done, or the repercussions, or even the stark reality of the Hannibal to which I'd so briefly returned, but that I had the ability to plan. To put it in the terms of the obnoxious self-help books Rocky and I held dramatic readings from when we did inventory: I'd been a fish in the current so long, I'd forgotten I could swim.

So I breathed, and I planned, and then I drove to the Hannibal mall, where the stores would still be open. I found, as I knew I would, a Christian bookstore, as full of calligraphy as Darren Alquist and I could have hoped, and I found a magazine called *Born Again Teen!*, with an ecstatic skateboarder on the cover, midleap. It was perfect, and I bought two identical copies, smiling sweetly at the rosy-faced woman behind the counter, and I drove back to my building, where the actors were still saving their dummies. I sat at my desk and made a list. Then I made seven more. I found a glue stick in the top drawer, and I pasted each list onto a separate page of one magazine, careful not to let the edges of the papers stick out. I smashed the whole thing flat under my dictionary. And then—deliberately, joyously—I walked to the bathroom and flushed the toilet.

Tim was at my door in two minutes, eyes wide, grin wide, arms wide, and he actually picked me up when he hugged me. "I thought you'd been kidnapped!" he said.

"I was. Come in."

"I heard you flush, and I was like, 'Oh, Jesus, is that a ghost?' And they all made me come up and check. And it's *you*! You're *here*! We weren't in rehearsal, or I'd wring your neck."

"No, I know," I said. "That was your bat signal. I need your help."

Tim sat on the arm of my couch and bounced. He was still sweaty from the CPR, and when he plowed his fingers through his hair they left wet ridges.

I said, "Do you remember the boy who went missing? The one from the Bob Lawson thing?"

"Sure," he said, and started to say something, and stopped himself. My face must have spoken volumes, and I didn't care. I sat on the couch, my feet up, facing him. I tried to start at the beginning, but I wasn't sure what the beginning was. The day I met Ian, or the day I found him crouched in the stacks? So I started in the middle. I said, "One day he brought me this origami Jesus."

I told him the whole story. The short version, at least. I'm not sure why I knew I could trust him: because he loved drama, perhaps, or just because he was Tim, or because I could see him as a child, crouched on the floor of the library, reading *Bunnicula* and bouncing just like he was now. But I was right. I could trust him. I could have trusted him even if I still had Ian right there with me, still missing, still hunched under his overstuffed backpack.

"This is amazing," he kept saying. "It's just, like, *amazing*. I mean, we thought you were this mild-mannered librarian and everything. And there you are, all vigilante and shit, and risking your *life*!"

It was oddly irritating to be seen in such flattering light, and so I stopped him. "I need your help," I said. "You and only you, and you can't tell *anyone*."

I showed him the magazine, and I showed him the lists, and I told him what I needed him to do. "You can have everything in the apartment," I said. "Everything that's left. For payment. You can keep it yourself, or use it for props, I don't care. Or sell it." He looked around at the coffee table, the lamps, the oriental rug my father had sent me for Christmas. Nicer than most of the things in the prop room.

"I'd do it for free," he said, and I could tell it was true. He was pacing gleefully around the room, like I imagined he did backstage before each entrance. "You just gave me the best role of my *life*."

I slept in the apartment that night, as soundly as I had in months, and Tim knocked on my door at 10:00 a.m. to tell me he was "heading into battle."

"Seriously," he said, "Lucy, if that pastor is there, and I stab him with my keys, will that ruin everything?"

"Yes." I couldn't help laughing. "Stick to the script, Tim. And the pastor won't be there. You look great, though." He did. A gray suit from the costume department, a white shirt, no tie, scuffed dress shoes. His hair in a neat ponytail. He had a briefcase, and a clipboard with a pen and some kind of form on it. I looked more closely: it was one of the theater subscriber forms from the lobby, with the top folded back. The magazines were tucked under his arm. "You know which one is which?"

He nodded. "Most definitely."

"Break a leg."

I spent the next hour cleaning, not because I thought Tim or the next tenant would particularly care how vacuumed the carpet was, but because it was the only thing I could think to do. I wiped the windows with vinegar, and I scrubbed the rotating plate from the microwave, and I emptied out the medicine cabinet.

Finally there was Tim, banging on my door with both palms, racing in—out of breath and red and jubilant—and galloping circles around my coffee table.

"I was brilliant!" he said. "Lucy, I was fucking *brilliant*, and there wasn't a single reviewer there to see me! But I don't care! I was fantastic, and yes, for the record, that kid is definitely one hundred percent queer. Flaming. You should have seen me! I'm like, 'Ma'am, I have a free trial subscription here for you,' and she's about to just take it out of my hands, and so I go, 'Listen, I actually get in trouble unless I give this directly to someone who's in our target demographic,' and then I say that I saw the basketball hoop outside, surely she has a teenage son, and she goes 'No, he's only eleven,' and then suddenly he's behind her in the doorway going 'What? What?' It was *perfect!*"

I said, "Did he look okay?"

"What, like healthy? Sure. Kind of, like, high-strung though. I would say maybe agitated. But he wasn't bleeding or anything. They actually let me into the house. I'm standing there in the front hall, and the mom is asking what our affiliation is. So I say evangelical. I didn't even know if that made sense, but apparently it did. So then I say exactly the part you said. I go, 'Yes, we're based in Vermont, but we also have offices in Iowa, Ohio, and Oahu, Hawaii.' You should've seen the kid's face. I think he thought I was about to out him. He was *glaring* at me, from behind the mom. And then it's like I could see the wheels turning, and he's figuring out that the only one who knew that was you. Meanwhile, the mom is going on and on about what's our philosophy, who's our publisher. So I hand her a copy, the clean copy, and I say, 'You don't have cats, do you? My eyes are watering.' The kid goes, 'No, just a guinea pig,' and I say, 'Oh, I grew up with ferrets.' The mom is busy reading the magazine by this point, so I'm able to just wink at him, but then he *gets* it, you can tell he just completely gets it, and that's when I hand him his copy. I say, 'Look it over, see if you find something in there to relate to. Just really spend some time with it, when you have a moment to yourself, and see if it speaks to you.' He practically crams it up his shirt. Didn't want the mom to get it. That woman is *completely* anorexic, by the way."

Tim was still circling, and I was still sitting, shaking, watching this strange windup toy I'd set in motion. I said, "Tell me what the house looked like."

"Normal, I guess. There weren't any huge crucifixes or anything, if that's what you mean. It was really, really clean. I could see a piano in the living room. It was all very, like, Pottery Barn, but kind of cutesy. It was the kind of house that would've had needlepoint pillows of sailboats. Not that I saw any."

This was comforting, for some reason, this vision of normalcy. Or maybe it was just nice to have *something* to picture. I said, "So then what?"

"Then check this out: I go, 'So can I get your subscription today, or will you be filling out one of the cards in the center of the magazine?' And the mom is in the middle of making some excuse about wanting to look it over some more, and Ian goes, 'Mom, can I go upstairs and read it?' I got the feeling she almost wanted to say no, like she wanted to check it out more first, but I was standing right there looking hopeful, so she says yes and shows me out. The kid was up the stairs before I even made it to the door. I'm betting he ran up there and locked his room. If he's smart." He stopped his pacing and held his arms out. "So? Did I do good?"

He was probably just looking for applause, but I got up and hugged him. "You're amazing. And you will *never* tell *anyone* about this."

After Tim left, I grabbed a few more things and walked in a daze to my car. It started raining as I headed out of town, and I drove by the Drakes' quiet house once more, honked three times, and left Hannibal forever. I imagined Ian, up in his room, peeling back the magazine cover. He'd recognize my sloppy handwriting right away.

What I'd written, sitting there in my ransacked apartment, were reading lists: "Books to Read When You're 11" was the first one. It began with *Danny, the Champion of the World*, that charming paean to civil disobedience, and included the Oz series ("But make sure they're by the real L. Frank Baum!" I'd written. "Not just plain Frank!") and ten more books that I couldn't stand the thought of Ian *not* reading, that I'd have piled on his outstretched arms if I were still his librarian.

"Books to Read When You're 12" started with *The Giver* and *The Golden Compass* and ended with *Lord of the Flies*.

It was hard to picture Ian at fourteen, Ian at sixteen, but as the lists filled I could see his mind taking shape, and I could see that the fifteen-year-old Ian who'd just fallen in love with *The Catcher in the Rye* would be ready next for *A Separate Peace* and *The Things They Carried* and large doses of Whitman.

I told eighteen-year-old Ian to read *David Copperfield* ("Whether I shall turn out to be the hero of my own life, or whether that station will be held by anybody else, these pages must show"), and I told him to read *Middlesex* and A. E. Housman and Jeanette Winterson.

I'd wanted, in those later lists, to include something more directly helpful, some books that would tell a sixteen-year-old how to reason with the father who wanted to throw him out of the house, or the mother who insisted he was going to hell—but all I knew were novels. It gave me pause, for a moment, that all my reference points were fiction, that all my narratives were lies.

After I finished the lists I'd tried, I really had, to write something of my own in there—a note, an encouragement, anything— but I couldn't. The pen refused the paper.

Because what it's come down to, after that whole messy spring, that whole tortured summer, all the time since, is this: I no longer believe I can save people. I've tried, and I've failed, and while I'm sure there are people out in the world with that particular gift, I'm not one of them. I make too much of a mess of things. But books, on the other hand: I do still believe that books can save you.

I believed that Ian Drake would get his books, as surely as any addict will get his drug. He would bribe his babysitter, he'd sneak out of the house at night and smash the library window. He'd sell his own guinea pig for book money. He would read under his tented comforter with a penlight. He'd hollow out his mattress and fill it with paperbacks. They could lock him in the house, but they could never convince him that the world wasn't a bigger place than that. They'd wonder why they couldn't break him. They'd wonder why he smiled when they sent him to his room.

I believed that books might save him because I knew they had so far, and because I knew the people books had saved. They were college professors and actors and scientists and poets. They got to college and sat on dorm floors drinking coffee, amazed they'd finally found their soul mates. They always dressed a little out of season. Their names were enshrined on the pink cards in the pockets of all the forgotten hardbacks in every library basement in America. If the librarians were lazy enough or nostalgic enough or smart enough, those names would stay there forever.

If a Book Lacked an Epilogue,
Ian Would Frequently Offer His Own

I am the mortal at the end of this story. I am the monster at the end of this book. I'm left here alone to figure it all out, and I can't quite. How do I catalogue it all? What sticker do I put on the spine? Ian once suggested that in addition to the mystery stickers and the sci-fi and animal ones, there should be special stickers for books with happy endings, books with sad endings, books that will trick you into reading the next in the series. "There should be ones with big teardrops," he said, "like for the side of *Where the Red Fern Grows*. Because otherwise it isn't fair. Like maybe you're accidentally reading it in public, and then everyone will make fun of you for crying." But what warning could I affix to the marvelous and perplexing tale of Ian Drake? A little blue sticker with a question mark, maybe. Crossed fingers. A penny in a fountain.

But in real life, I won't be in charge of those blue stickers ever again. No more deciding if a book is fantasy, or if it's appropriate for the fragile youths of Hannibal. I found my new job after a summer at home—far from Hannibal and far from Chicago, and that's all I really cared about. Here, twenty-year-olds check out books on feminist theories of vegetarianism or contemporary criticism of Hemingway, and no one ever asks me for salvation. All they need me to do is scan and stamp, scan and stamp. I'm content here. I'm stable. Or at least, I'm stationary.

If I ever go back to the Hannibal library, it will be as a ghost. Ian always believed the library was haunted, and perhaps he was right. Isn't it what all librarians strive toward, at least in the movies and clichés? Silence, invisibility, nothing but a rambling cloud of old book dust. My hands will still hold the book, will sweep the picture around the children's circle, left to right, but nobody's back there behind the spine. I'm the Nothing Hand. (Don't let the rabbits know where I'm hiding.)

Here are the pictures, then. Gather around and look close: runaways and borrowers, angels and aurochs and actors, crafty villains and small, scrappy heroes. Now, complain that the girl in front was blocking your view. Squint hard and ask why the artist drew it all wrong.

I'm practically a ghost here already after all, pale and haunted behind my new desk, and I've realized this is what happens to characters no longer central to the main plot, the ones whose greatest adventure is now behind them. This is what becomes of the Mad Hatter, the evil stepsister, the used-up genie. They sit at an empty table and remember the day something extraordinary blew through town.

For one brief moment that October, I was part of the story again—or maybe the story just caught up with me. Heading home from work, I got pulled over for speeding. I thought even then that it was all over, that Ian had turned me in. "Do you know how fast

you were going?" the officer asked. So fast you wouldn't believe, I
wanted to say. So fast that I haven't stopped moving in months,
not even in my sleep. I opened the glove compartment for my reg-
istration, and five thousand restaurant mints fell onto the floor
and the passenger seat and bounced off the gearshift into my lap.
So Ian had been prepared for the long haul. We could have stuck it
out another week, could have crossed some field into Canada half-
starved but with fresh breath. I handed over the paper and felt my
heart tighten and my bones break into a million sharp splinters:
at least for a while, Ian had believed we would make it and never
go back.

Come closer for the final page now, and push aside the girl who
keeps getting in your way. Demand to know first if it's a happy ending or a sad one, if the good are rewarded and the evil punished.
Peek at the last words. See if you can tell. Ask it again: Does it all
turn out in the end?

But I don't know. I don't know. It depends what you mean by
end. The end of my story, or the end of his? Here is all I know: I
still search for him, in the recesses of my computer, and I still come
up with the Cape Cod plumber. But if he gets out, when he gets
out, I'll be able to find what becomes of him. There are a million
ways it could all come out fine. There are a million ways it could
end very badly. He must be fifteen by now, and maybe I won't have
to wait much longer to see. I remind myself again and again that
in this day and age, we don't really lose each other forever. There
is no more Siberia.

Squirm on the carpet and look at the clock. Ask if this story
was true.

Here are the final pictures. Here are the helpful captions. Here are some hopeful last words for the peekers-ahead, the ones like Ian and me who couldn't help but read the last sentences first. (Perhaps I've misled them, the way I myself was misled—the way that deep down, I always assumed our courage was some kind of guarantee, that a happy ending was waiting for us, if only we could get there. Or perhaps I haven't. Because who can say that it won't still come true?)

So here, patient listeners: your soothing epilogue. Imagine him happy. Imagine him spinning in circles. If I couldn't believe it, I couldn't get out of bed in the morning. Imagine him hiding those lists for eight long years. Imagine his heaven, where he can float through characters and books at will. (Let's dream him up a king, a giant, a boy who can fly.) Imagine him already there, under his covers with the flashlight. For a blissful eternity, such a world should suffice. For now, it should save him.

Let's say that it does.